There is no friend as loyal as a book."
- Ernest Hemingway

The Wicked Chase

Houston Cullen Series:
Book One

By

Karen Sue Burns

Copyright

ISBN 978-0-9896027-9-2

Credits

Cover — Cajunflair Publishing

Note

This book was previously published in 2012 by Crimson Romance under the title *In Hot Pursuit*. It has been updated and re-edited with new scenes added.

Dedication

The Wicked Chase is an updated/revised version of my first book published in 2012 by Crimson Romance under the title *In Hot Pursuit*. My mother was so very proud of me for my first publishing contract and showed a print copy of the book to everyone who worked at the facility where she lived. She passed in 2013 and I do think she would enjoy this new version of the book.

Love ya, Mom!

ONE

THE STABLE LIFE OF DALLAS WELLS encountered an unexpected detour on an afternoon in mid-May—one of those close to scorching afternoons when office workers shuffled paper or checked movie times, waiting for the clock to tick-tock to going-home time. She considered herself productive that afternoon, color-coding her accounting files for the upcoming fiscal year end.

The detour began when her office phone rang.

It was an outside call, from First National Bank. Her hand hesitated over the receiver, but she was a sucker for a ringing telephone.

"It's Lynne Harris."

"How are you?" Dallas said.

"Confused. We haven't received the wire yet. I couldn't reach Scooter."

"What wire?"

"The wire for the twenty-five million dollars from the Bridge Foundation. Can you check on it?"

Dallas had no idea what Lynne was talking about—and no way would she let Lynne know that. It was embarrassing to once again not know beforehand, about the arrival of a major gift to the university.

"Give me a few minutes and I'll get back to you."

Dallas replaced the phone, shook her fists at the ceiling. A twenty-five million gift had been wired today? What the hell? She jumped out of her chair and headed for the office of her boss, the vice president of finance. Surely, he knew about the wire. She rushed down the long hallway and found his assistant, Ellie, at her desk.

"Is Scooter here?"

Ellie looked up from a paperback novel. "No. I came back from lunch and he was gone. Calendar says he's at a meeting and should return in half an hour."

Dallas blew a slow breath, worked at calming her frustration. "Please, let him know I need to talk with him as soon as he returns."

She debated what to do next. Should she wait for Scooter or should she call Development, the department responsible for soliciting gifts? Would Scooter be upset if she didn't wait for him?

Back in her office, she turned her chair away from the desk and her eyes moved to the CPA certificate on the wall. She'd worked her ass off to pass the exam and earn that credential. Ten years ago, she hadn't worried about making the wrong decision, she simply went with her gut instincts. She picked up the phone to call the executive director of development.

"Rebecca, I need to ask you about a gift that was wired today."

"You mean the one from the Bridge Foundation?"

"That's the one. The bank called and the funds haven't arrived."

"That's strange. The wire should have been sent first thing this morning. We sent over the wire instructions two days ago." Rebecca's voice was calming. "Let me contact the donor and I'll call you back. I'm sure it's a simple mistake."

While Dallas waited for the return call from Rebecca, she shuffled files on her desk, then dug an antacid tablet out of her purse. The taco she had for lunch was talking to her. She chewed the tablet and stared out the office window. Friday classes at Houston Cullen University were over and students rushed toward the parking garage down the street. The weekend would officially begin at five o'clock.

The phone rang. Rebecca's name appeared on the digital read out.

"I called the director of the foundation. He said he talked with their brokerage firm this morning and the wire was sent as planned." Rebecca was strangely still calm.

"Something is wrong." Why wasn't she freaking out like Dallas was about to do?

"Don't worry," Rebecca said soothingly. "I'm sure it's some glitch within the bank. They're all having computer problems these days."

"Right, thanks for the information."

Something was definitely wrong. How did twenty-five million dollars disappear? Dallas' head was hot. Where was Scooter? He should be the one calling the bank. But Lynne had called Dallas, so she'd do her duty and follow up. She punched in the number and Lynne answered on the first ring.

"The Bridge Foundation says the wire was sent this morning," Dallas said.

"You're sure?"

"That's what our Development Office told me." She wiped sweat off the back of her neck. "What should we do to locate the funds? This can't happen every day."

"No, it doesn't, and not with such a large sum. I'll call the Foundation's brokerage firm, Gregory James, and get the transaction number for the transfer so we can trace it through the Federal Reserve System. Should I follow up with you or Scooter?"

"Would you mind calling Scooter?" Dallas knew he'd want to hear it from Lynne himself.

"No problem, I'll call him as soon as I have an update."

Dallas next called Ellie to find out if Scooter had returned . . . not yet. Now what?

She stacked the color-coded file folders on the credenza adjacent to her desk, then decided to clean out her e-mail. The distraction of busy work kept her from guessing why the gift might be missing. She glanced at the time in the corner of the monitor—3:27. Surely Scooter would return any minute.

She first went through her inbox and deleted messages she'd already read, jotting reminder notes on a yellow pad. She clicked through the list and checked the time again—3:51.

Where was Scooter? This *would* be the day he was late

coming back from a meeting.

Dallas next focused on the spam folder, a total of 112 messages. She worked her way through it to those dated today, then she stopped, her fingers clutching the mouse. This was strange, a message from Gregory James, Inc., the brokerage firm used by the Bridge Foundation. Why would they send her an e-mail? She double-clicked and read the message. Her throat squeezed shut, and she couldn't catch a breath.

Holy shit. The message confirmed a change—her change—to the wire instructions for the Bridge Foundation's gift. The receiving bank and the associated account number had been updated as instructed . . . by the controller of Houston Cullen University. She swallowed, then sucked air in her lungs. *What the hell?*

She jumped out of her chair and rushed to the office door, closed it quietly. Then the shaking started, from her elbows to her knees. She began to pace her office from the small window to the door, fifteen steps, back and forward. As she walked, the shaking lessened. Although her brain spiraled in a state of shock, her limbs began to regain their memory of function.

After a few minutes, she stopped pacing and sat back at her desk, ready to deal with the message, still open on her monitor.

The e-mail was an error. She had made no change to the wire instructions. How could she? She hadn't known about the gift until two hours ago? The message implied she stole the twenty-five million by changing the HCU wire instructions. It was a mistake or a joke. Someone had a sick sense of humor.

She sighed and printed the e-mail. She debated telling Scooter about the message but concluded it was best to keep it to herself for now. She grabbed the paper off the printer and folded it in half, then half again, small enough to slide into her wallet. She tossed the wallet back into her purse. She'd analyze the impact of the e-mail later and then determine the right thing to do.

Even a lousy plan was better than no plan at all.

$ $ $

Scooter Taylor finally returned an hour later and informed Dallas he'd already called the police. Rebecca had already informed him about the missing funds.

"Dallas, this is all your fault," he said through thin lips. He sat at his huge oak desk scowling at her. Late afternoon sunlight filtered through the window blinds, creating prison-bar stripes on the honey-toned wall behind him.

"What? My fault?"

"Yes." He squeezed the bridge of his nose with two fingers. "You should have verified the wire was received this morning. But you didn't and now the funds are missing."

"I didn't even know about the gift." She blew a slow breath. The Gregory James e-mail popped in her head and she pushed it quickly to a back corner.

"You would have known about the wire if you were on better terms with Development. But, oh no, you're always picking at them." He lowered his voice. "They don't like you, so they don't talk to you."

Of course, Development didn't like her. The by-the-book procedures she routinely insisted on placed them on opposite sides of most issues. How did that relate to a missing gift? She crossed her arms over her chest. "Maybe we're not all besties, but that doesn't mean this is my fault."

"It doesn't matter now. Locating twenty-five million dollars is what's important." He glared at her again, shook his head. "I expect you to be a team player."

"I *am* a team player," Dallas reminded him, on the edge of pleading, even though they were in familiar territory. He reminded her every few months to get along with Development.

"Damn it, you better be."

"I'll do whatever I can to help. Just tell me what to do."

"Good. I—"

A campus security officer knocked on the door. "Mr. Taylor, Houston PD is here." She nodded at Scooter, then left.

Dallas took another slow breath. The police had arrived real fast. The situation was now a bona fide disaster for HCU.

A tall man wearing jeans and cowboy boots entered Scooter's office. He surveyed the room with a calm face. He had that ruggedly appealing look that screamed *don't tangle with me.*

"Good evening, I'm Roddy Phillips from the Burglary and Theft Division, HPD's Financial Crimes Unit." He pulled a small notebook from his jacket pocket and flipped it open. "We received a call from a Mr. Taylor reporting missing funds."

"Yes, detective, I'm Scooter Taylor, vice president for finance here at HCU." He walked around his desk and shook the cop's hand, then turned toward Dallas. "This is Dallas Wells, our controller."

"Good to meet you, Mr. Phillips," Dallas said. He nodded in reply.

Scooter directed the detective to the round conference table across from the desk and waved a hand to Dallas to join them. Rebecca Holland from the Development Office, accompanied by a man who looked like he stepped off a New York runway, hastened into the office.

"Rebecca, you're here," Scooter said, smiling.

"Looks like we made it in time." She pointed to the man beside her. "This is Logan Rice, the executive director at the Bridge Foundation."

Scooter made the introductions and hustled everyone to sit at the table. Dallas turned her chair around to join the group. She had a good view of both Logan Rice and the detective, each a good-looking man. But looks were often deceptive, as her ex-husband had taught her.

"Mr. Taylor, tell me about the missing funds," the detective said.

"A twenty-five-million-dollar gift to the university is missing," Scooter explained. He waved a hand toward Logan. "The Bridge Foundation, one of our most prominent donors, electronically transferred the funds to a HCU bank account this morning. They used wire instructions e-mailed to their office by Rebecca's assistant."

"I can verify our brokerage firm used those instructions," Logan added.

Dallas' stomach performed a loop-da-loop. How could Mr. Rice be certain the correct wire instructions were used?

"The problem is that the wire was instigated correctly but the funds were never deposited to our bank account," Scooter said.

"Okay," the detective said. "Why was the transfer made today?"

"The date has been set for two weeks," Scooter explained. "HCU is in the middle of a six-year capital campaign to raise one-hundred million dollars. The foundation's cash donation was the premier gift for the campaign."

Her breathing hitched. This could prove to be a nightmare for HCU. She wished she had worked harder at getting Development to understand the importance of her accounting procedures. Maybe then she wouldn't have received that mysterious e-mail. Would the detective suspect her? Her face was hot and her left leg tapped a steady rhythm on the carpet.

"This is terrible," Rebecca said. "What are we going to do?" She ran a hand through her blond hair, artfully mussing her perfect bob.

"Our bank officer told me she would put a trace on the wire using the transaction number from the brokerage firm," Dallas replied.

"That's good. But, Detective, Rebecca is right, this is terrible for the university. What do we do now?" Scooter said. "My God, twenty-five million dollars gone . . . like that." He snapped his fingers.

"This is ridiculous," Logan spat out, glaring at Scooter. "How in the hell, in this electronic age, does your bank lose our gift?"

Scooter's eyes widened at the outburst. "Mr. Rice, please, we need to stay calm. Like Dallas said, First National is tracing the wire."

Logan glanced at Dallas and their eyes locked. In that instant, she felt her heart flutter in her chest. Then he broke his gaze and dismissed her with a curt nod. What was that? He pulled a business card from a pocket of his suit jacket and slid it across the table to Scooter. He rose. "I have to go. My grandmother needs to hear about this before it hits the local news. Please contact me with any updates." He quickly exited the office.

Detective Phillips jotted in his notebook. "Will do. Mr. Taylor, before I leave, I'll need a copy of the wire instructions, all the contact names at the Bridge Foundation, their brokerage firm, and your bank."

Scooter nodded, his face a grim mask.

Dallas felt the tension in the room crawl along her arms. She knew Scooter worried about the potential negative impact on donors. Would this mess cause them to reduce their giving to HCU?

To make matters worse, neither the university president nor Rebecca's boss, the development VP, were even on campus. They were traveling somewhere together, trying to raise more money. Neither executive would be happy when they heard about the theft and the possibility that the Bridge Foundation might publicly blame HCU. Dallas wondered if either executive had been notified.

"Also, I'll also need a list of names, work locations, and phone numbers for employees in the Development and Finance offices." The detective's eyes focused on each of them, one at a time. "There will be additional requests if we get into an investigation. I hope that won't create any difficulty for y'all."

"Not at all," Scooter said, glancing at his watch. "We'll do everything we can to help with your investigation. I'm sure our president will want to talk with you as soon as his plane lands. I'll leave a message for him"

"Good." Detective Phillips handed out business cards. "We'll put a trace on the wire transfer to verify it's not a bank error. You'll hear from me once I know something."

"I realize we don't know if there has been a crime," Scooter explained. "But I wanted to alert you as to our concern."

The detective nodded. "We'll see."

"Scooter, can I help you get anything?" Dallas asked.

"No, both you and Rebecca can head on home. I'll give you a call tomorrow since I know you're scheduled for vacation next week."

"My vacation can wait," Dallas said quickly.

"Let's see what happens." Scooter rose and went to his desk. They were dismissed.

Rebecca and Dallas left quietly and walked down the hall to the front of the Finance Office.

"This is a freaking nightmare," Dallas said, chills snaking down her back.

"Or a really bad horror movie. I hope the police arrest whoever did this."

"Me, too." Dallas also hoped they didn't consider her the number one suspect once they started the investigation.

$ $ $

Logan parked in the circular driveway in front of the Rice family home. No doubt about it, he'd rather be drinking a beer at his favorite neighborhood bar. Telling his grandmother about the loss of the gift would not be easy. She'd probably blame it on him.

He found her in the study, watching a ridiculous reality show on television.

"Good evening, Gram." He bent down and kissed her cheek.

Sarah Rice, the regal matriarch of the Rice family, beamed at her grandson from her seat on the luxurious leather sofa. "Logan, what a surprise." She lowered the television's volume. "What brings you here? No date tonight?"

He sat across from her. He knew she wouldn't appreciate any hedging on his part for visiting her unannounced on a Friday evening. He got right to the point.

"I had a meeting at Houston Cullen University thirty minutes ago. There's a problem."

"A problem?"

"The Foundation's gift didn't make it to the University's bank."

"What in the world do you mean?"

"The money is gone, possibly stolen."

"How could someone steal a wire transfer?" She rose, anger flashing across her normally composed features. She walked to the fireplace with a slight limp, her back to her grandson. After a long minute, she turned. "How could you let this happen?"

He ignored her question. "I don't know how a wire transfer goes missing."

"We need to call the police."

"Taken care of. Remember Roddy Phillips? The guy I trained with for the Houston Marathon a couple years ago."

"Yes, of course, a nice young man."

Logan nearly rolled his eyes at the "nice young man" comment. Roddy was tough as nails with a wicked sense of humor.

"He's the detective working on the case. I just met with him."

"I need to talk to him. This situation is totally unacceptable." She returned to the sofa. "Logan, the Rice family does not allow this type of thing to happen." She punched a small pillow, her lips a thin line. "I expect you to find the bastard who stole our money. Then bring him to me. I'll make sure he pays for his crime."

"Gram, please, the police will take care of this."

She looked at him with steel in her eyes. "They damn well better do their job then. The Rice family will not tolerate anyone taking advantage of us."

Logan changed the subject and asked his grandmother about her spring garden. She loved planning the colors every year. The change in conversation should also help maintain her blood pressure at a healthy level. At least he hoped it did.

He left an hour later, after assuring her that he'd provide updates on the police investigation. As he drove away, he congratulated himself on convincing Gram that he'd deal with the theft and she didn't need to be hands on. After all, she had a full schedule running the family and he did have some experience with police matters.

He called Roddy on his cell phone.

"Man, what a surprise to see you at HCU. I thought you were working homicide."

"Switched a few months ago," Roddy said with a chuckle. "Sorry this happened to your family. You guys have been good to Houston over the years."

"Whatever. Do you have any suspects yet?"

"Hell no, we don't even know if there's been a theft. We're starting with a bank trace and we'll go from there. But if it is a theft, who would be on your suspect list?"

"I don't know. How about everyone working at the school?"

"We'll start with the ones who knew about the transfer."

"I'd start with that controller, Dallas something," Logan said. "Rebecca told me she said she didn't know about the transfer. That doesn't make sense considering her position."

"I agree."

"There was something strange about her, like she was nervous or on edge. What could be the reason for that?"

$ $ $

Dallas started her ten-year-old Volvo wagon, adjusted the air-conditioning to neutralize the heat of the day. She dug her cell phone out of her purse and called her best friend, Ruthie.

"Something awful happened at work and I'm not in the mood for a noisy bar."

"No problem. We can get together next week for happy hour."

"No, come to my house," Dallas said. "I have alcohol and I'll make you dinner."

"You are so predictable. You always cook when you're stressed."

"And lucky for you, I'm a good cook."

"All right, I'll be there in an hour."

Dallas drove on autopilot down the Southwest Freeway to Sugar Land, an upscale community southwest of Houston, her thoughts on the Gregory James e-mail. She didn't know what to do. The obvious answer was to show the e-mail to the police. Of course, they would then consider her the thief. Whoever had changed the wire instructions and sent the fake e-mail had probably covered their tracks and all guilty roads would then lead to Dallas.

She was better off keeping her mouth shut and pretending she'd never received the damned thing. Although staying quiet didn't feel right, it felt dishonest. She'd see how things went with the police. That was the best she could do for now.

She turned in the driveway of her townhouse and hit the button to open the garage. Once inside, she shed a layer of stress and turned on the lights. She headed up the stairs to her bedroom, threw her purse and tote on the bed, then went into the closet, pulling off her summer suit.

After donning a T-shirt and shorts, the doorbell rang and Dallas hurried down the stairs. She swung open the front door and enveloped Ruthie in a fierce hug.

"I'm so glad you're here."

"You really did have a bad day."

"You have no idea. Come in the kitchen and I'll give you all the details."

Ruthie sat at the granite island, in her favorite leather stool, while Dallas retrieved a bottle of wine from the under-counter cooler. She held it up. "Cabernet okay?"

"You bet."

Dallas uncorked the wine, then poured two glasses, handing one to Ruthie. "How about pasta and a salad for dinner? I made pesto sauce last night."

"Sounds great. What can I do to help?"

"Nothing right now, this won't take long."

"Tell me what happened. I'm dying to hear."

As she cooked, Dallas explained the events surrounding the theft. Starting with the phone call from Lynne Harris to walking out of Scooter's office with Rebecca, everything except for the Gregory James e-mail. That was too awful to reveal. She ignored the guilt battering her heart.

"I thought you didn't care much for Rebecca?" Ruthie said.

"I don't. She seems fake to me but everyone at HCU loves her." Dallas sipped her wine and thought about that. "Maybe I don't know how to get along with others."

"That's not it. You're just prickly at times." Ruthie smiled, eyes crinkling.

"You're right, I guess. But this is awful for the university. That Logan Rice was a real piece of work, leaving in a huff. The police detective was so calm it was eerie."

"You can't blame Mr. Rice for being upset. That's a lot of money to lose."

"Of course, it is. I'm not thinking straight. Scooter wasn't thinking straight either, saying it's my fault."

"You two have had a bit of a love-hate relationship the last ten years."

Dallas dropped linguini in a pot of boiling water and stirred the noodles. "He's so unpredictable. I've always wondered if his marriage is good. He never talks about his family."

"Neither does my boss. Maybe Scooter is simply a moody guy."

Ruthie always made good sense. "You're probably right. Would you mind putting the salad together? I'll put garlic bread in the oven."

Ten minutes later, the dinner was served and the wine glasses refilled.

Ruthie waved her fork in the air. "I was thinking. What if Scooter meant it, that he truly thinks the theft is your fault?"

"Why would he seriously think that?"

"You're the only one who claims she didn't know about the wire transfer. You know that old saying, she who protests too much is guilty."

"That's ridiculous."

"Just playing devil's advocate. If I thought it, you can bet the police will as well."

"And that thought is downright scary." Dallas wanted to shout the words but kept her voice low. She couldn't forget the e-mail. "This is a terrible blow to HCU but I didn't cause it. Scooter said he'd call me tomorrow. I figure my vacation next week is history."

"Do you suppose the police will want you to stay in town?" Ruthie's lip twitched, then she burst out laughing.

"Stop that," Dallas said. "This is a horrible situation."

"Sorry, trying to keep your spirits up. I realize HCU has a rough road ahead."

"You can say that again. I'll do whatever I can to help Scooter. He may not be boss of the year but he deserves my support."

"Good for you," Ruthie said while patting Dallas' arm.

"I wonder who really did it. The thief had to know a wire transfer was ordered along with all its details." Dallas drummed her fingers on the granite counter.

"Exactly, and you know what?"

"What?" Dallas said.

"The thief had to know how to change those details."

"Damn, we're smart . . . unless some hacker in cyber space got lucky."

"Not likely," Ruthie said.

"Okay then, that means everyone at HCU, First National, the Bridge Foundation and their brokerage firm is a suspect."

Ruthie finished off her wine. "Look at it from the bright side. The more suspects there are, the less chance of the thief being you."

Dallas threw a dishtowel at her.

Ruthie left after a cup of coffee, a brownie, and a good laugh. Dallas turned on the dishwasher and headed upstairs to bed. After washing her face and donning a cotton nightgown, she climbed in bed and clicked on the television. The glare of the local news cast shadows across the bed and she snuggled in a pillow. A story about the upcoming hurricane season nearly put her to sleep. Then she heard "Houston Cullen University" and rolled back toward the screen.

The newscaster stood in front of Brennan Hall, the main

administration building on campus, and provided the bare essentials of the theft. No one on campus was interviewed. Dallas didn't know if that was a good thing or a bad thing. It seemed strange that the theft of $25 million from a local institution hadn't generated more interest from the media.

She clicked off the TV, rolled over, and punched the pillow. Damn, what a lousy day. Would the police eventually find the Gregory James e-mail? Would Scooter or the police actually consider her a suspect? Well, hell, she'd prove them all wrong.

$ $ $

Scooter called mid-morning on Saturday. And bless him, he didn't mention yesterday's chewing out but he did say that Detective Phillips had contacted him and the police now considered the loss of the $25 million a crime. Dallas agreed to meet him at the office on Monday morning. He would need her around for moral support.

After loading the dryer with towels, she left for a noon spinning class at the local Sugar Land fitness club. The club bordered the Southwest Freeway on the edge of the Sienna Colony Shopping Center. She parked on the freeway side, a minor miracle for a Saturday, then stepped on the sidewalk and stopped. What the hell was this? Exiting through the mall doors were Bill Jenkins, the VP of development at HCU and Rebecca Holland, holding hands. He must have returned to Houston last night.

Bill disengaged his hand when he noticed Dallas.

Rebecca spoke first. "Hi, how are you?"

"Hey y'all, didn't expect to see you in the suburbs." Her curiosity was sparked instantly as neither Bill nor Rebecca lived in Sugar Land.

Bill lifted a shopping bag. "We picked up some donor gifts from a specialty shop in the mall. Looks like you're on your way to the fitness club we passed."

"Spinning." She glanced at her watch. "I'm late. I'll see you on Monday."

"Enjoy your class." Bill pulled Rebecca's elbow and they moved to the parking lot.

Rebecca turned to look Dallas as she walked away. Their eyes met, then Rebecca grinned.

During the class, Dallas thought about Bill and Rebecca and why they were shopping together, and in Sugar Land rather than Houston. She didn't believe their explanation about donor gifts as most of HCU's local vendors delivered. Plus, she didn't trust Rebecca, and Bill was so damned charming. But . . . they were both unattached and could do whatever they had a mind to do, including canoodling with a co-worker.

She arrived home within an hour, invigorated from her workout and drenched in sweat. After a quick shower, she pulled towels out of the dryer then scratched out a grocery list. Her pantry needed restocking and she had a new recipe for stuffed chicken breasts she wanted to test. Once in the car, she decided to visit her grandmother as she hadn't talked to her in a couple of days. She headed to Houston, rather than the grocery store.

Nana had lived in the same southwestern ranch house for forty years. Dallas' grandfather had built the home for Nana, the love of his life. He'd only been able to spend a decade in the it, before dying of a heart attack. Dallas had many wonderful memories of her grandmother and the house, especially the aroma of baking bread and pumpkin pies and brownies. Holidays were her specialty. Nana ensured the first view of Santa's gifts under the tree on Christmas morning was magical. Plus, she was a school bake sale queen with her peanut butter cookies.

Dallas knocked her usual three short raps before letting herself in through the side door. Nana stood at the kitchen counter dressed in a bathrobe, fussing with a coffee pot.

"Nana, are you feeling okay?"

She jumped then turned. "What are you doing here? I don't remember that you were coming by today." She belted the robe a notch tighter and smoothed a hand over her short silver hair.

"Spur of the moment decision."

Nana did a thing with her mouth, eyed the level of coffee

grounds in the pot. "Very sweet but you really should call first."

"Sorry. What's with the bathrobe in the middle of the afternoon?" Dallas' stomach twirled. Good Lord, was Nana hiding an illness—cancer, heart disease, or Alzheimer's?

A man she'd never seen before walked in the kitchen. His bathrobe matched Nana's. Huh? He walked over to her, kissed her cheek then noticed Dallas. "Uh, sweetie, I didn't realize we had company." Surprise, then apprehension crossed his face.

"Bob, this is my granddaughter, Dallas." Nana patted his arm. She nudged her slight body against his. "Dallas, this is Bob Marshall."

She shook Bob's hand while a dozen questions zigzagged across her mind. Who was this man? What did he mean to Nana? Was she dating?

"Nice to meet you, Bob." Dallas wondered why she'd never heard about him. She tamped down her concern with a plan to call her grandmother the next day for all the details on Bob. "I dropped by to see if you had gathered those pictures yet."

Nana scrunched her face.

"Remember, the ones you took of the twins in high school for the collage, the collage for my study."

"I remember," Nana said. "We just talked about it on Tuesday. I haven't gone through all my prints yet. I'll do it next week."

"That'll work."

"Would you like some coffee? It's Dutch Chocolate." Nana was a connoisseur of flavored coffees.

"No, I better get to the store." Dallas turned to Bob and his blue eyes twinkled. "It was a pleasure meeting you. Any friend of Nana's has my full attention."

"You're just as Mary Anne described you. Enjoy the produce section." Bob was one crafty charmer with those blue-blue eyes.

Dallas kissed Nana good-bye and left through the kitchen. She'd Google Bob when she got home. Nana's welfare was her responsibility and she'd not let some charming senior citizen take advantage of her grandmother.

TWO

Monday, 7:16 a.m.

HER HCU OFFICE WAS QUIET when Dallas arrived on Monday morning. After loading the coffee pot, she settled at her desk for an e-mail check. The Texas section of the *New York Times* daily news link included an article about HCU: "Houston Cullen University Discloses Theft of $25 Million Gift." Dr. Arnold, the HCU president, had wasted no time in issuing a press release once he returned to Houston. Dallas agreed that going public sooner rather than later was a good strategic move. She tapped a red pen against the desktop. Being honest showed they weren't hiding anything and that should make their donors happy.

She scrolled through the remaining messages, replied to a couple and deleted the rest. Grabbing a mug off the credenza, she headed to the coffee bar. She poured a cup, leaned against the counter sipping the coffee, and considered the obvious.

Development hated her, Scooter didn't support her like he should, and the Gregory James e-mail had yet to be resolved. On the plus side, she had proper accounting controls in place and she wasn't responsible for the theft. But she was curious how it had occurred.

On the way back to her office, she decided to check on the newest addition to the accounting staff who was alone in the accountants' office.

"Good morning. I suppose you've heard the news." Dallas stopped in front of the desk.

"Sure did, on the Saturday evening news. Wow, twenty-five million dollars." The new accountant was young and still learning her job.

"I agree. It's hard to believe." She sipped the coffee. "I think we should verify that no other gifts are missing, even small ones. I need to review all the gift analyses through April. How far have you gotten?"

"March," the newbie said.

"Great." She was surprised and relieved at the progress. "Have you found anything that doesn't look right?"

The newbie pulled out a green pressboard file, rifled through it, then selected a single sheet of paper and placed it in the center of her desk. The paper was a printed schedule with columns of dates, names, and dollar amounts. Pointing to it she said, "I can't locate the matching cash receipts for these gifts recorded by Development."

Dallas leaned over the desk. The dollar amounts ranged from five-hundred to twenty-thousand dollars. She recognized the names of consistent HCU donors.

"The gift dates go back to January, about the time your predecessor left." She studied the schedule. It showed gifts recorded but no cash and a dollar total of sixty-five thousand dollars. Coincidence? "May I have this copy?"

"Sure, I'll have April done by tomorrow. I'm faster now that I've figured out the process." The young accountant chuckled and handed Dallas the schedule.

"You're doing a great job. It takes time to learn the steps. E-mail the updated list once it's finished." Dallas gave her a thumb's-up and returned to her office.

The first task was to e-mail Rebecca concerning the gifts on the schedule. She hoped Rebecca might feel some pressure to continue to be cooperative, considering the theft of the $25 mil related directly to her department. Dallas typed the newbie's list and pointed out that the Finance Office hadn't been able to match bank deposits to Development's gift input. Would Development be reversing the gifts, or did she possess additional information? No screwing around, were they legitimate gifts? Where was the cash?

She clicked send and the phone rang. Scooter summoned her to his office. She slurped coffee, realigned her new energizer bra, and gathered her usual red pen and spiral notebook.

He wasn't alone. Detective Phillips lounged at the small conference table, chewing on a coffee stirrer. Coffee sloshed in her stomach. Was he there to question her?

Scooter waved her into the office. "I'm sure you remember Detective Phillips from the other night." Scooter's face appeared flushed, no doubt his blood pressure was rocketing. She didn't want to heighten his stress level so she'd be on her best behavior.

"Good morning, Detective Phillips." She plastered on a nervous smile.

He smiled, sort of, the left corner of his mouth moved upwards, revealing a dimple. He nodded in her direction.

She joined them, ready for the detective's interrogation. Sitting across from him, she placed her hands in her lap. No need for the two men to witness the tremors.

"As you can imagine, there is a considerable amount of detailed work in getting to the bottom of this theft." Scooter stared at Dallas as he spoke. "We feel it would be in our best interest to have someone familiar with University procedures to work directly with the police. Dr. Arnold and I have thoroughly discussed this." His gaze moved to an empty clay bowl in the center of the table. "We both believe you are the most logical choice. You know both the treasury side and the gift side." His focus turned back to Dallas and his head bobbed. "We expect you to be our point person with the police."

Point person! He thought she was a damned hunting dog? Wait, the detective wasn't there to question her? Relief rolled over Dallas . . . whew and thank you, Lord. Maybe this could work to her advantage. Keeping up with their activities would help with her own investigation. If she solved the theft, she'd be the toast of the University, could prove that the Gregory James e-mail was bogus, and maybe, just maybe, Scooter would realize she was a team player. Fine, she'd be the HCU point person—woof, woof.

"I'll be happy to help. What exactly does a point person do?"

"Mr. Taylor, I'd like to answer that." The detective folded his hands on the table. "Miss Wells, I need to understand all there is to know about these donor gifts. Who, what, how, in one word—everything."

"I'll do whatever I can to assist you." She had to play nice so she could pump him for details of his investigation.

"Good. And call me Roddy," the detective said. "I'd like a tour of the Finance Office and an overview of the University's gift process."

"Scooter, I'll show Roddy around the office. Also, I'm flexible about working this week."

"Thanks. Your number one goal is to help the police with their investigation." Scooter's obvious relief at her agreement pleased Dallas. It felt good. To be honest, she wanted to find the thief before Scooter had a stroke. As his subordinate, she'd be out of line in telling him he should see a doctor, but he should.

Roddy stood. "Are you ready?"

She rose and moved to the doorway. "It's time for the ten-cent tour."

She heard his footsteps behind her as they moved down the hall. The next problem was to ditch him, without him becoming suspicious. She had some poking around to do before becoming the perfect point person.

"How many people work in the Finance Office?" he asked.

"Let me think." She counted noses on her fingertips. "Thirteen."

"Small office. Anyone who doesn't fit in with the group?"

Didn't he have a better question? "Yeah, me, I'm the odd ball, too smart for my own good."

She paraded through the various points of interest, introducing Roddy to the treasurer, to the student counselors, and to the procurement staff. She managed to keep her mouth shut as well, offering no extraneous information.

The last leg of the tour led to her office. Roddy plopped in a guest chair and she sat behind her desk, ready for his questions.

"Fire away. What do you need to know?" If Dallas were

asking the questions she'd want to know . . . well, never mind, this was his show.

"What's your favorite brand of food?" he asked.

"Brand? You mean like Mexican or Italian?"

"Yeah."

"Mexican, I suppose."

"I'm hungry. Let's get lunch." He stood, waited for her to follow. She remained in her chair.

"Detective—"

"Roddy."

"Roddy, we can talk here," she said.

"I'm hungry. Let's go, my treat."

Could she decline a free lunch offered by a police officer? No. They left even though it was barely past eleven o'clock. She figured a one-hour meal wouldn't be so bad and maybe she'd learn about all the evidence and clues thus far discovered by HPD.

They agreed on Café Taco, a trendy Mexican eatery a few blocks from HCU. Although the food was delicious, it wasn't a favorite of Dallas'. During her divorce, she learned her ex-husband would meet his girlfriend of the month at the restaurant. She told Ruthie that the frozen margaritas inspired extra-marital sex—molto spicy.

The waiter arrived as soon as they were handed menus. Within ten minutes, she eyed a taco salad and Roddy, beef fajitas.

Dallas swallowed one bite of salad before the questions began. Detective Phillips wasn't a man to waste time.

"Tell me about the Bridge Foundation."

"Don't know much. They've made small and large gifts to HCU over the past few years. None of the checks bounced. That's about it."

"I need more detail. Have you had contact with anyone at the foundation?"

"No one, other than Logan Rice the other night. The Development Office deals directly with donors." She wanted to find out what he'd learned about the theft since Friday. The best way to get him to open up was to play it smart and help him along.

"Perhaps it would help if I explained the process to you." Although she'd offered the clarification, her brain groaned in protest. This had to be the thousandth time she'd explained the gift process. With a new audit staff every year and Scooter's lousy memory, she labeled herself a talking monkey, babbling accounting procedures.

"Good idea. Fire away." Roddy was one agreeable cop.

"This is the short version." She took a sip of iced tea, gathered her thoughts. *Keep it simple.* Her monologue began as though she were training a new accountant.

He interrupted her immediately.

"I need to know the whole process. Don't worry about it being too detailed. I took a year of accounting in college so I know a debit from a credit."

A man intimate with debits and credits—a dream come true.

"You asked for it. I won't short you on the details," she said.

"Start." He stuffed a flour tortilla filled with beef, onions, and cheese into his mouth.

After a calming breath, Dallas once again launched into training mode.

"As you already know, the Development Office is responsible for soliciting donations from individuals and organizations. We receive gifts as cash, checks, a stock certificate, and once in a while a work of art or real estate. And, on occasion, a wire transfer is used for a cash donation. We—"

"How do you determine the value of a piece of land or a stock certificate?"

Excellent question. He was listening while devouring his lunch.

"For real estate, we obtain an appraisal. For a stock certificate, we use the ending market value on the date of the certificate. Okay so far?" She forked a bite of salad for energy. It was nerve-racking explaining a complicated process in such simple terms.

"Yep, makes sense." Roddy poked his fork in the air. "Keep going."

"Development receives the gift, knows its value, and records it in their computer system according to its purpose like a scholarship or the annual fund. The cash and checks are walked over to the Finance Office daily along with a printed list of the gifts entered that day."

Roddy scrunched his eyes for a second. "How do you know all the cash and checks received by Development are processed and sent to the accounting office?"

Damn. Why the hell did he ask that?

"We assume HCU employees are honest. Donors call if they don't receive an acknowledgment for their charitable tax deduction. The donation received letter is automatically created once a gift is input to the donation system."

He rubbed his chin. "A phone call from a donor is the only verification a gift wasn't received and put in the system?"

The detective wasn't a dummy. His question mirrored an issue she'd struggled with more than once with the Development staff and a lack of good controls. One of the reasons they butted heads.

"I guess you could say that but we've had very few problems with gifts not being recorded. The—"

"What problems have you had?" Roddy's smile lost the dimple.

"If you keep interrupting me, we'll be here until midnight."

"No problem. I get off at five, so then we can order a beer." He smiled, dimples re-emerging. Then cop mode skidded back into place. "What problems have you had with missing donations?"

"Every once in a while, a gift check isn't sent to Development. The Finance Office cashier inputs it as something else, usually as a student payment." Roddy didn't interrupt so she rambled on. "Eventually the error is discovered and the information is sent to Development."

"I'll accept that for now." He pushed his chair back, drummed his fingers on the table. "How do you know the Finance Office gets all the cash for gifts entered in the donation system?"

Dallas' dilemma in answering the question ricocheted between evading it all together and overloading him with detail. She sipped her tea, folded, then unfolded the napkin on her lap. Might as well tell him everything.

"We have a process. One of the accountants receives the checks and the list of gifts from Development. The accountant verifies each physical check is on the list and notes the correct bank account. The checks are handed over to the cashier who inputs them to the cash system then deposits them to the bank. Okay so far?"

"Yeah, but that's all?" He munched a chip. "You don't have any other procedures to make sure all the cash is deposited?"

She blew out a breath. Did he think they were all dummies in higher education? She was paranoid about proper accounting procedures but had no control over Development, unfortunately. She might as well answer his question directly.

"We have other procedures. At the end of each month, we reconcile gift revenue to the bank deposits. It's performed through our gift suspense accounts. When the gifts and cash are recorded separately, the other side of the transaction is the same gift suspense account. We verify each gift has both a debit from the gift and a credit from the cash deposited to the bank." Dallas placed the folded napkin on her plate, settled into her role as the HCU point person. This would work out fine. "Remember, debits equal credits. The dollar amount for the gift revenue and the cash deposit must agree. You know how accountants are, everything must tick and tie."

"I get the picture." Roddy looked at his watch. "Want dessert? I've got several more questions."

"No thanks." She scooted the chair back, crossed her legs. "By the way, I have a couple of questions for you. First, what have you looked at so far—HCU employees, the wire instructions, the bank's involvement? What exactly? And second, do you have a forensics team on the case?"

"Forensics?"

"Yeah, they always do that on television." As soon as the

words tracked over her lips, Dallas' face heated like a sparkler on the Fourth of July.

Roddy ignored it. He waved to the waiter, who arrived with the check. "You don't need to be one bit concerned about police procedures. That's why I'm here."

"I want to help you. To do that, I need to understand the full scope of your investigation. I can handle the truth of whatever you uncover."

"I don't doubt that." He studied the check, met her gaze. "Truth is, I'm police, you're civilian." He shrugged. "That's the way the system works."

"Will you call in the FBI?" she asked.

"That's classified for civilians." He flashed a grin.

Damn. He refused to answer every question she threw at him. Maybe he did think she was the thief and he was playing with her. Did he already know about the Gregory James e-mail? She wanted to shout she was innocent.

Instead, she lowered her voice. "I understand you have procedures. Give me something to work with. Let me help you." She leaned over the table. "I can't help the police if I don't have a complete picture of what's going on."

"That's the way we, meaning the Houston police, work. I ask, you answer."

Dallas opened her eyes wide and shot him her most earnest look. "Don't forget, I'm the HCU point person."

Rather than agreeing with her, Roddy doubled over in a fit of laughter. She wondered if he was in pain considering the tears in his eyes. He finally noticed her glare and the clatter of her tapping foot.

"Sorry." He leisurely wagged a finger in front of her face. "You just looked so damned . . . forget it." Silence. After a couple of beats, he grinned, dimples winking. "Okay, I see your point."

"Thank you. Can't you give me an update?"

"Yes, ma'am," he said, stirring his iced tea with a straw. "We have nothing concrete, no major suspects, and no smoking gun. We're in the investigative part of the investigation."

Dallas could imagine his excuses revving up. He wouldn't say a damned thing to help her. "Are you saying that nothing—"

"As I was saying, we're basically doing legwork now. Today, we sent a technical team to First National and we're looking into the background of everyone who had prior knowledge of the wire. It's all standard procedure."

"Glad to hear standard procedure is still in vogue."

"Don't be snippy, Dallas."

"Wouldn't think of it, detective." It was her turn to grin. "Are you looking at the financial background of HCU employees? For instance, has anyone made a large purchase lately?"

"Absolutely." Roddy stood, threw some bills on the table. "I've got work to do and so do you. Let's go." He grabbed her elbow, directed her to the door

"But . . ." She had several more questions. Apparently, they would have to wait. He ushered her to his police-issue vehicle and drove quickly back to campus. After dumping her on the sidewalk without a thank you for the information she'd provided or even a good-bye, he roared down the street. At lunch he moseyed along like molasses running down a spoon, and now he was in a hurry? Did their conversation give him a great idea to investigate? An idea he didn't bother to tell her. Damn that cop.

Back at her desk, Dallas stared at a blank computer screen. What was her first step to locate the missing money? She transitioned from a somewhat confused point person to accounting mode and pulled out a yellow pad. Her best thinking was always on paper.

She jotted down an initial check list: review wire instructions, obtain phone numbers for donors of missing gifts, research electronic fund transfers, review updated gift suspense analyses, consider who at HCU might be involved, talk to First National and the Bridge Foundation.

She stuffed the paper in her purse, then called Daniel, the nice guy in the Development Office who performed the daily data entry. As usual, he was as sweet as jelly beans and accessed the phone numbers she needed from the donor records. She jotted them down along with the home addresses he threw in as a bonus. Check one on the to-do list. She had already made progress.

The office phone rang.

"It's Rebecca."

"What's up?"

"I've been looking into the list of gifts you e-mailed earlier. It'll take me a couple days to thoroughly review each one. Daniels's researching a couple of them for me."

"Glad to hear that. Some of these missing checks might be related to the theft. You've got to admit, it's quite a coincidence."

"I hadn't considered they might be related to the missing gift. I assumed it was a paperwork mistake. But not to worry, we'll get to the bottom of it." Rebecca sounded sincere. "I'll get back to you as quick as I can."

"Thanks. The sooner the better for all of us." Dallas was skeptical of Rebecca acting nice with her. The last couple of days weren't typical of their interactions.

"I'll do my best to have something by Wednesday or Thursday at the latest. I know this is important."

Dallas *knew* Rebecca was playing with her. She'd never before been concerned about Dallas' convenience in the eight years they'd worked together. Maybe Dr. Arnold or Bill had given her orders about cooperating with the accounting staff—about damned time.

She left a voice mail for Scooter letting him know she'd talked with the detective. She stuffed the campus directory in her purse and headed home. She didn't feel right doing internet research on HCU employees at the office. It made her feel a bit slimy even though Scooter had asked her to assist the police. If she did uncover a clue implicating someone at HCU, she'd rather be at home, where she could scream at deaf walls.

$ $ $

Dallas poured a glass of iced tea, then fired up the laptop in her study and logged onto the internet. She needed to know the nitty-gritty of how electronic funds transfers were completed. After a few queries, she knew the basics. The transfer from the Bridge Foundation was a wire transfer and the funds were good on the day of the transfer, i.e. ready to be credited to the HCU account at First National Bank. This meant the window of opportunity for interrupting the transfer was narrow.

"I'd make a great detective," she muttered.

She felt certain her earlier conclusion was correct—the thief had to be at the bank, the foundation, or the brokerage firm.

She continued her online search and learned that certain information was required for a wire transfer: the originating institution's ABA routing number and the sending account number, the receiving bank's ABA number and the recipient's account number, and of course, the dollar amount of the transfer. There was a protocol as to how the originating bank organized all the various pieces of information.

The Bridge Foundation knew all the necessary bits of data as did their brokerage firm. Ta-dah, her fist thumped the desk. The instructions must have been changed at either the brokerage firm or First National, not at the university. Dallas jumped out of her chair to perform the happy dance then headed for the kitchen.

Her stomached growled but nothing sounded appetizing. She stared at the contents of the refrigerator for a good thirty seconds then pulled out an open bottle of wine. She poured a glass of chardonnay and went to the living room to watch the news.

A local channel had an update on the HCU theft. Roddy's face appeared on the screen. He looked good on TV. She turned up the volume to hear the interview.

"Detective Phillips, this is a most unusual theft for an institution like Houston Cullen University. When did you start your investigation?" The newscaster shoved a huge microphone in his face.

"Last Friday evening," he answered.

"Have you determined how the theft was carried out?"

"We're pursuing several leads at this time." The microphone wiggled beneath Roddy's chin.

"Do you have a list of suspects yet?" The newscaster smiled at the camera, not at Roddy.

"We're pursuing several leads at this time," he repeated.

"Detective, please tell our viewers about your investigation. Will you be making an arrest soon?"

Amazing that Roddy could remain calm in front of such a nitwit reporter. His rating went up a notch.

"Ma'am, we're in the middle of several things right now and nothing is firm. You'll be the first to know once we're ready to make an arrest." Roddy smirked to the camera while the interviewer turned away from him and faced the camera alone, ending the spot.

Not for a minute did she believe the police hadn't made progress. They weren't about to tell the news media, or her, what had been discovered. Roddy had been a real zero at lunch. She'd answered all his questions and presented a good review of the Development and Finance offices but he hadn't told her one meaningful thing about the investigation. Well, other than the fact that the police were investigating. Duh.

She wondered if he he'd uncovered anything derogatory about the finances of HCU employees. Dallas knew her own situation wouldn't provide much to keep him amused. What about everyone else? She had access to the annual salary of every employee and knew that no one, other than Dr. Arnold, was getting rich working at a private university. Perhaps that alone translated to a motive for grabbing the money—stealing from your employer because you thought your salary was too low. The reasoning seemed lame, but then again, Dallas wasn't a crook.

Comparing a person's salary to their standard of living would require some effort. The easiest approach would be to concentrate on employees who appeared to be living beyond their HCU salary—those with a home in a ritzy neighborhood or owning a fancy car. She could obtain the house values from the local appraisal district and a list of employee vehicles from campus security.

Dallas went back to the kitchen for a snack—red grapes,

wheat crackers, and a wedge of brie. The phone rang as she poured another glass of wine.

"Mom, what's up?"

"Liz! How are you feeling?" Dallas knew pregnancy was a natural thing for a woman but nevertheless, she worried about Liz, the somewhat spacey half of her twin daughters. Early on she had concluded that worrying is a mom thing. Only four more weeks to go then she'll switch her fretting from Liz to her first grandbaby.

"Mom." She imagined Liz rolling her eyes. "I'm fine. I had an appointment with Dr. Bender today. I'm right on schedule for my due date."

"Sleeping okay?"

"Good enough. What's up with that theft at HCU?"

"Not much to tell, the police are involved. I had lunch today with the lead detective."

"I saw him on the news, kinda cute in an old guy sort of way," Liz said. At twenty-four she had yet to realize she would age past thirty.

"I don't see the cute part but I guess he knows his stuff. Make sure Dirk takes out the trash, not you." Dirk was a corporate attorney, a bit on the anal side but she couldn't fault his husband skills, except for the trash.

"Moooom," Liz said with a huff. "I'll talk to you later."

With the phone still in her hand, Dallas called Ruthie.

"Guess what? I'm the University's liaison with the cops on the theft." It sounded dumb saying that out loud.

"No kidding. Are you working with that cutie of a detective I saw on the news?" Dallas could hear Ruthie's cupid wheels revving up. One of her favorite pastimes was finding dates for Dallas.

"Uh-huh, he's a cutie all right. We went to lunch today and I couldn't get one piece of information out of him."

"Talked too much, huh?"

"No, hell no. I was a good HCU employee and answered all his questions. He refused to answer mine. He's police, I'm civilian. Total crap." Just telling Ruthie pissed her off. She needed to work on her temper. Surely, she wasn't menopausal. Forty-four was much too young to even consider it.

"Sorry lunch was a waste for you."

"Me, too, but that's not why I called. I have a couple of technical questions for you." Ruthie was an IT manager for an international oil company downtown. She'd be a good source for brainstorming about the wire transfer.

"Ask away."

"I'd rather talk to you in person. Do you have time if I stop by your office tomorrow?"

They ended the call with Ruthie's agreement to a meeting time.

Dallas made a bee-line for the study and reviewed her to-do list. It reminded her of Rebecca, who she doubted would actually provide any useful information about the missing gifts. Dallas would dig it out herself by calling donors first thing in the morning.

The last chore was to send an e-mail to the HCU security chief for a list of registered employee vehicles. She indicated the data was needed first thing Tuesday morning since she was sending the request at Scooter's directive. That should ensure a quick turnaround.

Dallas pushed back from the desk, stared at the computer monitor. Was she wasting her time with all this research? Could she really investigate the theft on her own? After all, what did she know about investigating a cybercrime? Not much, but her to-do list was a start. And she was one hell of a fast learner.

$ $ $

Houston, Monday Evening

The doorbell rang, once then twice. A bright blue door opened, inviting the entrance of a co-conspirator who was also a lover. Rebecca Holland strutted to the middle of the living room and glared at Bill Jenkins pouring a drink at the wet bar.

"Fuck it. Fuck it." She slammed a palm on the bar counter. "This is getting out of hand. That bitch is asking ridiculous questions about checks not being deposited. Who gives a shit? And catch this, she's the *point person* for the university with the Houston police. How lame."

"I heard, but it's no big deal. I'll do something to slow her down. Champagne?" He pushed a flute in her hand.

She accepted the glass. "Thanks for the offer. But I'll take care of her myself. It might be fun."

"I thought you were getting jumpy."

She noticed his cool appraisal of her. She composed her face with a charming smile. "I was earlier, but now, I've discovered the key to staying calm." She drained the glass and held it out for a refill.

He poured more champagne while chuckling. "There's a key to keeping your cool? I've always considered it a personality trait. Either you've got it or you don't. Do you?" He walked around to her side of the bar.

"How tiresome of you to even question me." Her eyes sparked briefly with anger then she moved a step back from him. "Of course, I do. I'll stay cool knowing this is almost over and the money is ours. Little Miss Dallas is nothing more than a temporary inconvenience."

"Good, keep that attitude. Did you pick up the airline tickets for Zurich?"

"Sure did. We leave Saturday afternoon just as we've planned all these months." She winked at him over the rim of her glass.

"Remember to keep your normal schedule." He began to pace along the length of the bar. "We don't want to blow this at the end."

She watched him, loathing filled her every pore. "Who's getting jumpy now? Believe me when I say I'm as cool as a cucumber."

The pacing stopped directly in front of her. He poked an index finger against her chest. "You better be cool. I don't want this fucked up. It's taken too long to plan. You'll take care of Dallas, right?"

She winked at him. "Are you ready for the real deal?" She casually pushed his finger down and back against his chest.

"What the hell are you talking about?" he barked, placing his hands on her forearms, bearing down. "Don't you dare push me."

She was strong and her arms broke free. She reached to her back. A knife blade flashed in the glare of the bar light and in front of his surprised face. It slashed down, again and again, slicing his chest and abdomen. His body made a slow assault to the oak floor. Blood gurgled from his mouth and chest and began its inevitable passage into the grain of the wood.

Rebecca studied the wilted body—disgusting. The sight of him made her want to vomit. A revolting example of a man, let alone her so-called partner. She had much, much better taste than a pansy like him. She kicked the side of his hip, careful to avoid blooding smearing her shoe. Nothing, no movement. Good.

She was so sick of him. One life had ended, and more importantly, her life had finally begun. She deserved it.

THREE

Tuesday, 6:03 a.m.

DALLAS WOKE AT HER NORMAL time the next morning. It was too early to start contacting donors of the missing gifts. She considered watching the news in bed, but guilt won. She grabbed a bottle of water from the refrigerator and headed to the treadmill in the study. Some exercise should curb her annoyance at having to wait three hours to make the calls.

Running was a favorite activity, next to TV movies, and reading mystery novels. She'd solved many a problem the last couple of years striding along the endless road of circulating rubber track.

She walked, then jogged watching the morning news while gulping water and sweating out her last color job. After a while, she stopped listening to the repetitive news of terrorism, congress, and the transgressions of Hollywood celebrities. Her mind wandered back to the HCU theft and her earlier question. Why does someone steal in the first place? Because it's easier than working? out of desperation? because they can? to get attention or to prove something?

After an hour, she punched in a cool down code on the treadmill. It was time to get her butt in gear and do something useful.

She loaded the coffee pot, then showered, and ate a piece of toast smothered with raspberry jam. After three cups of coffee and yelling at the television about a stupid news story related to secret tunnels on the south Texas border, she heard the kitchen clock bong nine o'clock.

In the study, she leaned back in her scratched leather chair and dialed the first number on the donor list.

"Good morning, may I speak with Mrs. Graves?"

"This is she."

"This is Dallas Wells from Houston Cullen University. I hope it's not too early to call."

"No, I've been up since five." Her voice reminded Dallas of Nana.

"Glad I didn't catch you too early. I need to ask you about a $2,000 check you sent in this past March for the annual fund."

"I remember the check. Is there a problem?"

"No problem. I was wondering if the check had cleared your bank and if I might get a copy of it."

"I'm sure it came through but I don't get my checks back. They're listed on the statement." She paused. "Is this about the news story I saw on channel thirteen?"

"Yes, ma'am, we're checking a few gifts we've received as a precaution."

"Good for you, dear. Do you need anything else?"

Dallas repeated the same conversation another three times. Perhaps her idea that the gift checks had been deposited in a bank account other than one of HCU's wasn't such a dumb idea. But at this point, she had no evidence of what bank the checks had actually been deposited to. She had to get her hands on one of the cleared checks. Surely one of the donors on the list received cancelled checks with their bank statement.

She kept calling, emptying another bottle of water, all the while hoping her stomach could handle the stress of digging for a clue to the theft. She rummaged around in a desk drawer, found a couple of pink antacid tablets, chewed vigorously then shivered at the metallic taste.

She hit the lottery with Jack Franks and a $20,000 gift last February. Both of his children were HCU grads, apparently satisfied ones, thus prompting him to donate every year. HCU loved motivated donors.

Mr. Franks received cleared checks with his bank statement

since it was a business account and said he'd be happy to dig around for them in his home files. Dallas made an appointment to meet him around noon. She hoped the back of his cancelled check would have the stamp of the depositing bank along with an account number. If it wasn't HCU's, then whoever stole the $25 million might be involved with this missing gift. At least that was her working theory.

She grabbed her purse and headed for the garage. She had enough time to swing by First National before meeting Mr. Franks. Dallas knew Lynne Harris, HCU's account executive, on a semi-personal basis and hoped she'd be available without an appointment.

$ $ $

First National's main office was located in downtown Houston, occupying several floors of Mitchell Center. The lobby was opulent and screamed Texas oil rich. Green marble covered the floor and walls, while glass and metal sculptures depicting Texas history were scattered throughout the space. A twenty-foot tall oil derrick of twisted metal graced the lobby's center.

Lynne had worked with HCU for a number of years. Due to the bank's prominence in the Houston business community, she knew most of the movers and shakers on a first-name basis. Dallas hoped she would be straight about the bank's position on the theft. The receptionist ushered her into Lynne's office in less than five minutes.

"Thanks for seeing me so quickly."

"Not a problem. I need a break anyway. Balance sheets all look the same after the fiftieth one." Lynne was well suited for the role of a banker—poised, soft spoken, Harvard graduate. Her outward veneer of charming relationship builder disguised a smooth-talking shark when it came to bank business.

"I'm here about the theft."

"I figured as much. Take a seat and we can talk."

Dallas sat in a guest chair, ran through her mental list of

questions.

She scrapped the list. "Has First National uncovered anything concrete about the funds not reaching HCU's account?"

"The police detective asked me the same thing about an hour ago. I'll tell you what I told him." Lynne straightened a pile of manila folders on her desk. "We're checking into whether the wire reached the bank's federal reserve account. If it did, we'll have a better idea of where the change of instructions occurred."

Dallas interpreted that to mean that five days after the fact, First National was clueless as to how the wire instructions had been altered.

"How long before you'll know?"

"Best guess is some time tomorrow." Lynne fiddled with a binder clip. "I suppose you've met the detective."

"Couldn't miss him." Dallas rolled her eyes. "Since I'm the university contact working with the police, I've had more than one meeting with him."

"I think he's kinda cute." Lynne did that smile-thing girls do when talking about a guy they might be interested in.

"You have my blessing in working with him," Dallas said. The cop was the polar opposite of her type, whatever that was.

"You don't like him?" Lynne leaned forward over her jumbled desktop, her voice soft. "Do you think he's married?"

Good grief, why do smart ass men have such an impact on strong women like Lynne? Hormones, loneliness, lust?

"Don't know, don't care." Lynne was such a good person, Dallas softened her reply. "I'll see if I can find out. I'm sure he'll be bothering me soon."

"Thanks. If he's single, I may ask him out for a drink one evening after work."

Lynne must be desperate for male companionship or really, really lonely. Or, maybe she encouraged new things in her life— probably a good attitude for a single lady.

"I'll give you a call if I discover he's single." Dallas would ask him, too. She thought Lynne was nuts, but . . . you go girl. "Back to the theft, do you have any idea how the instructions were changed?"

Lynne shook her head. "Depends on where and when the change was made. Once we determine that, we'll have some possibilities for you. I'll call once I get any concrete information. What number?"

"Use my cell. I hope you find something soon. The longer this drags out, the worse the publicity." Dallas stood, repeated her cell number. "Thanks, again. I'll let you know about the detective's marital status."

"And you'll hear from me as soon as I hear from the fraud department."

After leaving the bank, Dallas headed toward the Memorial area of Houston to meet the donor, Jack Franks. It was a beautiful day for the twenty-minute drive from the high-rise towers of downtown to wooded residential neighborhoods intertwined with winding streets and cul-de-sacs. She rolled down the window and turned up the radio, enjoying Michael Jackson on an oldie's station.

After one wrong turn, she found the right street nestled between a tree-lined boulevard and Buffalo Bayou. The house was a sprawling ranch with a front circular driveway surrounded by lush landscaping. She parked behind a silver Mercedes coupe.

The massive front door opened after the bell's first chime.

A handsome blue-eyed man stood before her. She might change her attitude on relationships if she dated a man who looked like this one.

"You must be Dallas. I'm Jack Franks. Please come in."

She followed him through a red-tiled foyer to a wide hall. The southwestern décor—heavy furniture, bright colors, and a cow skull on a wall—reminded her of the Texas history museum in Austin.

He led her to a large, masculine study at the end of the hall. The bottom floor of her townhouse would easily fit in it with square footage to spare.

"Have a seat." He pointed to a pair of club chairs facing a gigantic desk.

"Thank you for seeing me on such short notice." She settled on the butterscotch leather with a sigh.

"No problem. Would you care for a drink? Wine or a Bloody Mary?" He stood beside a dark oak bar that dominated one side of the study.

"No, thanks." It was a bit early but that didn't stop him from pouring a generous amount of golden liquor, probably scotch, into a crystal tumbler. He settled in the other chair.

"Dallas, love your name by the way, what can I do for you?" He sipped the drink, smacking his lips. "You have a question about my gifts to the university?"

"Not a question exactly. If it's not too much trouble, I'd like to borrow one of your cancelled checks. I'll make a copy and promptly return it to you."

"Sounds easy enough. I'll make a copy right here. Sure you don't want a glass of wine? Lunch will be ready in fifteen minutes." He beamed, nodded his head toward the foyer. "Our Darla is an excellent cook."

"Lunch sounds wonderful but I have to get back to the office." She faked a check of her watch. His drinking before noon had put her on alert. "I have a meeting in thirty minutes."

"Another time perhaps?" He flashed a set of perfect veneers. "Does this relate to the story I saw on the news last night? Something about a large gift being stolen? I'll be damned upset if any of the money I've given to HCU ends up in some other pocket."

"This isn't related at all. It's for our annual audit. The auditors continue to invent new data requests. This year it's a handful of gift checks." Yes, she was ad-libbing and lying. However, the auditors could very well make this type of request in the future, especially if she suggested it to them.

He downed the rest of the drink and stood. "What check number?"

"It's number 10542 written on February 6th."

"Probably cleared in February." At the bar again, he poured more liquor, then moved to a bank of file cabinets hugging the opposite wall and sat his glass on the top. He opened and slammed shut a couple of drawers before finding the one he wanted and rifled through its contents.

"Here's the February bank statement. What was that number again?" He took another long swallow of liquor.

"It's 10542. May I help?" The process needed to speed up. The amount of alcohol Mr. Franks had consumed in less than fifteen minutes was unnerving. Her dirty-old-man radar began to ping.

"Nope, it's here somewhere." His finger scratched across a piece of paper from the file. "Here it is, cleared on February 25th. Want a copy of the back, too?"

She nodded and the copies were in her hand before she rose from the chair. She was dying to look at the back of the check but didn't dare risk it in front him. The less he knew about her real motive, the better.

"Thanks again for the time, Mr. Franks." With the copies safely stowed in her purse, Dallas started toward the study door.

"Are you sure you don't have time for lunch?"

She sensed him close behind. "I can't miss the meeting. It's with my boss and he's a stickler for punctuality." It seemed like a good ten minutes before she reached the front door. She turned to shake his hand and damn near knocked him over. "Oops, sorry."

"No problem at all." Franks grabbed her hand. "I'll give you a call in a couple of days."

She could smell the liquor on his breath.

"To see if you need anything else. We can plan a lunch then."

Surprise fogged her brain for one second only. This guy was not her type. "Thanks again." She pulled her hand out of his grasp and hurried to the Volvo.

Mr. Franks remained standing on the front step as she put the wagon in gear and drove off. She waved exiting the driveway. Good riddance. No way would she meet that man for any meal. He was too pushy and too pickled.

Once she was out of sight of the house, Dallas pulled over to the curb. She couldn't wait any longer. If her hunch was right, she'd be one step closer to solving the theft and starting her vacation. She pulled out the copies and looked at the back. The printing was faint so she had to find her reading glasses.

What she found on the back of the check could be the beginning of her own investigation and proof that the Gregory James e-mail was a fraud. She took a calming breath, donned the glasses and looked at the copy. She couldn't make out one word or number. The printing was too small and too faint.

Getting older sucked. Even with the discount-store reading glasses she couldn't identify the details. She'd have to use a magnifying glass at home.

Dallas shrugged off her disappointment and focused on tasks still to accomplish. Next on her agenda was a visit to the Bridge Foundation. She didn't have an appointment and hoped simple surprise might get her in the door. She headed back to downtown Houston.

The Bridge Foundation had been a Houston institution for at least fifty years. It was founded on profits resulting from the discovery of drilling mud in 1901 and its use in almost every drill hole around the world ever since. Adolf Ricenski and his brother Joseph formed Rice Brothers International in 1902, shortened their last name to Rice, and made billions selling mud to drilling operations.

The Rice's were a conservative family, both in business and in private, who believed their wealth had a higher purpose than merely accumulating in bank accounts around the world. The foundation commenced operations in 1953 and was named after its purpose rather than the family. The mission was simple—to provide a bridge to a better life or purpose for its clients.

Dallas didn't know any of the Rice family personally, although she'd observed them around town a few times at a play or the symphony. She remembered reading that two or three of the great-grandchildren worked for the foundation, Logan Rice being one of them. Guess the family was civic minded, with silver spoons in their mouths.

Rice Center was another beautiful Houston office building.

Its sixty floors housed both RBI and the Bridge Foundation and Ruthie's office as well. After parking in the visitor section of the garage, Dallas hurried to the first floor. Pink marble graced the lobby along with a twenty-five-foot tall oak tree. The pink and dark green were a startling contrast to each other. Dallas studied the digital floor directory. The foundation was located on the forty-eighth floor. It was after the lunch hour so she hoped Logan or another Rice family member would be available for a chat.

The elevator doors opened to an unoccupied receptionist's desk and the waiting area. The room was paneled in dark oak with wine-colored ceiling-to-floor draperies bordering a wide window behind the desk. Two high-backed chairs in a wine-and-gold striped fabric along with a matching sofa occupied the waiting area. A plasma television situated on a wall displayed a cable news program.

She tapped her foot in front of the reception desk, patience not being one of her strong points. Where the hell was the receptionist? The gods were listening; a door adjacent to the desk opened. A young woman in a cute summer dress entered.

"Sorry to keep you waiting. How may I help you?" The name plaque on the desk read Amanda Moore.

"Yes, Amanda, you may. I'm Dallas Wells from Houston Cullen University. I'd like to speak with Logan Rice."

"I suppose this is about the missing funds." She smiled, perfect white teeth gleaming.

"There are several things. Is he available?"

"Mr. Rice is out of the office right now. Perhaps our PR director can meet with you. If you have a moment, I'll see if he's available." She motioned to the sitting area. "Please take a seat."

Dallas sat on the sofa and did her best to appear serene. It wasn't easy considering her mind rolled over whether someone related to the foundation stole the $25 million. Meanwhile, Amanda picked up the phone and spoke to someone.

Paging through an entertainment magazine, Dallas learned that celebrities apparently keep their svelte figures by eating raw foods only. Yummy.

Amanda summoned her. "Mr. Billy Rice will see you now. Please come with me."

She followed Amanda down a short hallway with offices along the sides and double doors at the end. They stopped at the second office on the left.

"This is Dallas Wells from Houston Cullen University."

She stepped into the office and met the man as he came around a large glass topped desk. "It's a pleasure to meet you, Mr. Rice."

They shook hands. He motioned for Dallas to sit in front of the desk without saying a word, then returned to his chair on the other side. He steepled his fingers in front of his chest and spoke.

"Miss Wells, I assume this visit is about the missing gift. You're wasting your time. We've already had a long discussion with the authorities."

"Thanks for seeing me on such short notice. I realize you've already spoken with the police. Since I'm the university's contact working with them, I need to verify a couple of items about the transfer."

"You should probably talk to my cousin. He dealt with the approval of the HCU grant request and the actual transfer. I do the public relations for the foundation."

"This must be a nightmare for you." It sure as hell was for her and she wasn't out $25 mil.

"It's not one of our better stories. My grandmother is going nuts."

"Really?" If it were Nana, she'd be spitting bullets.

"The whole grant to a local university scenario was her idea." He flipped a hand out. "She's taken the theft a bit personally. She believes the money was stolen to embarrass her."

"I have a grandmother and I know she wouldn't be happy."

"I think she's way off-base. My theory is that some bastard hacker got lucky."

"You might be right." Dallas had nothing else to learn from this man. "I appreciate your time, Mr. Rice. I'll make an appointment with your cousin."

He walked her to the door and they again shook hands. She hurried to the waiting area and Amanda.

"I need to make an appointment with Logan Rice, as soon as possible, please."

"I'll check his schedule." Amanda examined the computer screen, narrowing her eyes as though she were concentrating on brain surgery. "He has a few minutes available tomorrow morning at eleven-fifteen. Can you come back then?"

"Yes," Dallas started for the elevator. "Thanks again."

She damn near had a skip in her step. She'd made an initial contact with everyone related to the theft except for the brokerage firm. Ruthie was next. She punched the elevator button for the tenth floor, then called Ruthie to let her know she would soon have a visitor. This was too convenient.

The elevator opened to another receptionist area. Dallas waved her way in and headed for Ruthie's office. They met in the hallway and walked down the hall.

If she'd said it once, Dallas had said it a million times, working for corporate sure as hell paid off with a fantastic office—antique desk, small oak conference table with upholstered chairs, paintings, and a view.

"Glad you were free," Dallas said.

"Always available for you. How's it going being a point person?" Ruthie's lips curved up, although she tried to maintain a bland face.

"Everything is fine. I've been the perfect police contact." Dallas lowered her voice. "I've been doing some investigating on my own."

"You're nuts. Leave it to the police."

"I am." She tucked a stray hair behind an ear. "But . . . I feel the need to look into this on my own, just a little bit. I want to help Scooter even if he thinks I can't play nice with Development. I swear he's close to a stroke."

"All right, what can I do to help?"

"I think I understand the basics of how a wire transfer goes from point A to point B. I need to learn the inside scoop on how one might be interrupted," Dallas said.

"That shouldn't be too difficult." Ruthie transitioned from friend mode to professional mode.

Dallas grabbed a note pad and red pen from her purse, moved forward in the chair.

"The easiest explanation is that someone at the Bridge Foundation or their brokerage firm replaced HCU's instructions." Ruthie played with a jade dangly earring. "Or, the money was received on schedule at your bank and the change was made there."

"I've thought of those options as well." Dallas tapped a finger on her bottom lip. "What if the answer isn't so obvious?"

"If it were me, I'd have some fun with it and—"

"What about a hacker?" Dallas interrupted. "Maybe there's a person, say in China, who happened on the transfer while illegally poking around on a server." At least she assumed that's what hackers do.

"Another easy answer, but I don't think so. Think about the logistics." Ruthie's hands orchestrated her theory. "When someone hacks into a system's server, hundreds of messages and code scroll across their monitor. Unless they slice into the guts of the operating system, they can't control the speed of the scrolling." She stopped, looked out the window. "I think it's unlikely someone just happened to read the message containing the wire instructions and in a split second, changed HCU's account and routing numbers. It's probably more than one in a fifty million chance."

"I think I understand, scratch a hacker. I guess that means the revision of the instructions was intentional . . . and planned." *Someone really did want to screw with HCU.*

"Exactly. Let's talk about how and when the change was accomplished." The desk phone rang. "Excuse me while I get this."

While Ruthie answered the call, Dallas zeroed in on what they had just concluded—the theft of the $25 million, as it was in transit to HCU's bank account, had been deliberate and very well planned. Her gut told her that whoever planned the theft had to be associated with the university—an employee, a student, an alumnus, or a donor.

Ruthie finished her call. "Sorry, we have a new software app rolling out this evening and everyone's getting jumpy."

"We were discussing how the wire instructions could have been changed."

"Right. We've ruled out a hacker and concluded the switch was scheduled. I assume you want to know how the modification might have been accomplished without a staff member at the foundation, the brokerage firm or the bank simply replacing the bank and account information."

"That's what I'm asking." Dallas' fingers tapped a staccato rhythm on the arm of the chair. "That's too easy to do and much too easy to discover. Who'd be dumb enough? Whoever stole the money wanted to make a statement or is greedy."

"Possibly."

"Or, to settle a grudge."

"Another good possibility," Ruthie agreed. "Let's go back to how the crook might have gotten away with it."

Dallas noticed the sparkle in Ruthie's eyes. She was enjoying the mystery.

Ruthie continued. "If we assume there wasn't any collusion between the foundation, the brokerage firm, and First National, then the change may have been made systematically, independent of the three."

"Systematically? You mean with a computer program?" Thank heavens Dallas was talking to Ruthie, her brain had regressed back to third grade.

"Consider how a hacker might gain access to your PC at home." The phone rang again. Ruthie shrugged. "Gotta take the call."

She talked for less than a minute. "There's a problem with the roll out. I have to cut our conversation short. Duty calls."

Ruthie walked Dallas to the elevator. "Sorry I don't have more time. My best guess is that the wire instructions were changed by a mole."

"A mole?" A furry rodent?

She snapped the fingers of one hand. "Come on, Dallas, we've talked about this several times—a targeted virus that's released into the computer system of either the brokerage firm or the bank."

A voice shouted down the hall.

"Gotta go. I'll try to call you later." She gave Dallas a quick hug, then hurried in the direction of the shouting.

What the hell did she really mean by "mole" or "targeted virus?" Since Dallas had no clue, additional internet research was in store. What a day. It was time to head home, relax with a glass of wine, and gear up for more time on the computer.

Dallas retraced her steps to the Rice Center garage and headed the Volvo toward the Southwest Freeway.

She soon arrived at her townhouse to savor that glass of wine and discovered she wouldn't be drinking alone.

FOUR

Houston, Tuesday Evening

LOGAN RICE WAS A MAN ACCUSTOMED to order and now, more duty—civilian duty and duty to his family, to his family's business, and to the business of giving away money. Many would say "what a charmed life, you're lucky, no money worries like the rest of the middle class."

He didn't see his life through that particular pair of glasses.

Sure, he lived with the trappings of his family's wealth, but damn it, he wanted his old job back. Gazing at the Houston skyline through the window of his office, he rubbed the day's growth of beard with the palm of his hand. No, he wouldn't go there. He firmly slashed any thoughts of his former life from his mind. Reminiscing about his life as a special agent only made it worse.

"Logan."

He turned. "What's up, Billy?" Logan's cousin leaned against the doorframe.

"Wanted to let you know that a woman from Houston Cullen University came by today. She had questions about the theft." Billy moved to the small bar in the corner. "Want a bourbon?"

"Sure, why not?"

Billy poured two fingers, handed the glass to Logan, then poured a second glass.

Logan sipped the liquor, enjoying the end of the day.

"I heard she was here," Logan said. He remembered his reaction to her the other night. Distrusting her on one hand, yet attracted on the other. Her sparkling green eyes challenged him, while her full lips and ample breasts screamed *touch me*. He shook off his reaction. "Amanda said she made an appointment for tomorrow. What did she want?"

"Not much. Told her the idea for the grant was Gram's." Billy shrugged. "She said she'd talk to you since you handled the details."

"I met her at HCU last week. I've already talked to the police and Dr. Arnold and Bill Jenkins. I've said the same thing so many times, I'm a talking puppet." Logan didn't want to rehash the theft with another HCU employee, he wanted action. "Gram is pissed as hell. She pinned my ears to the wall on Sunday, again."

"I know," Billy nodded. "The whole family heard."

"Everyone?"

"Yep, the library door wasn't shut. Sorry, dude. Gram can still knock us on our ass."

"Isn't that the truth?" Logan's mouth curled at the thought of eighty-year-old Gram raising hell with her grandchildren. She held the family together like a drill sergeant. And that was no easy task considering the continually increasing number of Rice family members. Although Logan had personally avoided that family tradition, his cousins and brothers and sisters were propagating like rabbits.

"She's taking this personally." Billy added more bourbon to his glass. "Do you suppose the theft was meant to embarrass either the foundation or the family?"

"You mean like revenge?" Logan sat on the edge of his desk.

"Possibly. What about the foundation's board? Do we really know any of the members other than what's on a resume? Maybe one of them saw an easy chance to make a killing."

"We've worked with these people for years. I don't buy that." Logan shook his head. "But I suppose it wouldn't hurt to do a little checking."

"I'll call Greg in the morning," Billy suggested. "His security firm can do some quiet inquiries for us."

"Good idea. What about the university's staff? We should probably include them. Do you know anyone?"

"You're the one that dealt with them on the grant application.

I've only met the president and a couple of people from the Development Office. But I do remember one strange meeting."

Logan set the empty glass on his desk. "What the hell does that mean?"

"The gal that works with Bill Jenkins, Rebecca something, reminded me of a girl I dated in college."

"College?"

"Yeah, we dated our entire senior year then she broke up with me, by phone actually. I never saw her again."

"You don't know why she called it off?" Logan asked.

"Not a fucking clue." Billy's mouth thinned. "And she took off with my gambling stash, over a thousand dollars."

"Nice girl. Why'd you think this Rebecca was her?"

"Her hair was a different color but the eyes and the voice were just like Holly. Whatever. Guess it was a coincidence." Billy checked his watch. "Gotta go, the wife is waiting for me. It's spaghetti night." He headed to the office door. "I'll let you know what I hear from Greg."

Logan shoved a couple of files in his briefcase and headed for home. The Houston Astros were playing that evening and he wanted to catch the game on TV.

FIVE

Tuesday, 5:19 p.m.

THIS WEEK HAD COUGHED UP one surprise after another.

Roddy waited in his car for Dallas as she arrived home. Wine bottle in hand, he sauntered into the garage after she parked. Thankfully, she wasn't the skittish type, so his looming shadow next to the open car door didn't set her into panic mode.

"Miss Wells, everything okay? You took that corner a little fast."

"Well, gee, I didn't know the police would be scoping out my driving habits fifty feet from my driveway." She slid out of the car and planted herself in the middle of the garage. "What are you doing here? I'm off the clock."

"Don't get your panties in a twist."

"Detective Phillips, do not, I repeat, do not take that attitude with me." She started for the door to the house muttering, "I hate arrogant, smart ass men."

"I heard that." He was right behind her. "Dallas, stop."

She turned to face him.

"I apologize, stupid squad room comment." He held up the bottle of wine. "Truce?"

"Aren't you on call or something?"

"Off duty." His lips twisted.

Damn, those dimples. She unlocked the door.

"Come in, I'm too tired to argue with you." They stopped in her living room. "Have a seat. I'll find a corkscrew and glasses."

Just what she needed, making nice-nice with a cop when all she wanted to do was put her feet up and forget about him for one evening. Yet with no other choice, she threw her purse in the study and went to the kitchen. Maybe he'd get chatty after a glass of wine.

Dallas puttered for a bit, pulling together a tray of cheese and crackers, and uncorking the wine. Roddy perused her collection of DVD movies as she set the snacks and wine glasses on the coffee table. She poured two glasses and tasted the wine, a nice cabernet.

"You have a nice collection of films." He accepted a glass of wine.

"It's a hobby of mine, cheaper than collecting cars or crystal." She settled in her favorite chair, swung her feet on the ottoman. "What's new with the investigation?"

"I'm off duty." He found a comfortable spot on the brown tweed sofa. "This isn't an official visit."

"FYI, every visit from a cop is official. Now tell me what you've been up to. I know you've interviewed several people."

"How do you know that?" He crossed his legs, as comfortable as a feline in a bucket of catnip.

"I have my sources." No way would she tell him whom she'd talked with the last two days.

"I bet you do."

"Stop being a smart ass. By the way, are you married?"

"I didn't know you cared."

"Believe me, I don't. Lynne Harris at First National wants to know." Damn. Why did she admit that?

"Really?" He tasted the wine, smiled. "You've been a busy lady. Who else have you talked with?"

"Let's cut to the chase. As HCU's representative to work with the police, I'm entitled to learn what progress you've made in solving our theft."

"I'm not married, by the way."

If his flippant tone was a barometer of enjoyment, he was having one hell of a good time playing with her.

"Peachy. I'll let Lynne know you're available. Come on, Roddy, talk to me." She offered the plate of cheese and crackers to sweeten her request for adult conversation.

"Yes, ma'am." He popped a cheese cube in his mouth, then pulled out his notebook, flipping through the pages. "We've talked with several employees at the university, the foundation, the brokerage firm, and the bank." He paused, drank more wine. "So far, no one has popped out as the primo-thief candidate. Usually, my detective skills work much faster. Guess I'm in a rut."

She couldn't help herself and laughed. Maybe he wasn't so bad after all. He had a great sense of humor. "I'll put my money on you being in a rut. Surely you have a hunch or two. Even I have a theory."

"A theory? I love it when civilians think they're smarter than the police. What's your theory?"

Dallas forced herself to hold back. She always did talk too much. What was it about this guy that made her blurt out silly questions and reveal her activities? Why not rent a billboard next to the police station?

"You go first," she said. "Tell me why you think the theft was committed in the first place—plain old greed or an easy way out of a nasty problem?"

"You do know how to crash right into the heart of an issue." Roddy's face transformed to unemotional cop. "We've concluded the motivation was intentional. We believe the theft wasn't a chance occurrence committed by a computer hacker."

Dallas nodded at that conclusion, way to go Houston police.

"This crime was well planned with advance knowledge of the wire transfer. We checked a national database for similar crimes within the past five years and came up with zilch. This wasn't a random theft. The reason could be—"

"Settling a grudge," she said.

He frowned. "That's one theory. Or, someone at either the university or the foundation saw an opportunity to make easy money and took advantage of the situation. That would explain the familiarity with the details of the gift. We're concentrating on employees as well as anyone else who knew about the transfer." He closed the notebook. "That's it so far."

Now they were getting somewhere.

She licked her lips, took a deep breath. "Who's on your radar at HCU?" She hoped he wouldn't point to her.

"No names right now. I'll let you know once we have something concrete." He topped off his wine glass, spread out on the couch. "Now, enlighten Uncle Roddy with what you've been up to since I dropped you off yesterday."

"What have I been doing the last twenty-four hours? Not much, but I did talk to one of our donors. A $20,000 gift from earlier this year is still outstanding on the cash analysis. I met with the donor and the check has been cashed."

"What's the donor's name?" He pulled out his cell phone. "I'll have the cancelled check picked up."

Geez, her big mouth again. She couldn't refuse to give him the name of Jack Franks. If she didn't tell him she had a copy of the check he'd get it anyway and then she'd look like a fool or a crook.

"I have a copy of the cancelled check. Let me get it for you."

Roddy's mouth went weird, not a smirk, not a smile.

She went to the study. While retrieving the copy from her purse, she concluded Roddy having the check could work to her benefit. The police would be able to locate the bank and account number where it had been deposited. If she sweet-talked him, hopefully he'd share the details. Of course, he'd share, they were a team. She grabbed the check copy and returned to the living room.

"This is the cancelled check, front and back."

Roddy peered at one copy then the other then back to the first one.

His gaze traveled to Dallas. "How does this check relate to the theft?"

Good, they were getting somewhere. "Did I say they were related?"

"No, but you wouldn't have gone to the trouble of tracking down this check if you didn't think there might be a connection." He picked up the wine bottle. "More wine?"

"Just a bit. I'm not one-hundred percent convinced this check relates to the theft. Maybe it's a coincidence the cash is missing." She sipped the wine. "It's not normal for cash deposits to be MIA. Guess I need to re-think our gift-cash procedures. There's obviously a breakdown somewhere."

"Maybe, maybe not. Don't beat yourself up just yet." He stowed his notebook and the check copy in his jacket pocket. "I'll get working on this first thing in the morning."

"You'll let me know as soon as you hear anything?"

"Of course."

She figured Roddy's good mood was due to an excellent California cabernet and decided to test the waters.

"I want to switch gears for minute." She pushed her hair back and dove into the deep end. "What progress have you made looking into the personal finances of HCU employees?"

"Like who?"

"Like the people who had access to the wire instructions, Scooter, Rebecca, Bill, and Bill's assistant, Sarah Evans."

"I don't have anything. We're still working on access to their bank accounts," Roddy said. "There are privacy laws so we can't barge in like a rogue cowboy."

"The police could rummage around my garbage disposal if it suited them. What about a search warrant?"

"As I said, there are laws and we don't break them. Probable cause is necessary for a search warrant, not there yet." He drained his wine glass. "Anything else?"

"There is one small thing, a favor actually." A bead of sweat rolled down Dallas' back. Simply mentioning this to Roddy made her feel like a gossipy teenager. She wanted to know the truth. "This isn't a big deal. It's probably inconsequential. Could you look into the relationship between Rebecca and Bill?"

"That's easy, they're co-workers."

"Don't be a simpleton." Just when she thought he was being open with her. "You should check them out."

"Why?"

"I saw them together at a mall in Sugar Land last Saturday. It was strange. Number one, both of them live inside the six-ten loop, Sugar Land is out of the way for shopping. Number two, I swear they were holding hands. And, number three, Rebecca threw me this out-of-the-blue smile as they left. It was totally out of character for her."

"That's it, holding hands and a smile?" Skepticism flickered across his face.

"Yes, that's it." She didn't blame Roddy for doubting her logic. The reasoning sounded lame to her as well. "I don't blame you if you I think I'm nuts. My gut tells me something is weird with those two. Won't you at least consider they might have more than a working relationship?"

"I'll think about it." He stood. "Gotta go. I need to visit my mother on my way home."

She followed him to the garage. "Please call my cell if you have any news."

"Sure thing."

He pulled his car in the driveway to turn around. After he backed out, he stuck his head out the window.

"Lynne Harris thinks I'm hot, huh?" He winked and drove off.

Men and their egos.

The phone was ringing when she returned to the townhouse.

"Mom, it's me. I'm finally home."

"Jane, how was your trip? Did you do any sightseeing?" Twin daughter number two was finally home from Washington, D.C.

"It was fine, tiring and boring. Training isn't one of my favorite things. And, yes, we managed to do a couple of tours on Saturday, the White House and the Capitol."

"Wonderful. D.C. is still on my travel list." In fact, Dallas had quite the list of cities, both domestic and international, that she hoped to visit on future vacations.

"You'd love it. I heard about the big theft at the university. It was in the local papers."

"We made the news in Washington? Not the best kind of publicity." She doubted Scooter or Dr. Arnold would be happy

HCU's problems were news outside of Houston.

"There's no such thing as bad publicity anymore," Jane said with a laugh. "Has anyone been arrested?"

"No arrests, no suspects. I'm working with the police for HCU. Interesting stuff so far."

She heard a typical Jane sigh.

"If you guys would use Texas South Bank rather than First National this probably wouldn't have happened."

"I've told you a million times, we're not changing banks. The Board will never consider it."

"Don't forget we have a more updated computer system. First National hasn't upgraded for at least five years. Maybe they were negligent in some way, considering they're so far behind, technology-wise that is."

"Who knows? That's up to the police to figure out." She wanted to know about her daughter's life. "What else is going on? Dating anyone I should meet?"

"Stop asking me that."

As usual, she didn't learn a single thing about Jane's love life and she wasn't even that nosy. A mother had the right to ask questions of her children. Jane rarely disclosed anything about her private life while Liz talked nonstop. How could identical twins be so different?

After the call ended, Dallas went to the study to check her e-mail. The HCU security chief had sent the list of employee addresses. She printed it out, intending to research the appraised values of homes owned by Rebecca, Scooter, and Bill. After accessing the Harris County appraisal district website, she entered the first home address for a property record search. Rebecca apparently rented as her name wasn't listed on the record for her home address.

She pulled a jackpot with the value of Scooter's home, almost a million dollars. The value topped what she suspected he could afford based on his salary. He'd worked at HCU for years so she doubted he'd received a windfall from a corporate severance package. Maybe his wife came from money or maybe they spent beyond their means. Hopefully, Roddy would know the answer.

Her cell beeped in her purse on the desk. It was Liz.

"Mom, where are you?"

"At home, I'm on the internet. Still feeling okay?"

"I told you we're rolling right along and on schedule."

"That's good." The closer to Liz's due date, the more Dallas worried. "What did you do today?"

"Not much. I did mention to Dirk about the Bridge Foundation. He knows the director."

"Did Dirk say anything about him?"

"Said he's a real nice guy, a 'straight shooter' per Dirk."

"I have a meeting with the nice guy tomorrow." He should be happy as hell coming from such a wealthy and prominent family. "Guess I'll find out how straight he shoots then."

$ $ $

A few minutes after ten, Dallas slid into bed and clicked on the television. She hadn't heard the news since that morning. Nothing was new, same old stories on bad weather, bad politicians, and bad criminals. She dozed off for a few minutes then woke up to a story on internet viruses carried by e-mails.

Turning up the volume, she concentrated on the newscaster's words.

"The Blaster Worm has again made its way through corporate America. E-mail servers have been shut down across the country, stifling electronic communication and frustrating IT professionals. It's expected that more than 500,000 computers will be impacted before the worm runs its course. In other news—"

A worm? Bingo! She jumped out of bed and began pacing in front of the television.

A worm . . . of course. An article she'd read a couple of weeks ago described these nasty things as a computer virus triggered when an attachment to an e-mail message opened. Usually the virus screwed up the client computer it was received on, along with any servers the computer was networked with. It spread like a spider web crack in a car's windshield.

Dallas conjectured that a worm developed for the HCU theft would have a different purpose. When the attachment opened, a virus could have been sent through the server to the system managing wire transfers. The sole purpose would have been to alter the instructions and change the destination of the funds.

She stopped pacing, clenched her fists, felt a shiver along her spine. A message could have been sent several days before the actual transfer. Then waited for the Bridge Foundation's wire instructions to enter the system. Holy shit.

She sat on the edge of the bed. This was what Ruthie had been talking about. A mole, she said. Dallas looked at the bedside clock; too late to call anyone. First thing in the morning she'd contact Lynne at First National and ask her about recent e-mails from HCU employees.

She needed evidence, not a hunch or a great idea, before she'd talk to Roddy about this. She'd already played the hunch card with her suspicions about Bill and Rebecca. Her first step would be talking to Ruthie about her theory and whether there was the remotest chance it could be true.

Dallas knew she was close to discovering the "how" part of the theft equation. However, the "who" part remained open and would require the full extent of her detective skills. Scratch that, the "who" would require the full extent of her skills to be nosy and an obstinate pain in the ass. Somehow those "skills" would lead to an answer. That was the number one goal, regardless of where it might take her.

$ $ $

San Francisco, Tuesday Evening

Rebecca Holland stared at the towers of the Golden Gate Bridge poking through a bank of fog floating across San Francisco Bay.

They reminded her of the orange colored toothpicks her grandmother used to put in fluffy meringue to let her old biddy friends know the lemon pie she served every Sunday was sugar free. The panoramic view from the window of the boutique hotel filled her with calm. It displayed the darkness covering the city yet concealed the secrets the city harbored. San Francisco was a city to love and one in which to get lost. A new name and identity papers spawned a new life, a rich and rewarding life—one so well deserved.

The opulent suite—decadent with silk fabrics and Baccarat crystal—was the perfect initiation to a life of luxury, freedom from material worry, and indulgence of the body and mind.

It had been a good day. A meeting with a unique investment banker provided advice for ensuring a truly comfortable and worry-free life. And best of all, Bill Jenkins was dead and would not ruin her plan with his ridiculous arrogance, the audacity of the man. She sipped from a champagne flute, pushed a strand of hair off her face. In any event, Bill's pitiful role was over. He had nothing further to contribute to the success of the venture. Death was a just dessert for an impudent man.

Rebecca ordered dinner from room service, refilled the flute, and settled on the brocade sofa. She basked in the joy bubbling in her soul. It was delicious. She had scored the payback of the century. Twenty years in the making and now it was over. Poor little Billy Rice and his screwed-up family had received exactly what they deserved. Embarrassment, humiliation, loss—the perfect revenge.

She especially enjoyed the stress on that old biddy grandmother who thought she was so tough and so in control of her family. Yes, she had called the shots twenty years ago, but now Rebecca set the agenda. She hadn't yet made a decision on whether she'd send a second gift to Grandma Rice. The old bitch certainly deserved it for the hell she and Billy's father had dumped on her.

Thinking back to that scene so many years ago, Rebecca nearly broke the stem of the champagne flute. Somehow, they had discovered her pregnancy, not even Billy knew. They had come to her apartment two hours after the last final of her senior year at Southern Methodist University.

She had met the entire Rice family at Thanksgiving dinner that fall. She remembered a huge house in Houston and a throng of people. Billy had done his best to make her feel comfortable. It was an overwhelming experience for a farm girl from the sticks of west Texas. She had struggled through the dinner and clutched Billy's hand the entire evening.

The pain of that meeting in her apartment and its aftermath, including a painful miscarriage, were ancient history. She now had her payback against the Rice family. They deserved every single stroke of her strategy. Screw them to hell.

She rose and moved to the window again. The view was magnificent. The first of many devoted only to her pleasure. Las Vegas was the next item on her agenda. She had a man to meet along with silly fun to partake in before the real journey began. Oh yes, the best of her life was just on the horizon, all thanks to the Bridge Foundation. Payback was so very sweet.

SIX

Wednesday, 8:05 a.m.

FIRST THING ON WEDNESDAY MORNING, waiting for the coffee to finish, Dallas went to the study to check her HCU e-mail, hoping for a follow-up message from Rebecca. Nothing. Time to increase the pressure. She sent another message referring to the previous one and advising Rebecca's input was critical to the ongoing police investigation. Bill and Scooter were copied for good measure. If she didn't respond by the end of the day, then a third message would be sent to Dr. Arnold and most likely, the Pope.

Her cell phone rang as Dallas rose to return to the kitchen.

"Mom, I forgot to ask you something last night."

"Sure, Jane, what is it?"

"Are you free for dinner on Friday?" She hesitated a fraction of a second. "There's someone I'd like you to meet."

"You want me to meet someone?" Dallas' heart performed a loop-de-loop. Jane wanted her to meet a man friend.

"Don't start planning the wedding. This is merely a meet-and-greet. No big deal. Understand?"

"Of course, I understand. Meet and greet. What time and where?" Jane provided the details before ending the call. Jane had to be serious about this man if she wanted to introduce him to her mother. This was happy news and Dallas would hold off on thoughts about the wedding . . . until she met the man. Dallas poured a mug of coffee and checked the time on her phone.

Finally, it was after nine o'clock—time to call Ruthie, who was available.

"I have a quick question for you," Dallas said, leaning against a kitchen counter.

"What's up?"

"When we talked yesterday you mentioned that a targeted virus could have been used to change the wire instructions."

"Yes, that's a possibility." The clicking of Ruthie's nails on the computer keyboard accompanied her words.

"Could the virus have been launched by opening an e-mail?" Dallas hoped that wasn't a cyber idiot question.

"Sure, but usually something else is involved."

This was the confirmation of her theory. The coffee had made her stomach queasy. "Could an attachment be used to initiate the virus?"

"That's the most common way. It wiggles its way through the system and finds the target server. Then it carries out its mission," Ruthie explained. "Fairly simple if you know what you're doing."

Dallas performed a mental cartwheel then completed a fist pump. This was the "how" part of her premise.

"My working theory is that the wire instructions were altered by an attachment to an e-mail."

"Good possibility."

"Thanks, I'll call you later."

Dallas basked in the glory of their conversation for less than fifteen seconds. Before executing a happy dance, she called Lynne Harris.

"I need your help with something."

"Sure," Lynne laughed. "As long as it's legal."

"Not to worry. Would you check your e-mail log of messages received during the last week?"

"Won't take a minute. What am I looking for?"

Dallas heard the curiosity in Lynne's voice but she held off on sharing her theory until she had verification of any e-mail attachments. "Look for messages from any HCU employee."

"Let's see, last Monday there's one from Scooter Taylor, on Thursday one message from Rebecca Holland, one from Dr. Arnold and two from Scooter, then another from Rebecca on

Friday. That's it. Why are you asking?"

"Curiosity mostly. Is there anything strange or odd about the messages?" She turned and looked out the window above her kitchen sink. It was going to be another beautiful day.

"They all related to the gift transfer. Scooter and Rebecca both wanted to make sure the bank was alerted to the transfer. Nothing unusual."

"Who—"

"I almost forgot," Lynne said. "Bill Jenkins's assistant e-mailed the instructions on Thursday."

"Did any of the messages have an attachment?"

"Let's see, I'll have to check each one." Lynne spoke again after several seconds. "The message from Rebecca Holland on Friday had another copy of the wire instructions. That's the only attachment."

"Hmm, does anyone else routinely receive e-mails from HCU?" She had to be missing something. "What about your assistant?"

"Hold on a second and I'll go ask her."

It didn't take more than a minute for Lynne to return. "My assistant received an e-mail from Rebecca last Thursday. It was one of those silly jokes with a picture of a black cat in a pink bikini."

"Has she received them before from Rebecca?"

"Yes, they both like animals and send jokes back and forth. You know how those things get passed around."

"Sure do, I've received plenty myself." Was it possible, even remotely possible, that Dallas had stumbled on how the wire instructions were altered? "Any word yet on the bank's progress?"

"Nothing as of this morning. I hope to hear news later in the day," Lynne replied.

Dallas ended the call and began to pace from the kitchen to the study, around her desk, and back to the kitchen. Her nerves twitched, beating a steady rhythm against her elation that she may have figured out how the wire instructions were altered. A virus in the wire instruction or black cat attachment might hold the answer. She needed to talk to Roddy and went to the study for his number.

A greeting stated he was unavailable for the rest of the day. She left a plea for him to call as soon as possible. She itched to take action, then her eye caught the to-do list she had jotted down on Monday. The euphoria bubble burst. She had no proof that an e-mail virus had modified the wire instructions. She had no evidence a message from HCU carried the aforementioned virus. Maybe she should try a new hobby as a writer of crime fiction. Of course, she didn't have a murder victim to add to the plot so the book would be a bust.

$ $ $

Two hours later at the Bridge Foundation, Amanda greeted Dallas by name.

"Mr. Rice is running late this morning. Please have a seat until he's free."

While she waited on the sofa, her thoughts turned to Logan Rice. She pictured him as conservative, refined, a tad snobbish, and having a nasty temper based on his outburst in Scooter's office. She'd be lucky if she learned anything useful from him about the foundation's role in the transfer. But then again Liz's husband, Dirk said he was a nice guy.

Men were terrible judges of the character of other men. If a man could play hoops and drink beer, they were automatically included in the man club. More than likely Mr. Rice was spoiled by his family's money. She'd allow him an extra point for working with a charitable organization.

Her cell rang and this time it was Dr. Arnold. Uh-oh, this couldn't be good. How'd he know her number?

"Dallas, there are a couple of items I need to discuss with you. Since you're not on campus, could you meet me at Hermann Park? Would one o'clock work?"

"Yes, one is fine. Where in the park should I go?" What was this about? And why meet in the park and not his office?

He provided directions and ended the call. She was more than curious about the "items" on his mind. She'd rarely been in a meeting with him, as that was Scooter's territory. No doubt this meeting related to the theft, as had every breath she'd taken for the last six days.

Five minutes later, Amanda ushered Dallas to the office at the end of the hall with the double doors. She knocked, pushed on the half-open door.

Genuine surprise rarely crawled along Dallas' backbone. Not so today. Her breath momentarily halted, and she struggled to stifle a nervous giggle.

Not five feet from her stood a tall Bozo the clown, complete with orange hair, a red and blue striped blousy costume, floppy black shoes, painted face, and a large red nose in his hand.

"Excuse me." The first five seconds of shock had passed. "I must be in the wrong office. I'm here to meet Logan Rice and you don't look like him."

"Oh." The clown's shoes clomped half a turn to face her. "Miss Wells, you're in the right office. I realize this must look strange."

Her eyes closed briefly, allowing for a moment of pure humor. "I can say without reservation, this is a first for me."

"I'm substituting for a friend at Children's Hospital, last minute." He waved a red tie, smiled, displayed those million-watt teeth. "I'm sorry but we'll have to postpone our meeting. Are you free for dinner this evening? We can discuss the HCU business then."

"Well, uh . . ."

"Is seven good for you?"

"Uh . . . okay."

"Great. Give Amanda your home address. I'll pick you up. Casual, okay? I'll need to relax after this." He grinned. "It's my first clown gig."

"That sounds fine." What else could she say? "I'll leave you to your clown gig."

"I'll see you this evening, Miss Wells."

Dallas jotted down her home address for Amanda and retraced her steps to the garage. As she headed home, her mind wasn't on driving but on the clown named Logan Rice. A chuckle erupted at the memory of walking into his office. Even with the makeup, his grin was cute as hell, something she hadn't noticed last Friday. Her thoughts transitioned to what might be under the costume. Before her imagination could rev up, the cell phone rang, again. She was one popular girl.

Lynne's name appeared on the screen.

"I have information for you, but not a complete answer." Lynne's voice was steady and even. "When the wire first entered our system, the account information was per the HCU instructions. Somewhere along the way, the information was electronically changed and re-routed out of the system." She sighed, frustration laced her words. "Unfortunately, we don't know how the account data was changed or where the funds were directed."

"Damn. I had hoped for more progress. I appreciate that much though." Dallas switched her phone to the other ear. "I assume your IT folks are working on how the alteration was accomplished."

"Definitely. This isn't good for business so everyone is on red alert. You know how it goes."

"I do." Dallas debated about mentioning the possibility of an e-mail virus doing the dirty work. Oh, what the hell. "You might mention that the instructions could have been altered with an e-mail virus."

"That's why you were asking about e-mails."

"I was thinking out loud, trying to be creative. It's just a thought. Please call me when you have another update."

"I'll call if I have solid information. Hopefully, it won't be more than twenty-four hours."

"Thanks, Lynne." Dallas high-fived the steering wheel. Progress. "By the way, Detective Phillips is single."

"Cool." Her voice jumped two octaves.

Dallas made her way to Smith Street and the entrance to the

Southwest Freeway. She had the afternoon to rethink her logic and plan what she'd wear to dinner. The traffic was light for a Wednesday afternoon so she made good time. Halfway home she remembered the meeting with Dr. Arnold. Going the opposite direction of Hermann Park, she contemplated where to turn around when her cell rang.

"It's Roddy. We need to talk."

"Talk about what?"

"I've uncovered a piece of information on the cancelled check from Jack Franks. Meet me at the Starbucks on Gessner near the Southwest Freeway. How long before you can get there?" He sounded out of breath.

"Are you jogging?"

"Running down stairs. Damn elevators are too slow."

"Don't have a heart attack," she said.

"Very funny. How long, fifteen minutes?"

"I'll be there in ten."

"Good. Order a tall mocha latte for me." He clicked off.

Damn that man. Gessner was the next exit so Dallas swung over a couple of lanes to the off-ramp without noticeably ticking off surrounding drivers. The exit headed straight to the stoplight. She turned right and shortly swung into a parking space in front of Starbucks.

She ordered a café mocha for herself, the latte for Roddy, and settled at table in the corner of the store with an easy view of the entrance. Roddy soon arrived. She spied him before he glanced in her direction. More than one female head turned toward him as he wound his way through the tables. He looked frazzled. Was that a good sign or a bad sign?

He plopped in the metal chair opposite her. "One helluva day so far."

"What's up?"

"It's my mother and her——never mind." He eyed the coffee cup. "Thanks for the latte."

"You're welcome. What's the story on the cancelled check?"

"You sure know how to get to the point." He slurped the

drink.

"You called me," she said.

Roddy looked tired. His eyes didn't have the usual sparkle.

"That I did," he said.

"Come on, tell me what you discovered about the Franks check."

He didn't answer immediately. Her words floated in the space between them.

"It was not deposited to a HCU bank account." He grinned with those dimples waving. "Feel better?"

"Damn right." Relief slid down her shoulders. Her lungs filled with air and she blew a slow breath, it felt wonderful. "Where was the check deposited?"

"Banco Economico on the Grand Cayman Island. That's the easy part." He tore a hand through his short hair. "We know the account number but the bank refuses to release the name on the account."

"Can't you go through Interpol or the CIA or Homeland Security?" She couldn't believe it—a Caribbean bank refusing to give the Houston police important information.

"No." He chuckled deep in his chest. "Security is why people open accounts in the Caymans, and Switzerland, for that matter. We've contacted the FBI—"

"The FBI?"

"Yes, the FBI. I have a buddy in the Houston field office and he's helping with the account owner. I'm sure you'll be happy to know I have a strong hunch the Franks' check is related to our case." He chugged the latte. "Good work, by the way. This may turn out to be our strongest lead so far."

Oops, she needed to come clean. "By the way, there are, uh . . . other missing gifts."

"What?" Roddy's chest leaned over the small round table, his mouth a hard line, no dimples. "Talk to me."

Hopefully, confessing would ensure his continued help and good will. Her earlier relief evaporated and her stomach felt edgy. "The Franks' gift is the largest but there are two for $10,000. I talked to one of the donors but she doesn't receive her cancelled checks back from her bank. The second donor wasn't at home when I called."

"We'll contact both of them. I'll need a list of the missing gifts. I assume there's more than three." A grin flitted across his face. Robo-cop he was not.

"I've got it right here." She tore through her purse and pulled out the list and the notes she'd made when attempting to call each donor yesterday morning. "Here's the list and my notes." Was she the poster child for police cooperation or what?

"Thanks." He slipped the police issue notebook from his shirt pocket and began writing in it. "Which donors did you talk to?"

"Everyone except Lopez and Brooks."

"Good. We'll contact each of them and their banks. This may take a few days."

"Why so long?" she said. This was so frustrating. The police moved slower than Congress in an election year. "Can I do something to help?" Surely, she could do something to get this part of the investigation on the road.

"Nothing, I'll handle the details."

She snapped her fingers. "I almost forgot. I sent the same list to Rebecca on Monday and haven't heard anything other than a phone call. She's reviewing the gifts."

"Let me know when you hear from her."

"Will do. Any progress on the finances of Scooter, Bill, or Rebecca?" Dallas figured they were a logical starting point for unusual financial transactions in their personal bank accounts, especially Bill. As vice president for development, he should have known about the gift from the get-go and had plenty of time to plan how to steal it

"Why don't you tell me what you've discovered, and then we can compare notes." He popped a grin.

"Not much actually." She might as well show him she was fully cooperating. "I think Rebecca rents or leases a townhouse or apartment not far from the university and Bill owns a house in the Heights."

"What about Scooter?"

"The appraised value of his house is close to a million dollars. I don't understand how he can afford it based on his salary from HCU. But then again, I have no knowledge of his tax situation and other sources of income." She tilted her head. "But I bet you know all about his tax return."

"Right you are. Rebecca rents and pays her bills on time. Bill is frugal and also pays his bills on time." Roddy shrugged. "Not much to suggest a motive for stealing millions."

Damn. Why were they both such good credit risks? "What about Scooter?"

"I agree his house seems out of line with his income. We'll look into whether he's having financial problems."

"Being in debt doesn't make him a thief."

"No, it doesn't." Roddy finished the latte, wiped his mouth with a paper napkin. "We'll wait to make conclusions until we have all the facts."

"Understood." She saluted him. "Change of subject. Do you think First National could be negligent due to an outdated computer system?"

"Where'd you get that idea?"

"Thinking outside the box."

"Let's not make any assumptions until the techie guys file their report." His cell phone rang. He listened for a moment before stowing it back in his shirt pocket.

"Gotta go. I'll let you know when I hear back from the FBI." He stood and stretched his arms to the ceiling. "In the meantime, give some thought to your other coworkers."

"Like anyone who might have a grudge against the university?"

"Yep, that's the idea. Anyone whose demeanor has changed in the last year, isn't as friendly, or is more difficult to work with. You get the picture." He pushed the chair toward the table. "I'll see ya later."

She called out to his retreating back. "Hey, thanks for keeping me up to date."

He responded with a back-handed wave and continued to thread his way among the tables to the exit. He pulled out his cell and stopped walking. After a few seconds, he turned his gaze in Dallas' direction. He shut the phone, walked back to her.

"You forget something?"

"No, but we do have a new development." Roddy's mouth had a weird twist. "Bill Jenkins was found dead this morning with a knife in his chest."

What? Bill . . . dead? She sucked in air, digesting the information Roddy had just relayed. She shuddered. The mental picture of a knife in Bill's chest freaked her out.

Roddy departed immediately after dropping the bomb. She couldn't get her mind around it—Bill Jenkins, dead. He was the first person she knew who had been murdered. It seemed so grisly and repulsive to imagine Bill dying that way. It was one thing to watch a television cop show with a gruesome murder and quite another to have worked with a truly nice man who departed this world as a homicide victim.

Why had Bill been killed and by whom? Was it related to the HCU theft? Her gut screamed the murder was definitely related. The timing was too damned coincidental. He was such a regular guy and a harmless flirt. What a waste of a life.

Dallas trudged out of Starbucks and headed toward Hermann Park and the one o'clock meeting with Dr. Arnold. She'd be early and take a few minutes to relax in the sunshine. She called Scooter as soon as she headed north on the freeway.

"It's Dallas, I heard about Bill."

"Thanks for calling. Bill's death is quite the turn of events. How did you hear about it?" Scooter's voice was calm and soothing, a contrast to the obvious stress of last Friday.

"Detective Phillips told me. Do you know who discovered his body? Where was it?"

"Sarah found him." She had been Bill's assistant for years. "He didn't come to work on Tuesday or today so she got curious when he didn't answer his home phone. She went to his house this morning and let herself in. He was in the living room, lying on the floor. She immediately called nine-one-one.”

"That's terrible. Is Sarah okay?” Even imagining that picture of Bill sent a bolt of shivers along her spine.

"She went home after talking with the police. Her husband is with her. Dr. Arnold plans to stop by this evening.”

"I'm glad she's not alone," Dallas said.

"Me, too. More bad publicity." Scooter sighed. "It's hard to believe someone we know would kill Bill. Do you think he knew something about the stolen money?”

"I suppose it's possible. Hard to believe it though.” Surprise flooded through her like a spring rain. She and Scooter almost had a consensus for a change. "There's something else. Did you read the e-mail I sent to Rebecca this morning?”

"The one about gifts without matching cash deposits?”

"That's the one.” Her stomach growled. The coffee didn't substitute for lunch. "I visited Jack Franks yesterday, the donor of the largest gift. He gave me a copy of his cancelled check and I gave it to Detective Phillips. It was deposited at a bank in the Cayman Islands.”

"The Caymans . . . more bad news." Scooter's voice trailed off to a whisper.

She heard a man near the end of his bad news rope.

"Come on, this could turn out to be good news. I'm certain the missing gifts are related to the theft. The police are working on getting the name on the Caymans account.” She hoped her words were encouraging. "Also, they're contacting the other donors for their cancelled checks.”

"Damn it, this is terrible." Anger salted his words. "Dr. Arnold won't like our donors being contacted by the police.”

"It's a routine part of their investigation. The police have to do their job and we have no choice but to cooperate.”

"I know. But donors can be fickle.” He sighed again. His mood changed like a bouncing ball.

"Have Rebecca call them to smooth over any ruffled feathers. You know how they all love her.” She bit her tongue as she said that.

"She's not here, out sick the last two days."

"Really? How interesting." No wonder she hadn't replied to the second e-mail or called Dallas back.

"I'll talk to her tomorrow and she can call the donors then. Ellie is ill today, too. There's a bug going around."

Unlike Scooter, Dallas found it strange, downright weird, that everyone was suddenly calling in sick. Rebecca's absence from HCU on the very day Bill's dead body was discovered might be a sad coincidence or it might be something else.

Dallas ended the conversation, frustrated with Scooter. What had happened to his priorities? All he worried about was Dr. Arnold not liking the police contacting donors. What about the police finding the $25 million?

Fifteen minutes later she drove into the parking lot of Hermann Park, off Fannin Street and noticed Dr. Arnold by his car. She waved to him then locked up the Volvo.

"Let's sit over there." Dr. Arnold pointed to a bench a few yards down a sidewalk bordering the outer edge of the park. Live oak trees shaded their hike to the bench.

Sweat beaded on the back of her neck. She was nervous meeting the HCU president without Scooter. This wasn't the usual thirty second encounters she was accustomed to. She had no clue as to the agenda and waited for Dr. Arnold to speak once they were settled on the bench.

"Dallas, I realize this conversation is irregular. I'd appreciate you keeping it between the two of us." He stared straight ahead, the sun glaring off his glasses.

"I will. What did you want to discuss with me?"

"You will keep this meeting confidential?" He glanced at her briefly.

She nodded, her anxiety elevating. She stopped her foot from tapping on the concrete.

He pursed his lips. She guessed he'd made a decision.

"Scooter hasn't been himself the last couple of months." He glanced from side to side as though searching for an eavesdropper. "I'm worried about him. Have you noticed anything out of the ordinary?"

Two teenagers strolled toward them. She waited for the couple to pass and considered the best response to Dr. Arnold's question. Truth or dare?

"That's a difficult question to answer. Scooter is . . . inconsistent at times. He can change his mind a lot."

Dr. Arnold appeared startled for a moment then regained his composure. "Is that so?"

Not a question requiring a reply. She kept quiet and waited for him to continue, mental fingers drumming on the bench.

"I need your cooperation." He hesitated, rubbed his face. "I'd appreciate you reporting directly to me, rather than Scooter, on your work with the police. I realize this is an unusual request but I assure you it's made with the welfare of the university in mind."

Holy shit.

"I get the feeling there's something you're not telling me," she said.

"Very perceptive, but I need you to honor my request all the same."

Dr. Arnold had just asked her to ignore her boss and communicate only with him. Scooter would consider it insubordination while she considered it a no-win situation. Yet she had to do the right thing.

"I'll honor your wishes. However, Scooter expects me to update him on my progress." A trickle of dread trudged across her chest.

"I understand your dilemma. You may provide Scooter a high-level summary of your activities with the police. No details, though."

She squeezed her eyes shut. Less than thirty minutes ago she had blabbed to Scooter about the missing cash. She had to tell Dr. Arnold.

"I've already given Scooter the details of some missing gift checks," she said.

"What are you talking about?" he replied sharply.

A young couple pushing a baby stroller passed in front of the bench, providing a few moments of distraction while she gathered her thoughts. She had to tell him everything, and she did.

Silence for a good thirty seconds, which was a lifetime for Dallas as she sat on a park bench with her boss's boss and wondered how bad she'd screwed up as the HCU point person. She hoped Dr. Arnold wasn't thinking of his top ten ways to fire her.

"It's okay." He blew out a breath, patted her hand. "I know you're doing everything you can to help with this situation. However, if there's any other reason to contact our donors, speak to me before talking to the police. In fact, call me every day with an update on your activities using my cell number. If I don't answer, I'll call you back as soon as I have privacy."

Dallas' role as the HCU point person became exponentially more complicated. First, she couldn't be direct and forthcoming with her direct superior. Second, she had to call Dr. Arnold once a day to report her conversations with Roddy. And third, she couldn't contact donors without Dr. Arnold's permission. Just peachy.

She was an HCU trooper though. "Okay, I'll report in daily."

Damn, now she had three bosses—Scooter, Roddy and Dr. Arnold. Would the real boss please stand up?

SEVEN

Wednesday, 4:00 p.m.

ONCE BACK HOME, DALLAS PLOPPED in front of the television to watch the local news and escape from the past several hours. She needed a mental break from her borderline obsession with the theft. Her brain was overloaded with details swirling nonstop. It needed to spring a leak and empty her mind of stress.

The empty mind routine must have worked. She woke from a quick nap as a story began on Bill's death. She had expected local coverage, but not the lead story. His association with HCU was highlighted in the report.

An on-location reporter once again supplied the details live from the front of Brennan Hall. He stated the police were treating Bill's death as a homicide. They didn't yet have any suspects. It was an even juicer story considering the unknown whereabouts of the mega gift which was also mentioned.

She turned off the TV.

She was tired of HCU, missing funds, and running around Houston like a crazy person. At dinner tonight, she'd ask Logan Rice a couple of questions, then erase the theft from her mind for the rest of the evening.

She poured a glass of chardonnay, then went to her bedroom to draw a bath—girl time was in order. She doused the water with jasmine-scented bath oil, set the wine on the edge of the tub and slid into the water. Its warmth and the oil's aroma stroked her senses with the gentleness of a feather.

Her curiosity about Mr. Rice brewed as she sipped the wine. Who wouldn't be fascinated after meeting him in a clown costume? Even Ruthie's attempts at cupid-playing had never involved a clown. She chuckled at the memory of him in that outfit. Priceless.

After twenty minutes, the water was cold, and the wine glass empty. She dried off, then studied the contents of her closet for the perfect casual outfit.

She pilfered through pants, shirts, and summer dresses. Pulling out three of each, she coordinated various ensembles and ended with a mess of clothes on her bed. She checked the bedroom clock: six forty-five. Decision time—she threw on white jeans, a lime green silk top with a smidgen of cleavage, and silver sandals. She quickly applied foundation, mascara, lip gloss. She fluffed her air-dried hair, sprayed on Coco, and pirouetted in front of the mirror.

Grandma was looking good.

The doorbell pealed and she hurried downstairs.

After re-fluffing her hair, she opened the front door.

Oh. My. God.

Logan Rice resembled a movie star—sandy hair, blue eyes, square jaw, and that million-watt smile. His six-foot muscled frame sported a light blue Polo shirt and khakis. He looked good enough to eat . . . well, lick at least. A one-eighty from when she first met him in Scooter's office. Maybe it was the fact he had a smile on his face.

"Miss Wells, it's good to see you again."

"Mr. Rice, good evening." She stood in the doorway, statue still. She didn't invite him in, or offer a glass of wine. Where were her manners? Finally, her tongue became unglued. "Did you enjoy the event at the hospital?"

"Actually, it was fun. The kids were great and I managed not to fall over the floppy shoes." He unloaded the grin. "Are you ready? I'm starving."

"I'll get my keys." She picked up her purse, turned on a lamp in the living room, and hurried back to Mr. Rice. He waited on the doorstep, not a figment of her imagination.

While walking to his car, he mentioned she should call him

Logan and Dallas responded with the same. Things were definitely going well. They were on a first-name basis in less than three minutes.

She expected he'd drive a decked-out sports car, the typical ride for a hot-looking bachelor. Wrong. His vehicle proved that a person shouldn't make assumptions. Logan opened the passenger door of a mid-sized family sedan.

"My grandmother has a car like this." She groaned in silence. Her big mouth again.

"It's reliable." He glanced at her. "I hope you like Italian. There's a Carrabba's not far from here."

"That's fine. Turn right at the next corner." She cringed. Giving him orders already?

They arrived at the restaurant minus any further extraneous comments from Dallas—so far, so good. Logan talked about the Astros; he sounded like a huge fan.

Sunlight streaked the spring air so they settled at a table on the patio. Fairy lights, lush potted plants, and secluded tables evoked a mood perfect for romance—totally unnecessary for this dinner. After being seated at a corner table, shrouded from other tables by a large sago palm, Dallas experienced a momentary illusion of being on a date with a very attractive man. She gave herself a mental slap to ward off such ridiculous thoughts. This dinner addressed a business matter and nothing else.

They perused the menu and discovered a mutual appreciation for the same food and wine. Logan ordered a shrimp appetizer, grilled chicken and linguine for two along with a bottle of merlot. They discussed the weather and the national basketball playoffs until the wine arrived.

"Dallas, I'd like to propose a toast."

She raised her glass, curious as to what he'd say.

"Here's to a mutually rewarding experience." He lightly tapped his glass against hers.

What did he mean by "mutually rewarding experience?" Was he referring to the $25 million, to a good relationship between HCU and the Bridge Foundation, or something else?

"Logan, the reason I made an appointment with you is to discuss the loss of the gift funds last Friday. I'm now the HCU contact with the police and I—"

"I know that and we will have a conversation about the theft." He smiled. "Let's enjoy our dinner first, get to know each other. We can talk business later."

"I could use a break from the subject." She sighed. That was an understatement. "It's overtaken my life the past six days."

"I can only imagine. Put the theft out of your mind for now. Tell me about yourself. Who is Dallas Wells?"

"When I figure that out, I'll let you know."

A corner of his mouth hitched up. "I'm serious. Are you married, divorced? Have children, cats, dogs?"

He was serious, how cute. "You may be sorry you asked," she said, her stomach suddenly overrun with ribbons of angst. "Well . . . I'm divorced and I have twin twenty-four-year-old daughters. One is pregnant, with her first child due in a month. I'm almost a grandma."

"I can't believe that. You're much too young to have kids that old."

"Thanks." The arrival of their appetizer saved her from further sharing. They focused on the shrimp for a minute or two until Dallas had to ask a question. "Your turn, tell me about you."

"That's easy. Most of what I do revolves around my family—work, fun, socializing, you name it. These days there's a member of the Rice clan involved in most of my activities. I've never married and have no children so I give a lot of attention to my nieces and nephews." He laughed. "If I ever do become a father, I'll have plenty of experience at changing diapers."

Dallas was uncomfortable at the turn of their conversation to such personal topics. Their entrees were served and thankfully, they transitioned into less personal topics of conversation until the dishes were cleared and cappuccinos arrived.

"Are you relaxed enough to discuss the theft?" She might as well get the ball rolling. The reason for the evening was professional. The fact that she found him attractive as hell was irrelevant.

"Very relaxed." His mouth had a lazy smile before his tongue licked his lips. He again leaned forward with his elbows on the table, his gaze drilled into hers. "Ask me any question you have in mind."

"Does anyone at the Bridge Foundation have a personal relationship with a HCU employee??

"Not yet, but things are looking better."

"I'm serious." She had no idea Mr. Society Guy would be such a flirt. "Don't you think it's possible this particular gift was targeted not only because it's a lot of money but also because the Bridge Foundation was the benefactor?"

He moved back from the table, business persona back in place. "Meaning that someone has a major problem with the foundation? Sure, it's possible. But why? We give money away. Who would be unhappy with that?"

"Someone who had a request turned down?" She sipped the coffee, weighing the words on her tongue. "Or, perhaps it's not related to what the foundation does. Perhaps the theft was a personal matter, a grudge. Perhaps the real motive was to embarrass the foundation."

"You've got to be kidding." Logan leaned back in the chair, stretched out his legs and crossed one ankle over the other. "Who in the world would want to embarrass the foundation? We're the good guys. We help others advance their charitable programs with our grants. You're way off-base, Dallas."

He was wrong, so very cute and so very wrong. She was certain of it. "No, I'm not off-base. A computer hacker didn't get lucky so someone went to a lot of trouble to change the wire instructions. That takes knowledge and technical skills and a damned good reason to go to all the effort. I believe this whole scenario was personal and so does Detective Phillips."

He seemed startled by that piece of information. "I'll go along with this line of thought for now." The waiter arrived with the check. "The question on the table is whether there is an unknown connection between a HCU employee and one of ours."

"That's the question," she said. "Let's start with the original contact from HCU related to the donation. Who first approached the foundation?"

"It was a conversation between my grandmother and Dr. Arnold last summer. I think it was at a lecture on global warming. Gram is active in environmental causes." He sipped his coffee. "Rebecca Holland followed up with her and Gram agreed to add the topic to the agenda for our fall board meeting. As a rule, we first discuss the initial merit of any request over a million dollars before requiring the submission of a formal proposal."

Dallas caught herself listening to his voice, rather she felt his voice—melted chocolate softly flowing over her thighs. Oops.

"It was at that board meeting that you, I mean the board, agreed to review a proposal?"

He nodded.

"Did every board member agree?"

"Funny you should ask. I was surprised we had two negative votes." He must have noticed the question in her eyes. "No. I can't give you the names of the dissenting votes."

She made a mental note to perform an internet search on the foundation's board members.

"What was next?" she asked.

"I sent a letter to Dr. Arnold indicating our interest and requested a formal proposal. The letter included guidelines for the proposal's format along with the submission timetable." His voice was somber. "We're fairly strict in our requirements for such a high-dollar request."

"HCU receives the letter, kicks into high gear to write the proposal." She was thinking out loud. "There must have been communication related to preparing the proposal. Who from HCU made the contacts with the foundation?"

"My assistant and I talked to both Bill Jenkins and Rebecca Holland. It was all standard for this type of request. Nothing unusual comes to mind. The final proposal was received in March and the board voted in April. You know the rest."

"We're missing something. I can feel it." Her stomach rolled, too much coffee.

"You're concentrating too hard. Let's change the subject." He studied her for a moment.

She did her best not to squirm.

"Tell me something about yourself that your boss doesn't know," he said.

"There's not much to tell." She thought for a second, struggling with her attraction to him. "Promise me you'll keep this to yourself."

"I will." He crossed a hand over his heart.

"Well . . . my secret desire is to play serious poker at a Las Vegas casino with the big boys."

She saw the surprise in his eyes. Forty-something CPAs weren't the usual card sharks.

"No kidding. What do you play, five card stud?" he asked.

"Texas Hold 'Em. I'm quite the player in certain circles." He didn't need to know it was the twins, Nana, and Ruthie.

"I'm impressed." He signed the check, then stood. "I better get you home before they kick us out."

All in all, it had been a pleasant evening. Logan had provided new information about the donation. She mustn't forget the possible connection between a HCU employee and the Rice family. Better to question the obvious and dig into the details of what he hadn't said. But all that could wait until tomorrow. She was pooped and looked forward to slipping into bed and watching the late-night news.

A few minutes later, they turned the corner to her street. Lights flashed ahead. Someone's alarm had probably gone off. She realized quickly the lights were in front of her townhouse.

"What is going on?"

"Looks serious. I count three police cars," Logan replied.

He parked in front of a neighbor's house. Dallas ran down the sidewalk to her front walk. A police officer stopped her.

"Are you Dallas Wells?" the officer asked.

"Yes. What's going on here? Why is my front door open?"

Logan drew up beside her, draped an arm over her shoulder.

"Officer, what's the problem?"

The officer first eye-balled Logan then turned his attention to Dallas.

"Miss Wells, I'm sorry to tell you this, but your grandmother was attacked tonight, in your home. She's at the Sugar Land Hospital."

She became numb, like a statute with every drop of blood drained from her body. Logan's hand squeezed her shoulder.

"Oh, my . . . Nana—is she okay? Was she badly hurt? What hospital is she at? I need to go to her."

"Miss Wells, she's okay." The officer spoke in a soft voice. "She has a gash on her head and she was shaken up, but she's basically okay. Her friend called nine-one-one immediately."

"Friend? What friend?"

Logan squeezed her shoulder again. "Dallas, let him explain."

"Oh." Her lungs sucked in air. She swallowed hard, licked her lips. "Someone was with her?"

"That's right, he was an older gentleman." The officer dug in his pocket and handed Dallas a piece of paper. "He left his cell number and asked that you call him before going to the hospital."

She moved to the side for better light. "Logan, can you see this? I don't have my reading glasses."

"It says Bob Marshall. Do you know him?"

"I met him the other day. He's Nana's new boyfriend."

"Let's call him on my phone." He keyed in the numbers, handed the phone to Dallas. It rang once.

"Bob, it's Dallas. How's Nana?" Tears snaked down her cheeks.

"Dallas, I'm glad you called." He sounded relieved. "Your grandmother is fine. She has a bump on her forehead and a couple of stitches. The doctor wants to keep her overnight for observation." His voice became hoarse. "As long as nothing turns up, she can go home in the morning."

Her heart began to beat again. "Thank God it's nothing

more serious. I'm coming to the hospital right now."

"Please, wait, there's nothing you can do here. Let me stay with her. She's asleep and won't wake up for several hours."

"But, I need to take care of her."

Logan rubbed her arm, stood quietly next to her.

"I'll take care of her. I owe it to her." Bob's voice cracked. "If only I'd gone in with her. Maybe I could have stopped the guy."

"This wasn't your fault." She didn't yet know what had happened, but whatever the event, it had profoundly affected him. She followed her instincts. "I'll be there first thing in the morning to take her home. You'll be there all night?"

"I'm not moving more than a foot from her bed until I see you in the morning."

She passed the phone back to Logan, swiped away the tears, and took a moment to take stock of the situation. Nana was fine, that's all that mattered. But what prompted her to travel to Sugar Land this evening?

Logan must have realized she'd ask that question. He took her hand and they walked to the front door. The same police officer waited on the step under the glare of the porch light.

"What exactly happened to my grandmother?"

Logan positioned himself behind her, his presence a welcome comfort under the circumstances.

"According to Mr. Marshall, she stopped by to bring you photographs and cookies. When you didn't answer the doorbell, she used her key to enter the house. Mr. Marshal waited in the car. After several minutes she hadn't returned, so he decided to check on her. He rang the bell. She didn't come to the door so he entered and found your grandmother lying on the living room floor."

His explanation pounded against Dallas' brain, she slowly absorbed the cop's explanation. Tears again threatened. She now understood what Bob had meant when he said it was his fault Nana was hurt.

"You're saying someone was already inside when she

entered the house," Logan said. "Was it an interrupted burglary?"

"We don't think so. Miss Wells, I need to show you something." The officer motioned for them to follow him as they went upstairs to the master bath.

In a million years, she could never have predicted what the officer had to show them. Written on the mirror over the vanity, in what looked like dark red marker, were the words: *Back off bitch or you'll be sorry.*

Dallas' body stiffened in shock. Why would someone break into her home and leave this ugliness? She stepped back from the mirror and wished the words to disappear.

"Miss Wells, do you have an idea of who might want to threaten you?" The cop held the police-issue notebook in his hand, waiting for a reply. "Have you had problems or cross words with anyone lately?"

She shook her head and walked to the bedroom to perform a three-sixty survey. Nothing had been disturbed other than the mirror. The room was just as she left it with clothes strewn over the bed.

"I don't know anyone who hates me enough to break into my house and leave such ugly words." She glanced at the bathroom and a wave of apprehension swept through her. Some asshole had been in her house, uninvited. "I can't remember the last time I had an argument with someone. This makes no sense."

She ran downstairs and retrieved a bottle of water from the refrigerator, then stood with a hip against the counter and stared out the window over the sink. The streetlight near the corner of her front yard illuminated a large oak tree and the shrubs along the side fence. This was a well-lit neighborhood with little crime. She couldn't remember ever hearing about a home break-in or burglary.

The local constable patrolled regularly and almost everyone had an alarm system. Damn . . . she hadn't set the alarm when she left with Logan. Talk about the mistake of the century. If the alarm had been set, the jerk wouldn't have broken in.

She heard her name being called from the living room. Logan and the police officer were examining the lock on the front door.

"Have you found something?" she asked.

"The break-in occurred through the door on your patio. It has the marks of being jimmied. This one is clear." The cop shut the front door. "Your grandmother interrupted the guy going or coming. I'd guess it was shortly after he entered since there wasn't any damage other than the mirror." He mumbled in a walkie-talkie on his shoulder. "If a perp wants to threaten with a break-in like this, they normally tear up the house pretty good. I figure your grandmother spooked him and he took off."

Talk about too much information. Tears threatened Dallas.

"I wish I had set the alarm when I left." She wrapped her arms tight around her chest. "That might have scared the guy off."

The officer shook his head. "I doubt it. These guys know how to neutralize every home alarm on the market." He glanced around the living room. "We're about done here."

"What happens next," she asked.

"Have the lock replaced on the patio door," Logan answered.

"We need your finger prints to compare against the ones we've taken from the bathroom and the door." The officer smiled and opened the front door. "There's a mobile unit in the van. We'll give you a call in a day or two."

Logan stood by her side as the prints were taken. Within a few minutes the police departed and they moved inside to the kitchen.

Dallas washed her hands then poured shots of brandy and handed Logan a glass. They studied each other from opposite sides of the kitchen.

"Thanks for dinner," she said. "The ending was a bit unexpected, even for me."

"That it was. I'm glad you didn't arrive home to this alone."

"Me, too." A single tear etched her cheek.

Logan placed his glass on the counter, took three steps toward her. The maleness of him filled the small kitchen. His finger wiped away the tear, gently caressing her cheek. The scent of his aftershave sent a shiver down her arms. It had been so long since she'd been this close to a man.

"Are you sure you're okay?" His voice was husky, his eyes searched her face. "I don't like you staying here with a broken door lock."

She hadn't thought about that. "I'll call my friend, Ruthie."

He looked at his watch. "It's past midnight. There's no need to bother her. You can stay with me. I have a very comfortable guest suite."

Was Logan nuts or what? She hardly knew him. What would her daughters think?

"That's very sweet of you, but—"

"No excuses. Throw your things in an overnight bag and we'll be on our way." He gave her a quick hug and pointed to the door. "You have five minutes."

Dallas hurried upstairs to gather clothes and toiletries. She was too tired to analyze why she agreed so easily.

Within minutes, they headed north on the Southwest Freeway. The drive to Logan's home in the West University area of Houston was quick and uneventful. She paid little attention to the surroundings as he escorted her through the house and upstairs to the guest bedroom. He pointed to the master suite at the end of the hall, just in case of emergency.

The bedroom was lovely with muted peach and cream colors and rich oak furniture. The joining bath had a garden tub along with a spa shower. The elegance reminded her of the Four Seasons Hotel in downtown Houston.

"This is wonderful." She sat on the bed, stroked her hand over the duvet, admiring the luxury of the fabric. "I'm glad I came."

"I'm glad you came, too." He leaned against the doorframe. "At least you can't get in any mischief here."

"Mischief? I'll have you know, Mr. Logan Rice, that I don't get in mischief, I create mischief."

He threw his head back and laughed. "Well, don't create any here, unless I'm involved."

Not more than five feet from Logan, she could see the

strength emanate from him like the first breath outdoors on a frosty morning. At another time, she might have continued with the flirting but she was ready to call it a night. The past few crazy days, topped off by that ugly message, had drained her and she simply wanted to sleep.

"I promise to be on my best behavior. I'll see you in the morning." She moved to the door and placed her hand on the knob. "Goodnight, Logan, thanks again . . . for everything."

"You're welcome." He kissed her cheek then moved into the hall and turned back to her. "I've been thinking. Do you suppose the break-in this evening was connected to the HCU theft?"

EIGHT

Thursday, 7:39 a.m.

THE MORNING DAWNED DARK and dreary thanks to a spring thunderstorm. The storm's effects rolled through Logan's guest room with the occasional crack of lightening, reminding Houston residents that Mother Nature was indeed in charge. Hurricane season was just around the corner. Rain pattered against the window and French doors leading to a second-floor balcony. From its gentle rhythm, she concluded the worst of the weather had passed.

Dallas snuggled deeper into the warmth of the bed, unable to avoid thoughts about the events of last night. It seemed obvious to connect the dots between "back off bitch" and the theft of the $25 million. Was she going to listen to the threat and back off? No.

After a quick shower, she threw on jeans and a cotton top and applied a bit of color to her cheeks. Concealer helped mask the under-eye shadows caused by too much stress and too few hours of sleep. She packed her few belongings in the duffle bag, slung it over her shoulder, and headed for the kitchen and the coffee pot.

She heard noise coming from the first floor and hurried down the stairs and through a hallway to the kitchen. A television on the counter blared the morning news.

She stopped in the doorway, scoping out the kitchen. The layout was large and filled with tall cherry cabinets and stainless-steel appliances. With a restaurant-style range and oven it was definitely a cook's retreat. Perhaps Logan had another hobby he hadn't mentioned. She mentally hugged him. Men who cook garnered a high rating.

"Morning," she said from the doorway.

"Good morning. Did you sleep well?" He turned off the TV.

"Hmm, need coffee."

He poured from a carafe, brought a mug to her. "Try this."

"Thanks." She sipped the coffee; it tasted wonderful. She stepped into the room and stood across the counter from him. "Just so you know, I need coffee before I can speak."

"Understood." He nodded toward a mug on the counter. "My second cup. Have a seat. I made us breakfast."

She slid onto a forest green stool. "Do you make breakfast like this every day?"

"No, but you're special," he said, turning bacon onto a paper towel. "Usually my cooking is on Sunday with a large pot of coffee, lots of protein, and hours reading the newspaper."

He made a plate for her with a whole-wheat muffin, turkey bacon, and cantaloupe—most of the food groups. Granted it was more food than her standard vanilla yogurt but my heavens, a man cooked for her. She could easily be spoiled by the attention.

She transgressed for a minute, picturing Logan and herself lying in bed and reading the paper to each other. She'd read the sports page and he'd read the Sunday magazine. They'd toast with Mimosa's and plan the itinerary for the afternoon—a tour through the Museum of Fine Arts or perhaps the Arboretum in Memorial Park. The most enjoyable part of the day was being together. They would—

"Hey." Logan waved a hand in front of her face. "Are you awake or asleep with your eyes open?"

"I'm here." She laughed and it felt good. "Sorry, my mind took off for a moment. Thanks for the breakfast."

"You're welcome. Perhaps we can do it again when I'm not rushed for time." He checked his watch. "I have an appointment at the office in less than an hour."

"That would be nice. Breakfast I mean."

"Count on it. What are your plans for today?" He shoved his plate in the sink and ran water over it.

"That's right. Once I leave here I'm going to the hospital to take her home." She added her plate to the sink. "That reminds me, what did you mean last night about the break-in being connected to the theft?"

"Think about it. Twenty-five million is stolen from HCU and you're the HCU representative asking lots of questions. Crime isn't typical for your neighborhood yet all of a sudden, your home has a break-in." He moved next to her. "And don't forget those words on the mirror. My theory is that you've rattled the thief and he's trying to scare you off."

Dallas chewed her lower lip. "That's not going to happen. This is personal now." She swallowed hard, tamping down her anger. "Whoever did this doesn't know me very well. Screwing with my family doesn't scare me off, it pisses me off."

Logan nodded. "You should be angry."

Before she could reply, he moved a step closer, his blue eyes bored into hers. She broke the contact first; his body was too close. She pulled back and he moved with her. He placed his hands on her shoulders, gently pulling her to him. Then his lips touched hers.

A spicy tingle slipped down her spine while her heart threatened to explode, unaccustomed to the current activity involving her tongue. Logan was one good kisser. He pulled away then straightened his tie.

"I need to get going. Let's have dinner tonight. There are a couple of things I need to check out, then we can talk more about the theft. I'll call you this afternoon." He picked up his briefcase and suit coat. "A house key is by the phone and I've called taxi service to take you home. Give my best to your grandmother."

"Thanks for everything." She waved as he left. What was that? One minute he was kissing her like a long-lost lover and the next minute he was Mr. Businessman. Men were so weird.

She refilled her cup and sat at the counter to wait for the taxi, her head heavy with stress. Too much had happened in the past twenty-four hours, the past seven days. Frustration, no, anger washed over her.

A taxi arrived within fifteen minutes. Once at her townhouse, she used the outside keypad to open the garage door. She jumped in the Volvo and headed to the hospital.

The central information desk provided Nana's room number. Bob paced the hall in front of it.

"Bob, hey, are you okay?"

Bob whirled around and hugged her like she was the morning's first cup of coffee. "I'm so glad you're here. Your grandmother is ready to go and well, she's a little feisty."

Dallas smiled, that was her Nana. "Showing some attitude, huh? I better get her home then." She entered the room with Bob close behind. Nana sat on the edge of the bed flipping TV channels with the remote. Dallas took a deep breath as she noticed a small bandage near the hairline of her forehead and a large bruise on her right cheek.

"Nana, how are you feeling this morning?"

"Just fine. Now, take me home."

As soon as the attending doctor signed the release papers, they were on their way. Bob agreed to go home for the rest he badly needed. He wasn't happy to leave Nana but agreed to stop by her house for lunch.

Nana wasn't talkative in the car. Dallas couldn't blame her. The drizzly weather echoed varying shades of gray along the freeway.

Dallas was a bit blue herself, despite the fact Nana was fine and would suffer no physical effect from her ordeal. The doctor had insisted the only physical reminder of the incident would be a small scar. Dallas wondered about the extent of emotional impact. Nana took pride in her independence so Dallas knew she wasn't happy being caught off guard.

They exited the freeway and swung north to the South Wind subdivision. Ranch style homes on large lots were flanked by powerful oak trees, framing the street with a canopy. Pink and white azaleas bordered the walks. Even on a dreary day, the neighborhood evoked comfort from a thousand memories of Halloween, Christmas, birthday parties, and Nana's bear hugs.

Dallas parked in the driveway and hurried to help Nana from the car. Her grandmother shot her 'the look,' so she backed off. They entered the house through the front door. Nana headed straight to the kitchen with Dallas trailing behind like a lost puppy.

"Nana, I'll fix whatever you want." They stood on opposite sides of the center island. "What would you like?"

"Oh, poo, I can do it myself. I'm making coffee. That stuff at the hospital was gutter runoff." Nana retrieved a coffee can from the refrigerator while Dallas perused the mug collection in a cabinet. "Sit down, your hovering is making me nervous."

Fine, Dallas knew when to retreat and plunked in a chair at the oak breakfast table. It was a favorite spot. In high school and after her divorce, they had many discussions and disagreements at the table, usually with the coffee urn between them. The topics ranged from boys and make-up to the twins and the meaning of life.

After all these years and countless hours of plain old talking, they had yet to discover a subject off limits. Dallas remembered one winter evening when they agreed that a good marriage begins with the right two people. Nana had ample experience with that and, well, Dallas was clueless.

Nana puttered around the kitchen while the coffee dripped. She reviewed the status of the pantry and refrigerator, jotted down a grocery list, and didn't utter a word. Dallas knew enough to stay quiet. Within minutes, the fragrance of full-bodied French Roast filled the kitchen. Nana poured two cups and joined her at the table.

Dallas sipped and waited.

"Okay." Nana planted her mug on the table. "Tell me what is going on. Are you in trouble?"

"No."

"Then what the heck is going on?"

"I assume you're referring to your knock on the head at my townhouse?"

Nana rolled her eyes. "Of course, that's what I'm referring to. Why was some no-good jerk in your house?" Dallas didn't respond so she continued. "Was he there to hurt you?" A tear rolled down Nana's cheek.

"Oh, Nana." Dallas leaned over and hugged her. Her body felt so small and frail in Dallas' arms. "I won't lie to you. Yes, the intruder was there to hurt me, but not physically. At least I don't think so."

Nana's eyes blinked with confusion.

"I realize that sounds strange. He left a nasty message on my bathroom mirror. That was the purpose for his visit. The police speculate you interrupted him, he panicked and then hit you."

"My heavens, what a story. But I'm confused. Why would someone leave a nasty message for you?" She ran her finger around the top edge of the coffee mug. "You haven't been giving Jonathon a hard time, have you?"

Dallas laughed. "Not that he doesn't deserve it, but, no. Forget about the break-in. Are you really okay? Does your head hurt?" She pushed back a strand of silver hair on Nana's forehead.

"I'm fine. The doc said I'll probably have a scar, a reminder to call before I visit you." She patted Dallas' hand, then gave it a reassuring squeeze. "I'll take a nap in a bit, don't worry." She refilled their mugs.

"I'll do my best not to worry. Please make sure you rest every day for a while. And, if you feel dizzy—"

"Dr. Wells, I'll take it easy. Don't worry, I'm a strong old bird with lots of life left." She winked at Dallas. "Now tell me what the message said. There must be a reason why that awful person left it."

Dallas considered the best words to tell her grandmother the truth. On one hand, Nana was almost eighty and had been through a stressful ordeal, and on the other hand, she had survived a multitude of stressful events throughout her life. Dallas made up her mind, no sugar coating.

"I'll share with you what's been going on the past few days. More than likely, it's related to last night." She searched Nana's face for any signs of discomfort. "Let me know if you get tired."

Nana agreed with a wave of her hand. Dallas began her tale

with last Friday's meeting in Scooter's office. She mentioned helping HCU with the police and the encounters with Roddy and the dinner with Logan. She omitted her frustration with Roddy or the mind-blowing kiss with Logan.

She concluded with her suspicions that the HCU theft and last night's break-in were related and possibly Bill's murder as well.

"Now you know what I've been dealing with the past few days. Not my typical vacation."

"My word, that's quite a story. You're doing all this, uh, sleuthing, for the benefit of your boss and HCU?" Nana patted Dallas' hand again.

"Yep, that's my story."

"You know what you're doing. And who knows, your boss may come through for you once this is over. Are you close to solving the case?" She carried their mugs to the sink, turned back to Dallas. "You know, it seems to me, whoever took the money works at HCU. It's that simple."

Complicated was easy, simple was difficult.

Nana moved to the living room and Dallas soon heard a morning game show.

She closed her eyes, resting her elbows on the table with her head in her hands. Too much had happened in the past twenty-four hours, the past seven days. Frustration, no, anger seeped from every pore of her skin.

Nana could have been killed last night. Why had this happened? Dammit. Her eyes flew open and she clenched her fists, itching to hit something. She stopped herself from pounding the table. That would only alert Nana to the extent of her anger.

She needed to step back and review every fact she'd learned over the past few days. There simply had to be a common thread and if Nana was correct, that thread was HCU. Her stomach rolled at the thought. It was difficult for her to conclude that one of her co-workers was a thief and very possibly a murderer. She wished she'd been nosier about the personal lives of staff members in other departments, then she'd have more information to analyze— not being a snoop and a gossip was a big mistake.

She pulled out her cell phone to try Roddy and moved to the window. He answered.

"It's Dallas. My house was broken into last night."

"What?"

"That's right, and the asshole who broke in bopped my grandmother on the head and left a sweet note for me scribbled on my bathroom mirror—'Back off bitch or you'll be sorry.'"

"Did the Sugar Land police answer the call?"

"Yep." She glanced out the kitchen window. Sunlight penetrated the dreary blanket of clouds.

"Good, I'll give them a call. Was your grandmother hurt?" he said.

"A couple stiches on her forehead, she'll be okay. By the way, why haven't you returned my calls?"

"My mother had surgery yesterday, I've been with her."

"I hope she's okay," she said. "Sorry I gave you a hard time."

"She's fine and no problem. Have you heard from the Sugar Land police this morning?"

"Not a word. Have you heard from your friend at the FBI?"

"Not yet, but I'm hoping today is the day.

She heard a voice in the background.

"Gotta go," Roddy said.

Dallas pulled a small notebook and pen from her purse and returned to the counter. The simplest story was that a HCU employee committed the theft for reasons unknown and more than likely killed Bill because he knew too much.

She didn't have a shred of proof to support her assumptions. Clicking the pen, she made a decision. Even though she had no proof, she'd assume the thief was associated with HCU. She'd stick with that until she uncovered something else, or the truth.

Nana hadn't made a peep so Dallas tip-toed to the living room to check on her. Sure enough, she was sound asleep in her recliner. Dallas sat on the edge of the flowered couch and watched her breathe. She was the best grandmother a girl could have. There had never been a time when she didn't listen or transform a difficult situation into a learning situation.

She was the absolute best thing in the world after the death of Dallas' parents when she was sixteen. Dallas gave her grandmother plenty of trouble after their death. Something she regrets to this day. The absolute worst was eloping with her ex-husband, Jonathan, the day after she graduated high school. She dreamed of a secure future and he craved a cute young wife with big knockers. Enough said.

Dallas prayed Nana's lessons had rubbed off and would guide her in her own role as a grandmother. Liz was on the home stretch now, so it wouldn't be long before the grandma role would be official.

She checked her watch. Time to inform Scooter about last night's break-in. She called his office and Ellie answered.

"It's Dallas. How's everything going?"

"How's it going with you? Scooter said you've been busy on your vacation."

"I've talked to the police a few times and I'm doing my best to help. Is Scooter around?"

"No, he left on a trip today," Ellie said.

"What trip?" He didn't have a trip scheduled on the calendar. How could he leave in the midst of a crisis? "Where did he go? When will he be back?"

"I know, I thought it was strange, too. He flew to Las Vegas, said it was a family thing that had been planned for a while."

Yeah, right. "What hotel in Vegas?"

"The Grand Resort and Casino," Ellie replied. "If you're calling him, wait until later in the day. His flight is at noon."

"Will do. Do you know if Rebecca Holland is out sick today?"

"Yes, she is. I had a question for her earlier and Daniel said she's still ill." They ended the call.

Well, well, wasn't that interesting? Two people on the HCU list of possibilities out of the office at the same time. And one of them was Dallas' boss. She couldn't imagine being in a more uncomfortable situation. When this was over, she hoped Scooter wouldn't look at her as a traitor.

"Dallas, are you still here?" Nana called out. She rushed to the living room.

"Everything okay?" she asked. Nana played with the TV remote, flipping through channels. "Can I get you anything?"

"No, I'm just fine," she said. "You can go on home. Bob will be here soon with lunch."

She obviously preferred Bob's hovering.

They chatted for a bit longer then Dallas launched into a round of instructions to get plenty of rest and to eat healthy. Nana looked at her like she was performing a duck imitation and quickly ushered her to the door.

"I'm sure Bob is on his way so you can go on about your business." She kissed Dallas on the cheek then opened the door. "Now don't worry about me, I'm tough."

She no doubt looked forward to seeing Bob.

As she started the Volvo, Dallas wondered about Nana's relationship with Bob. They seemed genuinely fond of each other and enjoyed being together. Good for Nana, she deserved some fun.

She sat for a moment and pondered her next move. Should she go home? She pulled out the list she'd made in the kitchen. Rebecca's name was at the top. A face-to-face conversation with Rebecca should clear up any question of her involvement.

$ $ $

Dallas found Rebecca's home address in the campus directory. It was close to HCU and easy to find. Traffic was light on the freeway so she arrived in twenty minutes.

Rebecca lived in one of those large old houses divided into apartments. Trees and overgrown shrubs surrounded it. Her apartment was on the bottom floor with the entrance on the left side of the house. A brick path bordered by lush white hibiscus led to the door.

Dallas rang the doorbell, waited a moment, pushed the button again. Hopefully, Rebecca wasn't so ill she couldn't come to the door. Three newspapers were strewn over the front step. She knocked on the door. Still no answer.

The glare of a large window to the right of the entrance caught her attention. It was covered with sheers so she scrunched her face against the glass, shielding her eyes with her hands. She had a good view of the living room. Papers, books, and pillows were scattered over the floor. A lamp sat askew on the sofa and an overturned potted plant rested on an area rug.

This couldn't be good. Had Rebecca been hurt or even killed like Bill?

She raced back to the door and pounded on it, then rang the bell again. No answer. Should she call the police? She tried the doorknob and it turned. What idiot left their home unlocked in Houston? She didn't know if stepping into someone's house without being invited was breaking and entering but she took the plunge. Rebecca could be in trouble.

She shut the door quickly behind her and gazed around the front room. It was devoid of human spirit, as if the air had been sucked out.

"Rebecca, are you home?" Dallas yelled. No answer. "This can't be good," she mumbled and started to search the apartment. She called out Rebecca's name as she moved from room to room. It was a quick tour. She concluded Rebecca wasn't dead, merely not at home. She hadn't been there for two to three days based on the newspapers stacked on the front step along with the musty smell.

Yet she'd been calling HCU reporting in sick since Tuesday. She obviously wanted to give the impression she was in Houston. The twit had left in a hurry based on the condition of the living room and the unlocked front door.

Dallas spied a small table and a desktop computer in the corner of the dining room—the perfect place to start snooping. She wondered about jail time for a first B and E while the computer fired up. Maybe Roddy could convince the judge to be lenient on her. After all, she was acting on behalf of her employer.

Once the start page settled down, she reviewed the desktop

icons, and saw nothing unusual. She performed a document search on the hard drive, came up with zilch. Even the recycle bin was empty. If Rebecca had used the computer to plan the theft she had done an excellent job of erasing evidence of it. What was next? TV cops always did a search of the premises. Dallas realized her chance of discovering any proof was minuscule.

As she reached to turn of the computer, her eye caught the mail icon. She hadn't looked at an e-mail account. She clicked on the button. The user name and password were stored with the program so she had no problem opening it. There were only a handful of messages in the in-box and one was from United Airlines.

The message was a flight confirmation for a seven a.m. flight from Houston Bush to San Francisco this past Tuesday, then a second flight to Las Vegas yesterday afternoon. This was a one-way ticket. The date of the e-mail was early April.

What did this mean? Number one, Rebecca had lied about being ill. Number two, she had been in Houston when Bill was killed. And number three, numbers one and two had moved her to the top of Dallas' inventory of suspects. She froze, a chill slid down her spine. This could be the beginning of the end.

Apparently, Rebecca had plans. Dallas should call Roddy and tell him everything she'd just learned. That was the smart thing to do. But dammit, Rebecca had been dishonest to everyone and she shouldn't be allowed to get away with it. Dallas thought about those nasty words on her mirror. She fisted her hands. Discovering the identity of the thief was personal now. It was her duty as the HCU point person to follow Rebecca to Las Vegas.

How interesting that Scooter would be there as well.

NINE

Thursday, 1:16 p.m.

THE LAST HOUR HAD BEEN a whirlwind. Once she decided to fly to Las Vegas, Dallas called Logan. Why she thought of him rather than Nana or the twins was a mystery. However, she didn't call Roddy for fear of him throwing her in jail for breaking into Rebecca's house.

Once Dallas informed Logan of her plan, he arranged to accompany her on the Bridge Foundation/RBI corporate jet. Why the hell not? She agreed to meet him at Hull Airport in Sugar Land and rushed back to the townhouse to pack and rummage around for her sanity.

Packing a suitcase was one of her least favorite activities—right up there with going to the dentist and taking down Christmas decorations. She didn't have time to think logically about her outfits so she threw in jeans, shorts, slacks, tops, a couple of sundresses and a cocktail dress, in case the need might arise. She bumped the suitcase down the stairs and stowed it in the Volvo's trunk.

Heading north on Highway 6 to the airport, she called Dr. Arnold on her cell, hoping he wouldn't answer. No such luck.

"Good to hear from you."

"You told me to keep you informed of my activities." Dallas realized her voice sounded rushed so she slowed down. "I'm reporting in."

"What have you learned since we last spoke?"

"I'm not sure if this means anything . . . but Rebecca has been calling in sick since Tuesday and I believe she's flown to Las

Vegas."

"That doesn't sound like Rebecca. What does her misrepresenting her absence from the office have to do with the missing funds? Surely, you don't suspect her?"

That was exactly what Dallas thought. It had been rolling around in her head for the past two days and erupted with the flight confirmation. She didn't know if Rebecca possessed the skill to steal $25 million or to possibly kill Bill, but she intended to find out.

"Dr. Arnold, I don't know who's responsible at this point. The police haven't turned up any suspects. I wanted you to know I'm flying to Las Vegas. I intend to find Rebecca and talk with her."

"Are you sure that's necessary?" Impatience frosted his words.

"I do think it's necessary. Scooter is flying there this afternoon, too. Maybe it's a coincidence, but don't you find it odd?" Personally, she thought it was beyond strange.

"I suppose it is a bit unusual." She heard Dr. Arnold's sigh. "Consider yourself on official University business, not vacation time. I expect to hear from you twice a day. If you don't discover worthwhile information within two days, come home."

"That's fair. I'll call you this evening once I'm settled."

As she drove, Dallas acknowledged that flying off to Nevada was impulsive. She was leaving Houston without an action plan and that made her nervous. She wasn't good at winging it. And, concluding Rebecca was the guilty party, even though she'd been lying about being sick, was a gigantic leap in logic. But the timing came under the heading of "Too Damned Coincidental."

She arrived at the airport, parked, pulled out her single piece of luggage and headed for the one-story terminal building. Once inside, she glanced around the lobby and spied an information desk tucked in a corner. A teenaged boy with headphones glued to his head stood behind the counter. He bopped and weaved to the music pouring into his head.

"Excuse me." She waved her arms. "Excuse me."

He looked at her.

"I need to find a plane," she shouted.

"Gee lady, ya don't haft ta yell." He wrapped the headphones around his neck. "What plane?"

"It belongs to the Bridge Foundation."

"The what? The Street Foundation?" He riffled through papers on a clipboard.

"No, the Bridge Foundation."

He glanced up and grinned. Was every teenager a wiseacre?

"Can you tell me what hangar it's in?" She was wasting time.

"Sure, it's in F-20. There's a black SUV out the door to take you over. Any other questions?" The headphones were back in place before she could answer.

Dallas turned around and headed for a door in the back. The kid was right; the ride waited for her outside the terminal. A driver introduced himself and ushered her to the back seat. They skated along the edge of the tarmac to a collection of metal hangars. Many of the wide doors were open with planes perched in front.

They drove around the side of a light-blue hangar and finally she saw Logan, ambling down the steps of a gleaming silver plane. The SUV parked at its steps and she emerged.

"Dallas, you're right on time." He kissed her cheek. "We're ready to leave so let's get on board." He picked up her bag and she followed him up the stairs.

She expected the plane's interior to be luxurious and she wasn't disappointed. It set the bar high for future flying. Logan gave her the ten-dollar tour of the main cabin and the galley before they buckled in for take-off.

Once the plane achieved cruising altitude, the co-pilot strolled into the main cabin with a serving cart loaded with champagne, fruit, cheese and crackers. He parked it in the aisle next to their seats, locked its wheels, and disappeared to the front of the plane.

"It's a family tradition to bless every flight after liftoff." Logan filled two champagne flutes, handed one to Dallas. "We also have a traditional toast."

Her eyes widened. "A toast?"

"Grandma Rice started it with our first plane over thirty years ago. Ready?"

"You bet."

"Here goes: 'May the breath of angels lift your wings, may the brilliance of stars guide your way, keep us sound and safe, and let there be champagne for another day.'" He touched his flute to hers. "Gram has quite the sense of humor."

"I'll say. You toast every flight?" She had a suspicion he was teasing her.

"Yes, ma'am. Gram makes us swear we do the toast every time we fly. We've never had an accident, so," he shrugged, "I guess it works."

Dallas envied his casualness about the toast. "It's cute. Your grandmother obviously loves her family. Anything else I should know—rituals, eating or drinking contests?"

"The toast is the extent of our craziness." He pointed to the tray of food. "Have something to eat. It'll be several hours before we have dinner."

She made a plate of fruit and cheese and sat back to enjoy the company, the champagne, and the cocoon of luxury.

$ $ $

The plane rolled to a stop in front of a pink hangar. Once they climbed into the cool interior of a limousine, they set off for the Las Vegas Strip. Logan explained they had a ten-minute drive along Tropicana Boulevard to the Grand Hotel and Casino.

"Why did you select that hotel?" Dallas asked. Was it a coincidence Scooter was also booked at the Grand?

"Grandfather Rice went to Yale with one of the developers and bought a family suite before it opened. We all use it when we're in town. My brother, Max, and his wife were here last weekend. We should have the place to ourselves." He winked and displayed that killer grin.

"That's good, I guess." Asking about the number of

bedrooms sat on her tongue yet she swallowed the words. He called the room a suite, which implied multiple bedrooms.

"We've had some great times here. There's enough room for two or three families, kids and all. I think we've managed to stay every New Year's Eve for the last ten years. Gram loves the lights and the action."

"Your grandmother sounds like a hoot." Nana would probably like her, too.

They soon passed the Grand's towers, pink glass reflecting the afternoon sun, reminding her of cotton candy. The limo made a right turn before Las Vegas Boulevard and steered into the hotel's circular driveway. A uniformed valet welcomed them with a wide smile.

"Come on." Logan grabbed her hand and led her through the rotating glass door. "We'll be on our way once we pick up the key to the suite."

They crossed the dark marble floor of the lobby to the reception desk. Behind the desk, a huge digital screen played a U-2 video. The attendant greeted Logan by name and handed him a couple of card keys. After walking to the tower elevators, he punched in a code on the keypad and the elevator rose silently to the penthouse suite. The door opened to a small lobby with one large bronze door. Logan slid the card key in a security slot and opened the door.

They entered the foyer. Dallas stopped and gawked.

It was spectacular—black marble floors and red walls with framed artwork from floor to ceiling. She trotted behind Logan to the living room. The bold colors transitioned to muted tones of peach and green gracing the walls and furniture. He pointed out the bar to one side, a dining room and the kitchen around the corner, and the wing of bedrooms. He led her down a hallway to the bedrooms. It was wide and just as elegant as the rest of the suite. He opened a door on the left.

"This should do." Logan opened the window draperies, the late afternoon sun streamed across the light sage bedspread. The demeanor of the room was calming—a good omen for her first out-of-town investigation.

"This is beautiful. Let me take a minute to freshen up."

A bell bonged.

"Our luggage has arrived. Take your time," Logan said.

Once he left, she melted onto the bed. Her adrenaline rush had evaporated. The reality of Las Vegas, and Logan, and a hotel suite stung her eyes. She brushed away a tear.

On her fingers, she counted off her very good reasons for feeling off-kilter. Number one, she had no concrete evidence that Rebecca was the guilty party. Number two, she could be arrested for breaking into Rebecca's rented apartment. Number three, Dr. Arnold had been acting very chummy toward Dallas, not normal. Number four, rushing off to Las Vegas could end up being a huge disaster. And, number five, Logan Rice was too good to be true.

She rested for a moment, feeling uncertain and unsure and uncomfortable. At the same time, she knew without question that Rebecca was up to her designer eyebrows in something that didn't pass the smell test.

$ $ $

Dallas stood at the living room window gazing at the view below. The sun had almost retired and the lights of the Strip sparkled with a fairy-tale quality. She wondered about Rebecca's location amidst the perpetual illumination and glitter. Perhaps she was holed up in a hotel room or walking the Strip without a care in the world.

Dallas heard a noise behind her and turned. Logan moved to her side.

"Everything okay?"

"Just day dreaming." She stepped back from the window. "Do we need to call room service for a glass of wine?"

"Nope." He strode to the bar, pulled a bottle from an under-counter cooler and uncorked it. After accepting a glass of cabernet, she settled in a corner of the peach and cream striped sofa. It was time to coordinate their plans to search for Rebecca.

Dallas' cell phone interrupted and she pulled it out of her pocket.

"Nana, what's up? Are you feeling all right? Any problems?"

"I'm just fine, sweetheart. Bob has been taking good care of me." Nana's voice was strong and excited.

"That's good. You sound a little odd. Is something wrong?" She sipped the wine. Logan looked at her with a question in his eyes.

"Everything is fine. But I do have some news for you—"

"News! It's not Liz? She didn't go in labor?"

"Heavens no, this relates to me." Nana hesitated for a moment then continued. "I hope you'll be happy for me. Bob and I had a long talk this afternoon and we've decided to get married."

"Married?" Dallas' chest tightened, her Nana, Bob, what?

Logan mouthed to her "who?" She gulped and managed to whisper "my grandmother."

"I know it seems sudden to you, but Bob and I have known each other for over twenty years. Life is too short to live it alone."

Nana had made up her mind.

"I love you and I know you know what you're doing," Dallas murmured. "Congratulations. Have you set a date?" How could she not be happy for her grandmother and Bob?

"We're thinking maybe a month after Liz has the baby. Bob needs to give his kids time as well. One of his sons lives in Japan."

They discussed the ceremony for a few minutes then said good-bye.

"Are you surprised by that?" Logan asked.

"Totally, I first met Bob last weekend. I didn't even know they were dating. But Nana wouldn't agree to this unless she was one-hundred percent certain it was right for her. She's one smart lady." She looked at her watch. "I need to call the twins to tell them the news. I'll be just a minute."

"Go ahead, I need to call the office." He moved to the bar, cell phone in hand.

Naturally, neither daughter answered so she left voice messages. Logan was still talking. She picked up the suite's phone, dialed the operator, and asked for Scooter's room.

"Ma'am, we don't have a guest with that name."

"Maybe he hasn't checked in yet. Is there a reservation? He's my boss and I need to reach him." How weird, Ellie said he was leaving Houston at noon.

"We don't have a reservation in that name for this evening. Perhaps he's at another hotel."

"You're probably right." Wrong. Ellie told her the Grand Hotel and Casino.

"Right about what?" Logan had finished his call.

"Scooter isn't registered here tonight. This morning he told his assistant he was flying to Las Vegas for a family vacation but he's not here. She doesn't get these things wrong."

"There's probably a logical explanation. Maybe he switched hotels for a better room," Logan said.

"Maybe. I'm not sure."

"Do you suppose he gave Ellie the wrong information on purpose?"

"I don't know." That didn't seem like Scooter.

"You think he's involved in the theft?" Logan perched on the arm of a chair across from her.

"Not at all. But you have to admit it's weird he's here at the same time as Rebecca." Rather than finding answers, the list of questions continued to multiply.

"Perhaps it's a simple coincidence," Logan offered.

"No clue." She shrugged. "Maybe he did switch hotels." She stood and began to pace from the window to the bar and back, shaking down her nerves. "Let's talk about finding Rebecca. Should we go to the police?"

"I've thought about that, too. Max has a friend here who's a detective with the Las Vegas police. We could call him," Logan suggested.

"Why not? We'll tell him I'm helping the Houston police solve a $25 million theft. I've a hunch that a coworker has committed the theft. I came to this conclusion after breaking into her residence and her personal computer. My conclusion was based on an e-mail I discovered on said computer which I had no right to read, yet it provided a flight itinerary for Las Vegas. I immediately flew here in pursuit and I have not one piece of concrete evidence linking Rebecca Holland to the theft. Still want to call Max's friend?" She stopped pacing a few feet from Logan.

"I see your point."

"The Las Vegas police would consider me a nut job. That reminds me, I forgot to tell Roddy about my travel plans. I better give him a call."

"Go ahead. I need to make another call myself." Logan moved over to the bar again, this time sitting in one of the tall, bronze stools.

Dallas hesitated before calling. How much should she tell him? Spill the beans or filter the facts? She didn't *really* break into Rebecca's house; the door was unlocked. She'd opened it as she was overly concerned about her ill co-worker, bless her skinny cold heart.

She had her story and keyed in Roddy's number, praying he'd answer. The phone gods hurled good vibes as he picked up on the second ring.

"Glad you finally called, Miss Wells, I have good news," he teased.

"Yay, what?"

"We have the name on the Caymans bank account for the Franks' check. It's Holly Roberts. Ring any bells?"

"No, I don't know anyone with that name." The name had a curious sound though. "Did you get an address or the date of a $25 million deposit?"

"I wish. All the bank would release was the name on the account. We'll find something. We're searching every available database." He sighed, heavily. "What have you been up to?"

"I'm in Las Vegas with Logan Rice."

"What? Oh, that's right, your vacation."

"No, not my vacation." She swallowed, began pacing across the room. "Actually . . . I found an e-mail on the PC in Rebecca's apartment this morning confirming a flight to Las Vegas and here I am."

"What? Back up. Tell Uncle Roddy what the hell you've been doing since this morning."

She heard the impatience in his voice and spilled the beans, reciting her theory on an e-mail virus altering the wire instructions, who had sent e-mails with attachments to First National, and her earlier visit to Rebecca's house.

She told him the truth about traveling to Las Vegas to find Rebecca and to confront her. Roddy was not a happy camper with her last admission.

"Damn it, you can't go off half-cocked, looking for someone who you've concluded, without any concrete evidence, is responsible for a crime. You have no idea how dangerous she might be, assuming she's even associated with the theft. Are you out of your freaking mind?"

Her back stiffened. Here she was, using her vacation to help the Houston police. "No, I'm not crazy. I'm completely sane and a good HCU employee. I'm merely on vacation and if I happen to bump into a coworker while I'm here, well, gee, what a coincidence. Gotta go." She ended the call and that was that. It could have been worse—he hadn't zeroed in on the fact that she had entered Rebecca's house without an invitation. Small favors, thank you.

She glanced at Logan, still on his cell. She retrieved her glass from a table by the sofa and sipped the wine. Excellent bouquet. Good wine was one of her favorite things, along with the unnoticed observation of a handsome man. Logan finished his call and strolled back to the living room. She did enjoy the way he walked—a John Wayne swagger with Brad Pitt hips—but, she was not interested.

"What did the detective say? Surprised by our trip to Vegas?" He grinned and saluted her with his wine glass.

"Roddy did mention me being out of my mind. At least I was honest about the breaking and entering escapade. I can go forward with a clear conscious." She finished the wine. "Let's get this show on the road. I'll begin by making a list of all the major hotels. Do you have paper here?"

"That may not be necessary," Logan said.

"Why?"

"I talked to the head of the Grand's security, an old family friend. He agreed it was useless to go to the police and suggested we hire a private investigator, someone who knows Vegas and has plenty of contacts." He ran a hand through his hair. "I made an appointment with a JW McKenzie for tomorrow morning."

"We definitely need someone who knows Las Vegas." She thought about using a private investigator. "This is a great idea. Having a professional work for us is just what we need." She kissed Logan on the cheek. "Thanks. What did you learn about Mr. McKenzie?"

"Nothing other than he's one of the best PIs in Vegas and we won't be disappointed."

"I believe we have a plan," she said.

"That we do. Are you hungry?"

She shook her head.

"In that case, let's walk for a while. We can stroll the Strip, then have dinner at Spago at Caesar's Palace. It's another family tradition."

"You go to college with the owner?"

"My brother John is one of the investors in the restaurant."

"How many brothers do you have?" His family tree was getting complicated.

"Three, and two sisters as well."

"Of course, you do." As an only child, large families were difficult for Dallas to get her head around. "I'm taking a shower. I'll see you in a bit." She walked to her assigned bedroom wondering if Logan had any more family surprises.

$ $ $

Once Dallas shut the bedroom door, Logan pulled out his cell phone and clicked on Roddy's name under the contacts list. The detective answered immediately.

"Jesus, Logan, are you crazy?"

"No."

"Then why the hell are you in Vegas with Dallas Wells?"

"To keep an eye on her. I told you I don't trust her."

"You may be wrong about that."

Logan chuckled. "What? You've changed your mind about her."

"Yeah, maybe."

"I haven't. She's a good actress." Logan wasn't sure he believed that one-hundred percent. "I called to let you know we're talking to a private investigator in the morning. What's new?"

"Ask Dallas," Roddy laughed. "Seriously, no major leads so far. Waiting for First National and the FBI. I'll call if anything major kicks me in the ass."

"Make sure you do that. I'll keep Dallas occupied."

"I bet you will. Make sure she stays out of trouble."

"Don't worry. I haven't forgotten how to do undercover."

TEN

Thursday, 7:07 p.m.

WATER PEPPERED DALLAS' SHOULDERS and back and felt wonderful. The double-sized shower had complementary shower heads at either end, perfect for a tired body. The pressure of the past few days sluiced away. She had twelve hours of down time ahead. No investigating, no list making, no thinking about Rebecca Holland.

Ignoring her lousy packing job, she pulled black jeans, a white cotton top, and black walking flats out of her suitcase. She fluffed her hair, applied the usual minimal make-up, and dug out a black sweater.

Logan waited for her in the living room. Dressed in gray slacks and a yellow shirt, he looked every inch the conservative businessman. She wondered if he ever had a bad hair day—he looked that good.

She watched him notice her as she walked into the room.

"You look rested," he said.

"You have good shower equipment here." She grinned. "I'm ready to explore."

"I made a dinner reservation for nine. We have plenty of time to walk." Logan donned a navy jacket and helped Dallas with her sweater.

They exited the Grand via a walkway over Las Vegas Boulevard. A miniature replica of the Statue of Liberty announced the entrance to the New York-New York Casino. They took the escalator to the street level. The statue's outstretched arm tugged at Dallas' patriotic heart. She hoped it was a good omen for her journey to Nevada. With Logan's hand at her back, they began walking the Las Vegas Strip.

After thirty minutes of comfortable strolling, they stopped in front of Lake Bellagio, an eight- acre man-made pond housing more than a thousand dancing fountains in front of the Bellagio Hotel. The bopping water, along with lights and music, performed a show several times during the day and evening. The spurting water traveled higher in the air as the music reached a crescendo then fountains rose from the lake, changing color as they danced across the lake's surface.

Logan placed his arm over Dallas' shoulder as they watched the show. It felt like they were a couple. For a moment, she allowed her mind to skip in that direction. Not an epiphany, but she did like the idea. But . . . she was in no position for romance. She had such a lousy track record with men.

A shout of laughter from a nearby group of teenagers interrupted her musings. The music ended. The water and lights faded to their dormant states along with any thoughts of Logan and her being a couple. She would not meander into that particular daydream again.

"Let's go across the street to Caesar's." Logan took her hand. "We can enter the Forum Shops from the sidewalk."

They passed by the Bellagio, then crossed Flamingo Road using another overhead walkway. Vehicles belching fumes and booming unrecognizable and overly loud music clogged the intersection.

Once inside the Forum Shops lobby, she spotted a three-story circular escalator. She felt like a six-year-old at her first carnival. Ten-foot statues of Greek gods were set in niches along the walls of the lobby and marble covered the floors.

They stepped on the escalator and rode to the second-floor entrance to the shopping area.

Excitement bubbled as Dallas looked from side to side, beautiful store fronts and a blue-sky ceiling with clouds and subdued lighting gave the illusion of being on a narrow Roman street. Without a doubt, the Forum Shops were awesome.

They windowed-shopped their way past Gucci, Hermes, and Brooks Brothers, then past the Fountain of the Gods to Spago. After they were seated, the waiter appeared with a wine list. Logan studied it before ordering. She didn't recognize the name of the wine he selected, another indication of the huge difference in their lifestyles.

"Since we both like wine, I thought we'd try something different." He squeezed her hand on the table. "Are you tired? It's been a long day."

"I'm all right. It's nice to relax." As the words left her mouth, any lingering stress evaporated. "One night off is pure luxury."

"Glad to hear that. After dinner, we can go back to the Bellagio and gamble."

She'd never gambled outside of Louisiana and family poker games. It would be fun to try something new.

The waiter arrived with the wine, i.e. champagne; the label read Cristal. Dinner with Logan Rice was not the typical dining experience; he seemed so sophisticated. Still, she found him attractive. His mother was no doubt one proud mama.

"Is champagne another Rice family tradition?" Dallas figured they had a tradition for every event.

He laughed. "No. This night needs a touch of the bubbly." He once again touched his glass to hers. "To a peaceful evening with a lovely lady."

"Thank you. You're not half bad yourself," she murmured. She opened the menu to side-step the conversation from going in a direction she had no business going in.

They ordered their entrees, then discussed the weather.

Logan placed a forearm on the table and leaned toward Dallas. "Forget the weather. I'd rather focus on you."

"That's a mistake. Like I told Roddy, I'm too smart for my own good. Don't do well outside of the twins and my job." She sipped the champagne, raised an index finger, "Nana and Ruthie, too. That's me, simple girl, small world."

"You know what? You don't see yourself as others see you. You're far from simple."

Dallas was strangely flattered by his interest yet relieved when they moved to less personal subjects—the Astros baseball season, the stock market, and their favorite dessert. From the beef tenderloin to the raspberry soufflé, they chatted.

After a cup of coffee, they departed back across Flamingo Road for the Bellagio. The western night was beautiful although the lights along the Strip masked the stars. Even though she couldn't see them, Dallas knew they were winking at Logan and her as they strolled. The sidewalk was crowded with gamblers and party-goers.

"Let's go through Via Bellagio on our way to the casino," Logan suggested. "You'll find great stores."

Strolling past Gucci, Prada, and Hermes, they gazed at shoes, handbags, and exquisite clothing in the window displays. Logan must be accustomed to shopping in such expensive stores, but for Dallas, the stores provided window shopping only.

While Logan checked out sunglasses in the window of Dior, Dallas wandered over to Tiffany's. A silver picture frame or baby spoon for her first grandchild would be a nice surprise for Liz. None were displayed in the window, so she walked into the store.

Standing by the window display, she happened to glance at the wide thoroughfare of strolling shoppers and gamblers on a break. What the hell? Scooter was out there. She leaned over the glass shelf for a better view. Yep, it was her boss! He moved toward the Strip end of the walkway. She scurried out the store and shouted his name. He stopped fifteen feet in front of her, turned, looked her square in the eyes, and took off sprinting toward the street.

"I just saw Scooter. Come on." She shouted to Logan, several feet away from her.

She ran in the same direction as Scooter and threaded her way through shoppers laden with bags, attempting to keep Scooter in her sights. He darted through the crowd, increasing the distance from her. Too quickly, he boarded the down escalator and reached the sidewalk, rushing to the right.

Dallas struggled to keep him in sight while on the escalator.

Once reaching the street, she took a step and ran smack into a bear-sized man carrying a large plastic cup. The cup shot in the air and rained liquid and ice cubes over the bear. He roared. She apologized and darted around him. Near the driveway to the Bellagio's hotel entrance, she stopped, praying for a glimpse of her boss. Her head whipped from side to side as she searched. No Scooter.

She dashed a few more steps and zeroed in on the crowds, searching for the yellow shirt he wore. She stopped again, bending over to catch her breath, and noticed a row of four or five taxis lined up on the street, waiting their turn to speed up to the hotel's entrance to catch a fare. She raised up and noticed a man in a yellow shirt open the door to a taxi in the middle of the line. It was definitely Scooter. She sprinted towards the taxi and shouted his name. The vehicle lurched out of the line, turned, and darted into the traffic flow on Las Vegas Boulevard.

Scooter had left the building.

Dallas stamped her foot like a three-year-old who didn't want to take an afternoon nap. She couldn't believe her eyes—Scooter ran away from her, on the Las Vegas Strip, at night. Why would he act like that? Why did he lie to Ellie about the hotel reservation? Damn him. He had just complicated her life by a thousand percent.

She bit her lower lip. What would she say to Dr. Arnold?

She turned a full circle on the sidewalk, attempting to get her bearings. Tourists streamed past her as Logan appeared.

"What are you doing? I couldn't hear what you said before you ran off."

"I saw Scooter outside Tiffany's." She pulled air into her lungs to calm her nerves. "I called his name." She placed a hand on Logan's arm. "He recognized me then he took off running. I followed him out here. Why would he want to get away from me?"

"No clue. Are you okay?"

"I'm fine other than being royally pissed."

Logan's arms surrounded her and provided a much-needed

hug. He held her, his hand stroking up and down her back. She hated to admit it, but the contact calmed her anger.

"Let's forget this for now. Do you want to go back to the Grand or put twenty bucks in a Bellagio slot machine?" He grinned. "You might get lucky."

Probably not. She couldn't wrap her head around Scooter running away from her. Why? He wasn't a thief. Really, he was too damned conservative for that.

"You're on. I won't let Scooter ruin my evening. Let's hit the slots." She desperately needed to relax and slid her arm through Logan's.

They walked through the casino's main entrance. The Bellagio had a totally different look from the Grand—light and airy versus dark and moody. Now she understood why Las Vegas was so enticing. It appealed to every taste. Logan knew the casino's layout and led her to an area of slot machines called "Wheel of Fortune."

"Let's try these slots. They're a favorite of Gram's." He moved down the row of machines to the end, pulled out a chair then sat next to Dallas.

"Your grandmother likes to gamble?"

He nodded. "She's the slots queen. She's kept track of her winnings and losses for twenty years. Right now, I think she's five hundred dollars ahead."

"Impressive, was she an accountant by any chance?"

"No, but she has the mind for it." He fed a twenty in each of their slot machines. "Interested in a little competition?"

"Like what?" she said.

"First one who loses the twenty, buys the first drink."

"You're on." She maxed the bet and hit SPIN. Let the games begin.

Logan and Dallas never did finish that bet. The game went from twenty dollars to two out of three to three out of five. Each hit a hundred-dollar jackpot that spurred on the competition. They took a break after an hour, settling on stools at a bar to the side of the casino. Logan ordered Irish Coffees.

"This is fun. Seems like the later it gets, the less I lose."
Dallas covered a yawn with her hand. "I'm too tired to accurately
count my money."

"Usually when we stay up late, we've not been up so early in
the morning. Guess we need to plan better for next time," Logan
said.

"Next time?"

"I think we owe it to ourselves to come back when we're
really on vacation, not searching for Rebecca Holland."

He spoke like they'd known each other for years.

"We'll see." Why did she say that? Dallas couldn't see herself
vacationing with Logan in Vegas or anywhere else. Regardless of
an occasional kiss or hug, their relationship was based on the
mutual need to solve the HCU theft. There was nothing personal
about it.

Shortly after midnight, Logan flagged a taxi to take them
back to the Grand. Sleep was number one on Dallas' mind. Once
back in the suite, she kissed Logan on the cheek and headed for
her bedroom. At the door, she looked back at him.

"Thank you for dinner. I appreciate everything you've done
today."

"My pleasure. Sleep tight, Dallas. Tomorrow will be a busy
day."

Absolutely. The day would be especially busy if she might
have the opportunity to circle her hands around Scooter's neck.

ELEVEN

Friday, 6:54 a.m.

THE NEXT MORNING DALLAS WOKE early and decided to take a run on the Strip. She left a note for Logan and headed north toward the Paris Casino. As she ran, she vowed to remain the cool and collected university controller. No one, least of all Logan, needed to know the toll the last week had had on her. Sure, she was tough but the scene last night with Scooter was surreal and just plain weird. She had no clue why he ran away from her. That wasn't the boss she knew.

She retraced her route back to the Grand. Within minutes, she pushed a key card into the suite's security slot and found Logan on the sofa, reading a newspaper.

"Good morning. Any chance we have coffee?" she asked.

"Good morning," he said, turning a page. "Coffee's on the bar. Breakfast will be here soon."

Dallas poured a mug, headed for the shower. "Back in thirty minutes."

She zipped through showering and dressing then appeared in the living room as a waiter rolled in a service cart.

"Your feast has arrived." Logan patted one of the bar stools. "More coffee?"

"Yes, please. I'm close to talking mode."

She lathered a waffle with butter and poured a healthy dose of syrup. After a couple of bites, her brain was firing and up to speed.

"Breakfast is great," she said. "What time are we meeting Mr. McKenzie?"

"Ten o'clock, in the lobby." Logan poured orange juice. "Did you bring a picture of Rebecca?"

She nodded. "It's in the campus directory. She takes a nice picture by the way."

"Good. That will make identification easier. Have you thought about what you'll tell Mr. McKenzie?"

"No, I'll wing it." Last night she decided to throw planning out the window and adopt a new Las Vegas operating method.

They finished the meal in silence. She was tired of thinking and tired of talking about Rebecca and the theft. And that was all she had scheduled for her immediate future, until they found Rebecca, which hopefully, would be soon. She remembered Nana's stiches and resolved to stop complaining about being tired.

She grabbed her mug and stood at the window overlooking The Strip. "I wonder if Rebecca is one of the people down there."

Logan joined her. He took the mug out of her hand, placed it on the windowsill.

"I didn't properly tell you good morning." He wrapped his arms around her while his lips kissed her neck, then captured her coffee-breath mouth. Her heart refused to beat while his arms encased her. She pulled back. He was too close, the setting too intimate.

"Good morning, again," she said lightly, her heart stroking back into rhythm. "I'll get my purse and then we can meet Mr. McKenzie." She stepped back from him, smiled, and hurried to the bedroom.

She sucked in air, attempting to calm down. Accepting a good morning kiss from Logan bordered on stupid. He was too tempting and this was not the right time to think about a relationship, not that she would ever consider a relationship with him. His kissing her did not mean he was interested in a one. So why was she even thinking about Logan and kissing?

She slid on lip gloss and gathered her purse, anxious to begin her first interview with a PI. Hopefully, they would forge a working rapport and quick. Rebecca could have already left Las Vegas. Dallas pulled her cell phone off the charger and stuffed it in her purse.

Logan and Dallas entered the Grand's main lobby at ten o'clock. Hotel guests waited in line at the reception desk and milled around the massive lobby. She imagined they were fighting the urge to visit the ATM machine located next to the casino entrance.

She expected Mr. McKenzie to come through the revolving glass doors at any moment. Someone behind them called Logan's name. They turned together.

"Mr. Rice, Logan Rice?"

"Yes," Logan said.

"Good, I'm JW McKenzie."

Shock silenced both Logan and Dallas. He started to speak then stopped. The private investigator they hoped to hire was not the male they assumed, but a woman, a hot-looking young woman. She was tall and dressed in black leather jeans and jacket, with a pink T-shirt. Her blond hair was pulled back from her face. Blue eyes gazing steadily at Logan.

This was the PI?

"Ms. McKenzie, I'm Dallas Wells." She offered her hand. "I'm the one who will be hiring you. Mr. Rice is here as an interested party."

"Nice to meet you, Dallas; you too, Mr. Rice." She waved her hand toward the casino. "Let's get a cup of coffee at the North Edge. It's quiet this time of day."

Logan and Dallas exchanged a "why not" look and followed her around the backside of the casino toward the bar. A bartender at the long sleek bar saluted them as they settled at a small table. JW moved to the bar to order the coffee. She returned shortly carrying a tray with three oversized mugs.

"This is my special recipe." She emptied the tray. "Enjoy."

Dallas tasted the brew. "This is good. What's the liquor?"

"That's a secret my dear mama made me promise never to reveal." JW's lips curved.

"You're not what we expected," Logan said.

"Really?" She laughed. "Is that because I'm young or

because I'm young and blond?"

"Actually, it's neither," Dallas said. "We incorrectly assumed JW McKenzie was a Mr. McKenzie. But that's not important. We need your help to locate someone here in Las Vegas."

"First, tell me why you want to find this person." JW pulled a pen and notebook from a leather backpack.

Dallas stole a glance at Logan. He winked and nodded. Her hands shook a bit so she clasped them in her lap. Telling a complete stranger her suspicions about Rebecca made them more real and more ridiculous.

"I assume you hear plenty of crazy stories in your profession." Dallas placed her hands on the table. "What I'm about to tell you isn't one of those crazy stories." She took a deep breath. "I believe a coworker stole $25 million from our employer, Houston Cullen University. I believe she's in Las Vegas right now."

"Let's start at the beginning." JW studied Dallas, her face neutral. "Tell me about the theft."

Dallas hesitated; it was becoming a habit. Should she tell JW the whole story or the edited version?

"I must clarify something." Dallas had to understand the rules. "Everything we tell you is in total confidence, right?"

"Yes." JW nodded at her, looked at Logan. "What you say to me goes no further than the three of us unless you give me the authority to share the information."

"Fair enough," Dallas said, relieved at the authority in JW's voice. "Logan, are you okay with this?"

"We need JW's help. Go for it."

The accountant in Dallas kicked in and she started at the beginning, one week ago. Accountants are both detail and process oriented so naturally she enlightened JW with the most important details in chronological order. It was a gift.

Logan chimed in to explain the Bridge Foundation's rationale for donating the money, highlighting his grandmother's role in the initial request.

Dallas finished her monologue with last night's chase after

Scooter.

JW wrote in her notebook, then looked around the bar. A group of men had settled at a corner table. They were laughing, high-fiving, and ordering pitchers of beer.

"We love our tourists." JW chuckled. "Who do you want me to locate— Rebecca, Scooter, or both?"

"JW, would you mind if I speak to Logan for a moment?"

"No problem. I'll be back in a couple of minutes." JW strolled out of the bar in the direction of the restrooms. She gave the beer drinkers a wide smile as she passed their table. They howled and slapped each other on the back.

Men are so easy.

"Should I hire her to find both of them or just Rebecca? I haven't even considered how I'll pay her. I need to call Dr. Arnold."

Logan placed a hand over Dallas' on the table. "First, I think *we* should hire JW to locate both Scooter and Rebecca. Second, the Bridge Foundation will take care of JW's costs. It's the least we can do considering what you're doing on behalf of the university."

"Fine and thanks," she said. "As long as Dr. Arnold agrees."

She found her cell and discovered it was turned off. Once it found a signal, she discovered four messages. They'd have to wait as Dr. Arnold had priority. He answered on the first ring.

"It's Dallas. I have something to discuss with you."

"Of course. Have you seen Scooter?"

She watched Logan wander into the casino. He sat at a random slot machine, fed in a bill. She swallowed, realized he was giving her privacy. Complete honesty was her only choice with Dr. Arnold. She explained about Scooter not having a reservation at the Grand and seeing him at the Bellagio.

"I don't understand why he acted like that."

"I think I do." Dr. Arnold's tone was solemn. "Over the past year or so, Scooter has changed and I have a good idea why. But anything is possible at this point."

It was clear Dr. Arnold withheld information from her and

that was the way it should be since Scooter was her direct supervisor. She didn't need to know everything. Damn.

"The real reason I called is to ask a question. Logan Rice and I talked to a private investigator this morning. Should she pursue Rebecca only or Scooter as well."

"Good idea. Tell her to search for both of them."

"Thanks. Logan said the Bridge Foundation will pick up the cost for hiring the PI."

"Tell him thanks, but no. We're in this together and the university will pay its share. Give me a call when you have news."

She clicked off then listened to her phone messages—Jane and Liz wanted her home, Ruthie had wonderful news, and Lynne Harris had a progress report from the bank. Neither JW or Logan had wandered back, so she called Lynne.

"You have good news for me?"

"Yes and no. We know the virus that changed the wire instructions was attached to an e-mail and the sending server was HCU."

"Excellent." Dallas crossed her fingers, hoping Lynne wouldn't say the sending e-mail address was hers. It would be another manufactured piece of evidence like the Gregory James message.

"Don't get too excited. The virus also erased the sending address along with the ISP address. Bottom-line, we can't determine the specific computer at the University that sent the e-mail. That's it. We can't go any further unless our IT group works magic on the server. The good news is that we know the wire was rerouted to a bank in the Cayman Islands. I've already given the information to the police and the FBI."

"That's great progress." Relief washed over Dallas. Lynne's news verified Dallas' theory of the missing gifts being related to the theft. Yet the guilt from withholding the false e-mail, bubbled over the relief. "Did you talk to Roddy?"

"Yes, and he didn't seem surprised by the Caymans bank. We're meeting for a drink."

"Tell Roddy I'll call as soon as something turns up here.

Thanks for calling."

Logan returned to the table along with JW.

Dallas turned to her. "Logan and I are hiring you together. We'd like you to search for both Rebecca and Scooter." She removed the campus directory from her purse. "Photos are in here. What else do you need?"

"This is a good start. I'll make copies at the front desk and then circulate the pictures to all hotels, restaurants, taxis and so on. We have a good network here. Do you have their social security numbers?"

"You'd better contact Dr. Arnold for that." She wrote his phone number on a napkin. "Do you check credit card records?"

"We retrieve information in a variety of ways," JW said.

"Everything is legal, right?"

"Nothing for you to worry about," JW replied. "I need your phone numbers." She wrote them in her notebook and handed out business cards. "Call me if you think of anything else. I'll make those copies now." She stood and slung the backpack over her shoulder. "Be back in five minutes." She walked toward the lobby.

Logan and Dallas looked at each other.

"That was easy," he said. "What do you want to do now?"

"I'm going to call Scooter's wife. Maybe she knows where he's staying."

"Why wouldn't she be here with him?"

"Let's just say I'm curious." She found Scooter's home number on her phone's contact list.

"May I speak to Mrs. Taylor?"

"This is she."

"Hi, Mrs. Taylor, this is Dallas Wells from HCU."

"Yes, Dallas, how are you? I hope you had a bite of the Easter cake I sent to the office."

"I'm just fine and the cake was delicious," Dallas said. "I need to talk to Scooter. I hope you can give me the name of the hotel where he's staying in Las Vegas."

"Of course, dear. It's the Grand Hotel. He's attending one of those accounting conferences he attends every year."

"Right." Dallas had no clue about any conference.

"He called last night and said he's staying over the weekend. One of his college roommates is there as well and they plan to play golf."

"Did he give you a phone number there?" Dallas asked.

"No. Call his cell phone if you need to reach him. Here's the number." She rattled off an unfamiliar number. Dallas grabbed a pen and a napkin.

JW returned and handed the campus directory to Dallas. "I'll talk to you guys this evening." She disappeared into the casino.

Dallas watched her walk away and felt good about their decision to hire her. She raised a finger to Logan. "I need to make one more call."

She dialed Scooter's cell number. No answer. Her stomach assumed that sinking feeling she remembered from a carnival ride that dropped a hundred feet in seconds. Scooter had lied to his wife and to Ellie and Dallas. It made no sense that he'd be so dishonest. It dawned on Dallas that she didn't know her boss at all.

He had to be up to something. She prayed it wasn't the HCU theft.

"Logan, we have work to do."

"That's why we hired a private investigator."

"Yes, we did. She's helping us, not replacing us. I can't sit at a blackjack table and pretend the next hand is all I care about. I need to do something." She pounded a soft fist on the table.

"Okay, all right." He raised his hands in mock surrender. "What's the next step?"

"We walk the Strip," she said. "I think better when I'm moving."

"Let's go then." Logan stood and pulled back her chair, always the gentleman.

They strolled through the casino, following the green carpet path along the edge of tables and machines. Gamblers were already sitting at slot machines. After a few minutes, they exited air conditioning and entered the hot, exhaust-fumed air on the sidewalk. Dallas settled sunglasses on her nose.

"Let's stroll." She took Logan's arm then realized she had automatically attached herself to him and stepped away. She put the sidewalk between them, swept an arm from left to right in front of her. "You watch on the left and I'll concentrate to the right. Remember, look for both of them."

They walked in silence for a long block past the Showcase Mall featuring M & M's World and the World of Coca-Cola, too sweet for her taste, too pedestrian for Rebecca. Logan seemed awfully quiet.

"What's wrong? Don't you like surveillance work?"

"Nothing's wrong," he said.

"Sure?"

"Nothing's wrong." He grabbed her hand. "Come on, Planet Hollywood is a couple of blocks down. We can walk through it for more surveillance."

After forty-five minutes of walking up and down, over and around rows of slot machines, craps tables, and blackjack tables, searching for a glimpse of two people, she was pooped. Logan hadn't said much, being intent on the surveillance and all.

They glanced at each other next to a penguin penny machine. She nodded and they exited the casino through the nearest door. Back on the Strip, she spied the replica of the Eiffel Tower at the Paris Casino. Perfect. They set off for another long walk.

A hotdog cart sat near the casino entrance under a wide green umbrella with a couple of tables.

"How about a hotdog?" Dallas said. "I'm kinda hungry."

"Good idea. What would you like?"

Logan stood in line for their lunch while Dallas grabbed a table. The day was glorious—bright sun, blue skies, and toasty. The dancing fountains at the Bellagio across the Strip began their first show of the day. She felt good, other than wondering what was up with Logan. He sure seemed moody.

Dallas sat back and watched Logan approach the table. Butterflies raced through her gut. He made her nervous. Granted, he was attractive, polite, and fun, but they came from opposite social groups. He had been born in money and she had yet to get serious about her retirement planning. She brushed off her musings as Logan set a tray on the table.

"Here's lunch."

"Looks good." She swirled a French fry in ketchup. "I was just thinking. Seven days ago, I planned on a vodka martini at happy hour and now I'm in Las Vegas searching for a coworker who I believe is a thief, and I'm questioning the integrity of my boss. What a crazy week."

"Agreed. But look on the bright side."

"There's a bright side?"

"Definitely." His lips twitched then he chuckled. "You met me."

Good point. If the Bridge Foundation donation hadn't been stolen, she wouldn't have walked into his office with a fistful of questions. The world does work in mysterious ways but this was a stretch, for any single lady, to meet a man. More important though, was that damned e-mail. She made her decision.

"Yes, I did meet you." And that made her happy. "I have something to tell you."

He sighed.

Dallas placed her hand on his, then withdrew it quickly. The contact increased her anxiety.

"Tell me," he said, his voice soft and measured. "What is it?"

She pressed her lips together, dug in her purse and removed the Gregory James message from her wallet. She unfolded the paper and pushed it across the table.

"Read this," she whispered.

His brow furrowed as he retrieved the paper. "What is it?"

Dallas stared at him with wide, thick-lashed eyes. She licked her lips then said. "It's not true. I didn't change the wire instructions. That e-mail is a fake."

Logan's attention returned to the paper, surveying it closer. "You're right, it's fake."

She flinched at his statement. "How can you say that so

easily?"

Logan smiled. "Did you notice the sending address?"

She shook her head.

"You should have. The message isn't from Gregory James. Someone is trying to freak you out."

"They did a damn good job."

"Did you mention this to Detective Phillips?"

She fiddled with a napkin. "No, I didn't tell him and I feel guilty as hell. I, uh . . ."

"Why?"

Anger flashed in her eyes. "Because, dammit, he'd consider me a suspect and then I couldn't look for the real thief." She pushed hair out of her face. "And then when Nana was hurt, I knew I'd made the right decision."

$ $ $

Logan's initial distrust of Dallas evaporated into the Nevada air. He'd heard earlier from Billy and the report from their private investigator came back clean. This admission proved to him she had nothing to do with the theft. It seemed strange though that she didn't know about the gift.

"We need to tell Roddy so he can check out of the sender of the e-mail."

"I hadn't considered that," she said

"I'll give him a call later. I do have a question." Logan figured she'd have a surprising answer. "Why didn't you know about the gift transfer?"

"Scooter is a lousy communicator and Development loves to play with me. They know I make sure gifts get to the right bank account so on large ones, they don't tell me until the last minute. It's just a stupid game." She shrugged her shoulders. "Girls don't always play nice with other girls."

He laughed as he deposited the remains of their meal in a nearby trash can.

"What's next?" he said. "Want to gamble a bit?"

"I doubt I'd have any luck."

"The more you play, the better chance you have of winning."

"I disagree. It's nothing more than chance, aka luck."

"I concede on slots," he said. "But surely you agree skill is involved in, say, blackjack?"

"Sure, the key is counting cards and a dealer can spot a card counter a mile away. You might win big and get thrown off the table." She stood, stretched out her arms. "I don't have enough experience at tracking cards."

"But you're an accountant."

"Who said accountants are good at math?"

Logan appreciated Dallas' sense of humor and quick wit. Much different from the women he usually dated. "You could try your hand at a poker table."

A look of panic flew across her face. "Uh, no, that would take time away from our mission of locating Rebecca."

"You're right. Let's check out the casino."

They entered the Paris Casino and stopped to watch a slots tournament in progress. A square, created by rows of slot machines, contained players pounding the spin buttons as fast as possible. A DJ encouraged the contestants to "spin, baby, spin." A couple of blue-jacketed casino employees walked the rows of machines, apparently to verify that bionic hands weren't hitting the button. Dallas stopped walking and watched the tournament with narrowed eyes.

She leaned over to Logan, whispered in his ear. "Look at the woman sitting at the end of the last row." She pointed to the last row of slots. "Doesn't she look like Rebecca?"

TWELVE

Friday, 1:32 p.m.

LOGAN NODDED AFTER FOLLOWING DALLAS' gaze across the rows of slot machines. He motioned with a pointed finger for her to move to the right and he'd go around the left side of the roped-off machines. They set off in opposite directions along the perimeter of the tournament.

As she walked, Dallas' eyes drilled into the blonde, whose head stayed down. Unfortunately, she failed to notice a cocktail waitress carrying a tray of drinks and ran smack into her. Wine, beer, and plastic cups rained down. The tray rolled along the carpet and clattered against the stool of a tournament player. He barely glanced at the commotion.

"I'm so sorry," Dallas whispered.

She scooped up cups leaking on the carpet and trotted after the tray. Once it was retrieved, she turned back and witnessed a small crowd gathered around the waitress.

"Are you okay?" she asked the young woman. "I'm usually not so clumsy."

"No problem, ma'am." The woman reclaimed the tray and cups from Dallas hands. "This happens once a week." She moved through the crowd and disappeared around a corner.

Dallas did her best to shrug off the incident—humiliating to disrupt the delivery of free drinks. She moved along the outside of the tournament and scanned the area where she last saw the Rebecca look-alike.

The stool was empty. Dammit.

She ran toward it and collided with Logan. Her heart galloped. "Did you see her leave?"

"No. I was watching you and the tray of exploding drinks."

"Wonderful, just wonderful. Our timing stinks."

"You do have a gift for running into liquids."

She rolled her eyes and swallowed a smart response—*play nice*. They began to question people standing next to the ropes. No one had noticed a blonde slip under them due to the drink fiasco. The DJ declared a five-minute break. Players stood, stretched their arms and wiggled their fingers. She didn't envy their stiff fingers or the stress.

A casino blue-coat moved past them.

"Sir, sir." Dallas hurried after him. "May I ask you a question?"

"Sure, but the tournament is closed." He looked about twenty-five with a cute grin.

"I think I saw an old friend who taught my daughter kindergarten. She moved away and we lost touch. She was sitting at that stool." Dallas pointed to the look-a-like's stool. "Do you have a list of players I could look at so I'd know for sure it was her?"

"Ma'am, that's not information we normally share with our guests." He planted himself in front of her, spread his legs, and moved his arms and a clipboard to his back.

"Please. It would mean so much to me." Logan appeared at Dallas' side, she hugged his arm. "Honey, tell him how upsetting this is to me."

"She's been a little, you know." He lowered his voice. "Hormonal if you know what I mean."

"I understand, sir." The blue-coat grinned. "I have three sisters. What's the name?" He pulled the clipboard from behind his back.

"Rebecca Holland. But she may have gotten married," Dallas said.

"Let's see," he mumbled as he scanned a paper. "No Rebecca."

What was the name on the Cayman bank account?

She snapped her fingers. "Holly? Her nickname was Holly."

The blue-coat reviewed the paper again. "There is a Holly. But the last name is Barry. Sorry, it's not your friend. Enjoy your stay at the Paris Casino." He melded between rows of slots.

Why would the woman leave during the break? She'd be disqualified. Maybe she went to the restroom, or was hungry, or recognized her coworker from HCU.

Dallas turned to Logan, pushed him gently forward. "Let's go. We need to check the casino floor. She might still be here."

They spent the next half hour trekking through the rows of slots and gambling tables, staring at women with blond hair. Dallas checked every stall in three ladies' rooms surrounding the casino area. She stamped her foot in frustration and wondered where she'd lost her sanity. The Rebecca clone had disappeared.

Unconvinced, they circled the casino again. The crowds had increased along with the noise level. The only item of interest was an ant-sized woman dancing next to a silver Mercedes Benz. The orange light on a slot machine sliced through the crowd engulfing her and reminded gamblers that jackpots were real.

Their search culminated along a row of dollar slot machines.

"She's not here." Logan flashed a lop-sided grin. "Let's regroup and mull over our next move."

"You're right, let's mull." She plopped on the stool of the nearest machine and considered why Rebecca had ventured to Las Vegas. Gambling, shows, hanging out at a pool?

"What's next?"

"I've been considering why Rebecca came to Las Vegas in the first place." She frowned. "There has to be something worth the risk for her to come here."

"I agree." Logan leaned against a Blue Diamond machine. "Maybe she was meeting someone. Surely she wouldn't travel commercially without having a very good reason."

"Or . . . she wanted to flaunt it." Dallas warmed up to that idea. "By not simply disappearing to say, Mexico or Japan, she's showing how smart she is and that she's not afraid of getting caught." Her enthusiasm for the theory grew. "Maybe she's playing a game with us."

"Not likely. She doesn't know we're looking for her."

"But she knows I'm working with the police on behalf of HCU. I told her that last Monday. If she is the slots blonde, then she knows I'm in Vegas."

Logan rubbed his chin with nicely manicured fingers. "If I suddenly had unlimited funds . . ."

She chuckled at that comment.

". . . I'd probably do some serious shopping. Human nature, don't you think?"

"Now you're talking. What would you buy?"

"Probably a very large boat or a fully loaded SUV."

Was he a guy's guy or what? "Very nice, Logan." She leaned toward him. "But Rebecca's a sweet Southern girl. I can't see her driving around in a Hummer."

"Good point."

She leaned back on the stool, imagining a credit card without a dollar limit. "I'd shop for chunky diamond earrings, a very fancy handbag, and Chanel sunglasses. And those cute girly shoes, Jimmy Choo."

Logan stood. "Okay, I'm convinced." He held out a hand to her. "Let's go shopping."

When a man says he wants to go shopping, Dallas wasn't one to dilly-dally. They exited the casino back to Las Vegas Boulevard.

Logan led the way. "Since the Bellagio is across the street and has high-end stores, let's start there. We'll ask if any of the clerks have seen her."

They crossed the street via the overhead walkway and entered the hotel shops through the same set of doors as last night. Dallas stopped a few feet inside to get her bearings. Logan bumped against her and she skipped to the side, the less contact with him, the better. He was starting to grow on her, especially after declaring the fake e-mail a fraud.

Her eyes turned away from his chest and she considered the

high-end stores where Rebecca might celebrate her new riches. Hmm, what would Rebecca buy first? Something extravagant but not too-over-the-top. Dallas snapped her fingers—Rebecca wore a scarf nearly every time Dallas had seen her on campus. And, who was famous for beautiful scarves?

A minute later, they entered the Hermes store. A solitary customer browsed the rich leather handbags and wallets, and colorful scarves elegantly arranged on glass shelves. Price tags were discreetly out of sight. A salesclerk busied herself behind a counter and that was where they headed.

"May I help you?" she asked.

"Yes." Dallas dug in her purse for the HCU directory, opened it to the picture of Rebecca, and placed it on the glass counter. "We're looking for this woman. Have you seen her?"

"Why?" The salesclerk looked first at Dallas, then Logan. She smiled.

"She's my sister. Left her groom at the alter a couple days ago in Des Moines. We need to make sure she's okay."

Discreet laughter bubbled from the clerk.

"What's the joke?" Dallas said.

"Sorry." The clerk rubbed her tongue over her lips. "No joke. This woman was in here yesterday and didn't seem the least bit unhappy."

"Why is that?" Logan said.

"She bought one of our new Birkin handbags."

Bingo. "Which one?" Dallas asked.

"A black leather tote with diamonds on the closure and studs on the straps. It's part of our spring collection."

"Was it expensive?" he asked.

Logan obviously knew nothing about Hermes.

The salesclerk brightened. "Yes sir, well over $100,000."

Dallas' not too-over-the-top theory evaporated. She imagined the gears in Logan's head crunching to a stop.

"For . . . a . . . purse?" he sputtered.

Definitely a sticker-shock moment. Dallas patted his hand then got down to business and convinced the clerk to give her all the information the store had on the buyer. Initially, she wasn't too keen on the idea. But Logan's look of disbelief instigated the "be helpful to strangers" button.

The saleslady explained the buyer's name was Rebecca Holland and she paid for the purchase by credit card around 4:00 p.m. yesterday. That was all. The clerk didn't know the name of Rebecca's hotel or much else. Apparently, Rebecca wasn't a Chatty Cathy while shopping. She just wanted the damned purse.

They expressed their gratitude for the information and strolled out of the store.

"I knew I was right." Dallas wanted to dance.

"Rebecca isn't afraid of showing off her money," Logan added.

Dallas considered that for a moment. Was Rebecca flaunting it or maybe she really didn't know they were looking for her. She *couldn't* know Dallas had started sleuthing with Logan. The woman at the Paris slot tournament was probably just a Rebecca look-alike. Rebecca had no reason to use a false name as she was unaware of their interest in her. Also, a woman who buys a Hermes Birkin handbag wouldn't be caught dead next to a slot machine. Diamonds were more her style.

And where would one go for diamonds? Tiffany's, of course.

Dallas punched Logan in the arm. "Come on, Mr. Rice. Let's go rock hunting."

She steered him along Via Bellagio past Prada and Dior to Tiffany & Company.

The signature granite façade along with an Atlas clock figure framed the wide entrance to the store. She felt the slightest twinge of anticipation. Tiffany's could do that to a girl. The interior of the store was modern and elegant in subdued grays and pink.

They marched right over to the cash register. A customer, gingerly carrying a blue bag, turned away from the counter, leaving the salesclerk free. They repeated the Hermes story and once again hit the lottery. This time Rebecca had held back a bit with four-carat diamond studs and a three-carat diamond-and-emerald bracelet.

Now she had fabulous jewelry and an exclusive purse. Did shopping her little black heart out yesterday, mean she was still in Las Vegas today? No.

They walked out of Tiffany's to Via Bellagio and stopped in the middle of the broad walkway. Dallas put a hand on a hip and stared into space. Knowing Rebecca had been out spending money didn't get them any closer to finding her.

Logan snapped his fingers in front of her face. "Earth to Dallas. Let's go find a place in the casino to sit down, relax, and talk. I need to think."

They continued along Via Bellagio to the casino entrance. Dallas loved the casino's décor. The cream background with an overlay of rich green plants and colorful flowers seemed lush and elegant. The combination of colors inspired tranquility and relaxation—perfect ambiance for gambling.

They wandered until they came to a cocktail lounge. Dallas naturally headed for the long, curved bar rather than the low tables. They chose stools on the left side, providing a clear view of gamblers walking by.

The bartender moseyed over and Logan ordered two cups of coffee. Dallas noticed he didn't ask her what she wanted to drink but kept quiet. Had they transitioned from acquaintances to bosom buddies in two days?

Once the coffee arrived, they lapsed into their own thoughts. She thought about a Birkin bag and four-carat diamond studs, if only—Logan interrupted her mental flow.

"I think we need to regroup."

"Sure, let's regroup. What's your plan?"

"I was thinking, Rebecca has bought girly things, things that create a momentary rush."

"Uh-huh."

"Don't you think she'd want to settle down and stay low for a while?" Logan said.

"Seems logical to me. Why make yourself a target for the police?" And HCU and Dallas.

"Exactly. If I were running with that kind of money, I'd get out of the country as quickly as possible once I had some fun."

He glanced past her. She could hear arguing, then it moved off. Logan again focused on her. The man had the bluest eyes.

"I'd go where there are lots of Americans, either as residents or tourists," he said. "Easier to blend in."

"Like London or Paris?"

"Yes, I think Europe is a better bet than say, South America or Mexico."

"No sun tanning on the beaches of Rio?"

"I'm not a psychic." Frustration floated across his face. "All I'm saying is that if I wanted to hide from the authorities, I wouldn't go where I was odd man out."

He had a good point. Hide out in the open rather than behind closed doors where the need to be hidden might draw attention. Logan was one smart guy.

"I guess we need to make a list all the cities in Europe with high populations of Americans," she said.

"Let's ask JW to check the passenger lists of outgoing international flights the last twenty-four hours."

"Good idea. I wonder if she's had any hits yet. I'll give her a jingle."

Logan made the call instead. It was quick. He slipped the phone in his jacket pocket.

"And?"

"It appears we've hired a thorough private investigator. JW is already looking at passenger lists for outgoing flights from Las Vegas, both domestic and international."

"Good. When will we hear back from her?"

"Two to three hours."

Dallas drummed her fingers on the bar counter. "We have to find Rebecca."

"Relax. You have to be patient."

She clenched and unclenched her jaw. "Please, do not tell me to be patient." She rubbed the back of her neck. "I'm not good at patient."

Logan shrugged. "Fine. Do your best. There's not much we

can do until we hear back from JW."

She chewed on that for about two seconds. "We could look for Scooter."

"Why?"

Why? As if parking their butts at a bar was getting them anywhere. One phone call to JW wasn't an action plan.

"I'm feeling useless again. I don't like it. I need to stay busy." She sighed, heavily. She hadn't flown to Las Vegas to wait for someone else to find Rebecca. She stood. "I can't sit here. If I'm walking the Strip and touring casinos, looking at people, at least I'm being useful."

"You're right." Logan threw a bill on the bar. "Let's walk the Strip back to the Grand. We can keep a look out for Scooter and Rebecca along the way."

They exited the Bellagio through its main entrance and walked along the lake to Las Vegas Boulevard rather than taking the quicker people mover. The dancing waters show began another set as they were halfway to the street. They stopped to watch.

Logan casually swung an arm over her shoulder and surprisingly, she did not pull away. She wasn't comfortable with the physical closeness he seemed to find so easy. Yes, she had some sort of hang up about it. If she were analyzing herself, she'd say her problem related to trust, trust of a good-looking and very eligible man. She hardly knew Logan. He could be a habitual heartbreaker for all she knew. He was forty and never married, that had to say something. At least all those magazine quizzes said so.

The water show ended and five minutes later they threaded their way through the nonstop swarm of moving bodies in front of Caesar's Palace. Her eyes searched for a familiar face in the crowd. It wasn't easy. She had about a second to search for a glimpse of Rebecca or Scooter among the faces rushing past her at warp speed.

They walked slowly, irritating people behind them. Tough. Dallas had nothing but time.

After thirty minutes of strolling, she pulled Logan over to the inner edge of the sidewalk, not far from the Grand. She was hot and frustrated.

"It's been fun avoiding the hordes of people trying to mow us down." She wiped sweat off her forehead. "I think we need to switch to plan B. This isn't working."

"You're the one who wanted to walk the Strip and look at people." Logan swept his arm in a wide arc toward the street. "There's the people."

She glared at him. He overflowed with masculinity and was cute as a button. Why did he have to be right? Her brain hesitated for a nanosecond, switched gears. She was more than willing to admit a temporary defeat. The situation was ridiculous. She started to laugh—a deep in the gut release.

After a couple of seconds, she gripped Logan's shoulder, glanced past him, and sucked in air. Her eyes caught sight of a familiar face at the street edge of the sidewalk.

"There's Scooter."

She shot into the crowd, bumping her way past tourists toward Scooter. He faced the Strip, his back to her. She touched his arm. He turned toward her, his face cloaked with bewilderment.

"Fancy meeting you here." Dallas sensed, rather than heard, Logan pull up behind her.

Scooter blinked, had that deer-in-the-headlights look, then his face transitioned to administrative mode. "Dallas, I didn't know you were coming here for your vacation." He looked behind her. "And with a friend."

"It was a spur of the moment decision. What are you doing here?" She searched Scooter's face for a glimmer of something, but he looked normal.

"The wife and I decided to do some gambling and take in a couple of shows."

Yeah, right. "Sounds fun. I saw you last night at the Bellagio shops. Even called out to you but you turned the other way."

"Really? We were at the Bellagio last night but I didn't see you." Scooter laughed. "Must have been my twin."

She nodded. "Yes, a twin." She pointed to Logan. "This is Logan Rice. Remember, he came to the meeting with Rebecca."

Scooter nodded and the two men shook hands and exchanged pleasantries.

"Would you and your wife like to join us for dinner this evening?" Logan said.

Scooter shook his head. "Sorry, we have plans. I must get going." He smiled. "Have a nice vacation, Dallas. I'll see you on Monday." He turned and melded into the throng of tourists moving toward Caesars' Palace.

She faced Logan. "What the hell was that?"

"Sounded like a story to me. He doesn't know you talked to his wife."

"Obviously. I need to think about this." She glanced from Logan to the cars grinding by. "Let's get back to the hotel suite." She fluffed hair off her neck. "I'm hot."

Twenty minutes later, she had her feet planted on the sofa ottoman, eyes closed, head resting on the sofa's fluffy back. She couldn't get her head around Scooter lying to her face-to-face. He was a straight-laced kind of guy. It made no sense, unless . . .

She bolted up. Her arm knocked a green pillow on the floor. Logan sat across from her in a club chair, reading a newspaper.

"Logan."

"Hmm?"

Dallas finally had the nerve to voice the thoughts that had been rolling around in her mind ever since Ellie told her Scooter was flying to Las Vegas. "I think there's a possibility Scooter is involved with Rebecca."

He folded the paper over his lap. "What's your logic?"

She started counting on her fingers. "First, he hadn't scheduled any vacation on the office calendar and he's a stickler about that. Second, he gave both Ellie and his wife the wrong hotel information. And third, he just lied to me, a trusted and long-time employee, about his reason for being here."

"Maybe he needed some time alone, to get away from the

pressures at work and at home," Logan suggested. "He could have given them the wrong hotel for privacy."

She rose and walked to the bank of windows overlooking the Strip. It was busy as usual. She turned back to Logan. "My gut is telling me something isn't right with him. Scooter lying to me, as well as Ellie and his wife, is off the charts out of character. He's too straight laced. Even though he's unpredictable at times, he's a by-the-book CPA. He's not a thief."

"Didn't you just say you thought he was involved with Rebecca?" Logan asked.

"Sleeping with her doesn't automatically translate to stealing twenty-five mil with her."

"Oh." He grinned.

She rolled her eyes. Men could be so dense. Their logic translated sex to everything. She flexed her arms up and down, shaking out the excess tension. She was sweaty.

"I need to take a shower. I'll see you in an hour or so." Dallas closed the bedroom door quietly behind her and flopped on the bed. She needed time to reflect on what she'd learned in the past two days. She needed time to think about the cuteness factor of Logan Rice. And, she needed time to think about why he was getting under her skin.

$ $ $

Las Vegas, Friday Afternoon

Rebecca Holland was a survivor, plain and simple, no discussion required. Over the last twenty years she had learned to act when necessary and to hell with the consequences as long as she got what she wanted. At the final curtain call, results were all that mattered. And she was loving the results after acquiring twenty-five million dollars. The money, safely transferred to a private account in Switzerland, would cater to and satisfy her every need. Ooh-la-la. Life was perfect.

Almost perfect, that is. The issue of Scooter Taylor was the one last nut in the bunch of bananas. Rebecca was so tired of irrelevant complications that the pores of her skin nearly shed tears in frustration. Yes, indeed, Scooter was a complication. She placed a finger on her lower lip. He was a mere pebble in her shoe that would soon be resolved. She willed the doorbell to ring.

The butler had opened a bottle of chardonnay a few minutes ago. She poured a generous amount in a Waterford wine stem. She closed her eyes and savored the vintage on her tongue, perfect bouquet. An excellent glass of wine was Rebecca's one vice. She rarely swore and didn't have promiscuous sex. Other than that one debacle in college, her first time actually, that had set the wheels in motion.

Had she made the right decision back then? She'd asked herself that very question many, many times over the ensuing years. She shook her blond locks. At this point, there was no need to ask such questions. The deed was done and her only choice was to go forward. Looking back? Unnecessary.

The bell at the suite's entrance chimed. Finally, the last annoyance had arrived. She opened the door and wasn't disappointed.

"Scooter, welcome, I'm sorry we didn't have time to get together yesterday." Rebecca took his arm and guided him to the suite's living room. "Would you like a glass of wine? I have a delightful bottle open."

- - -

Scooter looked around the suite, taking in the opulence of the décor. It was quite a contrast to his small room off the Strip. The difference in luxury didn't matter one bit. And it couldn't be avoided if they were to stick to their carefully crafted plan. Item after item had been checked off. The one surprise had been Bill's murder, unconnected, but a nuisance nonetheless.

He kissed her on the cheek. "Wine sounds perfect, my dear."

They sat in matching leather stools at the bar, clinked glasses, and smiled at one another. Scooter was truly happy to see Rebecca. It had been two days since they'd shared a dinner late

Wednesday night at a twenty-four-hour coffee shop off the Strip. It had been much too quick and he had missed seeing her the last two days. But it was for a good cause, their new life together.

Scooter squeezed her hand. "It's so good to see your beautiful face, my darling. I've missed you so much."

"I've missed you as well." Rebecca stroked his cheek with a finger. She sipped her wine and gazed at him over the rim of the glass. "The future is ours. I'm anxious to get started."

He leaned over and gently kissed her on the lips. "As am I, my love."

The doorbell chimed again.

"Are you expecting someone?" Scooter said, wondering if she had a surprise for him. She always kept him guessing, and it was usually fun.

- - -

Rebecca rose and gently smiled. "I'm hungry and ordered a snack from the kitchen."

She opened the door and waved in a waiter who rolled a room service cart alongside the windows, opposite the bar and Scooter.

Rebecca addressed the waiter. "Please place the food on the bar counter." The waiter took a large round plate off the cart and set it on the bar behind Scooter. He then removed the silver topper off the plate and set it on the cart.

"Scooter, dear, did I show you the diamonds I purchased yesterday?" Rebecca moved to a coffee table in the living room. She caressed the blue Tiffany's box before opening it. "Come look at my jewels."

Two seconds later, Scooter stood before her, gazing at the diamond earrings. He was oblivious to the location of the waiter in the suite, which was unfortunate.

The waiter seized a white cloth off the plate on the bar. He moved with assurance behind Scooter and jammed the medicated cloth against Scooter's nose and mouth. Scooter was no match for the strength of the waiter and the coma inducing drug and within seconds, he slumped to the carpet.

The waiter faced Rebecca. "He'll be out for at least a couple of hours, maybe more. Plenty of time to get his body outside the city limits."

"Excellent. The laundry cart is in the bedroom. Roll him out of here, quickly. I must catch my flight."

THIRTEEN

Friday, 6:35 p.m.

"DALLAS, IT'S BEEN A LONG DAY. I thought we'd order dinner from room service."

After a thirty-minute nap followed by a soothing shower, she was fully alert. She looked at Logan, then her cell phone. She had calls to make and eating in the suite meant she could stay in her shorts, always a plus.

"Good idea. Is there a menu?"

They discussed options for several minutes and finally decided on grilled salmon rather than steak as it was healthier. Of course, chocolate cheesecake would zap the saved calories.

While Logan placed the order, Dallas moved into the dining room and called Roddy.

"How's your Mom?"

"Good, thanks for asking. How's Las Vegas? Any Elvis sightings?"

"Not yet. What's new on your end?"

"We got a hit. The funds were transferred yesterday from the Cayman Islands to a bank in Zurich, Switzerland. We'll try to work our magic again."

Hot damn. "Was the transfer amount the whole $25 million?"

"Good question. I'll get back to you on that. What have you stumbled across?"

She could hear the smile in Roddy's voice and gave him the details about seeing Scooter and Rebecca's purchases at Hermes and Tiffany's.

"Good work, we'll contact the stores," he said. "I'll dig

deeper into Scooter's background and see if there's a connection with Rebecca outside of the office."

"Excellent," Dallas said. "By the way, how was your drink with Lynne?"

"Promising."

Ten minutes later, she listened to her messages and attempted to return all the calls. The most important being that Ruthie had gotten engaged and the wedding was planned for August. After leaving voice messages, she strolled back to the living room. Logan stood behind the bar, uncorking a bottle of wine. She planted herself on a stool across from him.

"Hey there, whatcha doing?" she asked.

"I thought chardonnay would work with dinner. Would you like a glass while we wait for room service?"

"Wine is my favorite food group."

"Any news from Houston?"

She shared the information from Roddy. "If some of the funds have already been spent, then that's proof Rebecca used the money for her purchases here."

"I agree, seems logical. But we don't have absolute proof." Logan handed her a glass of wine. "By the way, JW called while you were on the phone. She won't have any details on international flights until tomorrow. She's coming up for breakfast to lay out everything she's learned."

"Good. I need something concrete so I can plan my next step."

"What do you mean next step?" Logan frowned.

"I'm a dunce. I need to get smarter about searching for Rebecca, even think like her." She sipped the wine. "For instance, why did she steal the money in the first place? You have WiFi here?"

"Sure, why?"

"I can do a background check on Rebecca using one of those online services."

Logan patted her hand lying on the bar counter. "Dallas, you've got to relax. JW will have all that information for us in the morning.

Of course, he was right, that's what PIs do. She was such an amateur at this investigating business. She'd wait to hear from the expert—this one time. No promises it would happen again. Nana had told her more than once that patience was not her middle name. Regardless, she needed to settle down. If she became too stressed or strung out she'd make a stupid mistake and that's the last thing she wanted. She'd work at it. Well, she'd try.

"You're right. I'll wait for JW and her information."

The suite's doorbell sounded; dinner had arrived. After the waiter served the meal, Logan and Dallas sat at the dining table.

"The salmon looks delicious," she murmured. And thus, the small talk began. They managed to get through an entire meal without a mention of Rebecca or the theft.

After refusing a second cup of coffee and another bite of Logan's cheesecake, Dallas stood, stuffed to the small stones in her diamond stud earrings. "Logan, would you like to take a walk? I need some serious exercise to melt off this meal."

"Good idea. Shall we wander around the casino or the Strip?" Logan followed her to the door of her bedroom.

She grinned at him over her shoulder. "Casino. I'll put on some jeans and get my purse."

Fifteen minutes later, they slowly meandered around the Grand's slots area adjacent to the elevators. Almost every machine was in use. Dallas noticed the intense looking faces of the gamblers sporadically punching the SPIN button—nothing like a gambler with an optimistic attitude.

Anyway, it was ten o'clock on a Friday evening in Las Vegas and the Grand was hopping. People were jumping up and down at the craps tables and maintaining a stone face at the blackjack tables. She loved it. The noise, the lights, and the energy—intoxicating. Rebecca might feel the same way.

Dallas touched Logan's arm. "I can hear a video poker machine calling me. I'm going over there." She pointed to a row of video poker machines along the wall. "I'll meet you back at the North Edge Bar in an hour or so."

He squeezed her hand and turned towards the craps tables.

She fed a hundred-dollar bill into the cash slot of a poker machine at the end of a row. The location provided a good view in three directions, perfect to catch sight of Rebecca in case she might stroll along.

Playing video poker was so much fun. With each spin, she bet the max and took her time selecting the cards to hold, studying the faces around her before hitting a hold button. Surprisingly, thanks to a full house and a straight, she was up seventy-five bucks after forty-five minutes, unusual for her typical lousy luck. What the hell. She cashed out.

She decided to find Logan rather than meet him at the bar. She wandered toward the tables area, threading through the rows of slots and through groups of eager tourists. Along the way, she noticed a five-dollar slot tucked alongside a wheel of fortune machine. She'd never played a five-dollar machine so she pulled a twenty out her back pocket and sat on the stool in front of the machine.

She rubbed the surface of the bill in her hand as she studied the slot's details. The jackpot was three pyramid symbols and won ten thousand dollars. A max bet was fifteen dollars. Her stomach lurched as she'd never bet that much in one pull in all of her many visits to Louisiana casinos. Five dollars was her maximum bet on anything.

She closed her eyes for a moment. Just do it. She straightened out the bill and fed it in to the cash slot, four credits appeared. She first hit the button for one credit, then SPIN. The drums twirled, one cherry and two blank spots, absolutely nothing. She wiped her palms on her jeans. Three more spins or one big one? *Go for it, for heaven's sake*. Her finger hovered over the max bet button then she hit SPIN with the side of her fist.

The rollers spun in front of her then wound down to slow motion. A golden pyramid locked in first, then a red seven, her heart sank, white space was surely next. The third symbol locked in, a golden pyramid. The orange light on the top of the machine began to strobe. Her chest hiccupped. She had hit a jackpot!

She sat there, staring at the face of the machine, excited as a fifth grader with her first tube of lipstick. The fifteen bucks had paid off.

An older couple came up to her. The man asked how much she had won and she didn't know. He leaned toward the screen. After a minute, he said. "You're gonna be real happy with this. Looks to me like you've won five thousand dollars. How long have you played this machine?"

"It was my second spin."

He saluted her. "Nice going."

They moved off and others stopped to look at the screen then went on their way. A floor walker came by and told her to stay by the machine, someone would be there shortly. After ten minutes, a casino manager finally arrived. She turned off the light by reaching around to the back of the machine.

"Do you know how much you've won?" she said.

"I'm not exactly sure."

"It was a good spin for you." She smiled and looked at the screen once again. "Yes, you're seventy-five hundred dollars richer. Do you want the winnings in a check or in cash?"

Dallas did cartwheels in her head. "Cash, if it's quicker."

"Can do. Stay here and I'll be back in a few minutes." She hurried off and Dallas pulled the stool close to the winning slot machine. She itched to tell Logan about her good luck but dared not move until she had her winnings. Ooh, this was so cool. What should she do with the money? Save it, of course. That's was her logical brain talking. Her spontaneous brain said to blow it.

She stopped listening to her talking brain. Fortunately, the casino manager returned with another employee who watched her count out the money, seventy-five hundred dollar bills. She filled out a form, gave them each a tip and they disappeared. Stuffing the bills in her purse, she continued the search for Logan with a new bounce in her step.

After strolling around the craps table for a couple of minutes, she finally spotted him talking to a skinny blonde with a cast iron push up bra.

Dallas hurried to him and whispered in his ear. "Guess what?"

He jerked. Guess he'd been concentrating on, uh, something at the table.

"What?" he said.

She noticed the blonde move to the other side of the table. Good. "I won a jackpot on a five-dollar slot."

"I thought you didn't like high dollar bets."

"Whatever." It was exciting to tell him her good news.

"How much did you win?"

"Seventy-five hundred."

His eyes widened then he hugged her. "Nice going, ace."

"Thanks." She pulled back from him. "Would you like to celebrate my good fortune?"

"Absolutely."

Five minutes later, they sat at a secluded table in the North Edge Bar with a glass of champagne.

"Here's to you, Dallas. You're a lucky and a beautiful woman."

What a sweet thing to say. "Thank you. It's been a long time since I've been lucky at anything."

"Why is that?" Logan said.

"I believe more in hard work than luck." God, that was harsh. "Sorry. That didn't come out right."

"You're a woman who works hard for what she has. Don't apologize for being dedicated."

"I don't apologize for being me, ever." What was wrong with her? Logan was just being nice. But she couldn't get the picture of him talking to that blonde out of her mind. How stupid was that? He could talk to any dumb blonde he wanted. She'd only known him for a week. For some reason, it seemed like a decade.

"You're a complicated woman, Dallas Wells." He squeezed her hand and signaled to the waitress for more champagne. "This has been a tough week for you." He grinned. "Try to lighten up."

Dallas hardly knew this man and he could read her like a neurologist reading a brain scan. Scary. "You're right." She thought about the slot winnings. "Change of subject. I have the perfect use for the money I won."

"A new purse?"

"No, I'm going to throw Nana and Bill the best wedding reception seventy-five hundred dollars can buy."

"Great idea."

"One of my better ones, I think. I'll give her a call later." She fingered the stem of the champagne flute. "No doubt you've been to lots of society weddings in Houston."

"I don't know about society, but yes, I've attended too many weddings over the years, mostly for my family."

"Why too many?"

"Because the conversation eventually settles on me and why I'm not the groom. Gram is unrelenting."

She raised her glass. "Here's to the South's most eligible bachelor." She snuffed down a giggle while he sputtered.

"That's ridiculous."

"You look like good groom material to me."

"Very funny." He sipped the champagne and seemed pensive. "Let's talk about you. Why haven't you remarried?"

"Let me think . . . I remember now. I'm a lousy picker. If I stay away from men then I won't make another mistake."

"You'd never pick me?" He spread his hand over his heart.

"Nope. Consider yourself safe from my girlish charms."

After a third glass of champagne and not-so-subtle flirting, Logan and Dallas returned to the suite. She floated past him to the windows. Light from the Statue of Liberty at New York-New York streamed in the window, painting a pattern on the carpet. It was past midnight and the street was just as busy as it had been hours earlier.

The scent of his cologne announced Logan behind her. After a moment, his body pressed against her back, masculine arms wrapped around her middle, his chin rested on her right shoulder. Hmm, what was he up to?

"I know we haven't known each other for very long." His words snaked in her ear, long and smooth. "Surely you realize I'm attracted to you."

"Right back at you." The champagne said that, not Dallas. She closed her eyes and sank into the strength of his arms. It had been so long since she'd experienced anything approaching the comfort of being close to a man.

She turned to face him.

"Hey, you." She rested her hands on his chest. The heat from his skin warmed her palms.

"Hey, yourself." His gaze shifted from her eyes to lips. The moment his lips touched hers, she knew she was in trouble, deep trouble.

Logan cupped the back of her head, held still for a moment, then ground his lips on hers. She could taste champagne. She couldn't breathe. She couldn't think. His lips moved to her ear and he whispered, "Let's get more comfortable."

Within seconds, she found herself reclining on the sofa with Logan pressed tightly to her chest. His mouth again captured hers and she was off on a carnival ride. She enjoyed the scrape of his beard on her cheek, the taste of his tongue, and the sensations rocketing through her stomach. Logan's hand touched her breast. Her breath held for an instant then she pushed against his chest.

"Stop, stop. This is a mistake." She wiggled out from under him and managed to scramble off the sofa without landing on the floor.

Dallas looked down at a surprised Logan.

"I'm sorry," she whispered. "I'm not ready for this . . . you, you surprised me." She backed up a couple of steps and said, "I'm going to bed." She gasped with a hand against her mouth before rushing to her bedroom.

- - -

"What the hell?"

Logan slumped against the sofa cushion, not believing what had just happened—Dallas pushed him away. He threaded fingers through his hair, taking stock of the situation. What in the hell was he doing? Dallas Wells was a business associate, so why treat her like a potential girlfriend?

Easy. She'd gotten under his skin. She seemed so damned harmless and so damned earnest. And now he was second guessing himself. Maybe she wasn't as innocent as he'd earlier concluded. Why couldn't he believe her? Why shouldn't he believe her?

She'd done nothing the last few days but think about the theft followed by searching for Rebecca. And, she'd shown him the fake e-mail. He rubbed the stubble on his jaw. There was no reason to distrust her.

Right then, he was angry with himself for letting his guard down. Dallas was an attractive woman and he'd allowed that to get in front of what needed to be done. Yes, he would be more careful going forward. His attraction had to be pushed aside, for now. He needed to deal with this logically.

He rose and found himself at the windows overlooking the Strip. This seemed to be a favorite spot for Dallas. What was it about the street below that fascinated her? All Logan saw were tourists making their way from one casino to the next—nothing interesting or important.

He would work harder at getting to know Dallas, to understand her, to figure her out. It might be fun. And, he was very, very good at accomplishing whatever needed to be done.

Karen Sue Burns

FOURTEEN

Saturday, 7:15 a.m.

THE MORNING DAWNED BRIGHT AND lazy. Dallas pushed an eye open and looked at the bedside digital clock, errhgg, too early. She plopped back on the pillow. Her thoughts immediately focused on last night. Granted the details were fuzzy due to the champagne, yet she remembered pushing Logan away and running to the bedroom.

She did remember frolicking on the sofa with him like a teenager and then the fun becoming too intense. She pulled a pillow over her head. No doubt she'd embarrassed herself and Logan.

How should she handle this? Hmm . . . teenagers were good at blowing off negativity. That would be her approach. She threw off the pillow. There was no going back. She rose, threw on a robe, and headed to the kitchen.

Thankfully, a carafe of coffee sat on the counter. Logan had once again beat her to brewing the morning coffee. She poured a cup and wandered to the living room, her pink bathrobe flapping around her knees.

"Good morning. You're up early."

"I hope you slept well." Logan sat in a club chair reading a newspaper.

Moving past him, she smiled, ruffled his hair, then stopped at the windows. Sipping her coffee, her thoughts focused on the last week. Seven days full of surprise, revelation, new friends, and tragedy—events from one end of the spectrum to the other.

Of course, meeting Logan was virtually off the chart. She'd

never have met him if not for the HCU theft. And the fact that she
was in Las Vegas, in his family's beautiful hotel suite, and
enjoying his company, made her feel guilty as hell.

She had to admit that today, she wasn't any closer to
discovering Rebecca's whereabouts and the certainty of her guilt
than last Friday. Walking in Scooter's office, before the dinner
with Ruthie, seemed like a distant memory. An event that had
propelled her to stand at this window and wonder, will today be
the day to learn the truth?

Logan folded the newspaper, then said, "Would you like
more coffee?"

She shook her head. His cell rang and he walked to the
kitchen. He soon reappeared, mug in hand and joined her at the
window. "You look rested. Jackpots agree with you."

"I'd forgotten about that. Don't let me forget to call Nana
later today."

"Will do." Logan smiled at her and kissed her forehead. "JW
will be here in an hour. I'll have breakfast sent up."

"I'm anxious to hear what she's learned." She moved away
from him and toward the bedroom. "Be back in a few minutes."

Forty-five minutes later, Dallas paced the living room waiting
for JW to arrive. She prayed they'd learn Rebecca's location—
good news only. Since her divorce, Dallas hadn't endured such
negative drama as she'd faced over the last week. Traffic court
with her girls was a walk in the park compared to chasing after
wicked Rebecca.

The doorbell rang and the private investigator entered the
suite, along with room service. JW had dressed in black with a
lime green T-shirt. Dallas liked her style and fondness for pastel
colors.

"Good morning." JW shook hands first with Dallas, then
Logan. "I have much to tell you."

"We're eager to hear what you've learned." Logan motioned
toward the dining room. "Let's have breakfast while we talk."

The waiter set the table and placed the food in the middle.
They each took a seat and loaded their plates.

JW spoke first. "I've learned quite a bit about Rebecca Holland. I think you'll find it interesting. But first, I have some bad news for you, Dallas."

Her stomach dropped to the floor. The first thought was of Nana, then her daughters. "Bad news?" Logan reached for her hand on the table.

"There's not an easy way to tell you this. Scooter Taylor was found dead at a rest stop on Interstate 15 early this morning. The police believe it's a drug overdose, possibly heroin. The ME will verify the cause of death in a few days."

Dallas froze, her lips formed an O, and she held Logan's hand in a death grip. This couldn't be true. After several moments, she composed herself. "Are the police sure it's Scooter? I simply can't imagine him being a drug user."

"I agree, it sounds awfully farfetched based on what Dallas told me about him," Logan said.

"The ID was conclusive. LVPD authenticated his Texas driver's license. I'm sorry. It can't be easy hearing your boss was found dead along a highway." JW half-smiled, half-grimaced.

"Do you know if his wife has been notified?" Logan said.

"The police have already talked to her. I believe she's flying out here to claim the body."

"I'm so sorry for her," Dallas whispered, wiping a tear off her cheek. She had a good measure of sympathy for Mrs. Taylor.

"This is the second death of an HCU vice president in a week," Logan said. "Do you suppose they're related to the theft?"

Dallas disengaged Logan's hand. "If they aren't, it sure is a coincidence."

"That was the bad news." JW's gaze moved from Logan to Dallas. "I don't have a lot of time so on to the other news. I've learned a bit about Rebecca Holland. She has an interesting history."

"Can't wait to hear it." Dallas poured a glass of orange juice.

JW pulled a spiral notebook out of her backpack. She flipped through a few pages and began. "I was able to trace her history as far back as college. Rebecca graduated from Southern Methodist

University in the late eighties and has a degree in English."

"My cousin Billy graduated from SMU around that same time." Logan picked up his coffee cup.

JW nodded to him. "Actually, they knew each other, quite well in fact. I believe they dated all of their senior year then broke up around graduation."

Logan sat his coffee cup down so fast that coffee slopped on the tablecloth. "Are you sure? Although . . . Billy did mention he met her at a donor event and she reminded him of a girl he knew in college."

Now, that was a connection Dallas had never considered. Her one quick meeting with William or Billy, at the Bridge Foundation office didn't ring any bells. He gave no indication that he knew anyone personally at HCU. Maybe Rebecca was the girl he dated at SMU. Was this a clue to the theft?

Logan sopped up the spilled coffee with a napkin as JW continued.

"My sources tell me the relationship didn't end amicably. I don't have the details yet, but I will soon. Rebecca goes off the radar for about ten years. She emerges working for the Mitchell Foundation in Houston in the early nineties then transfers to Houston Cullen University working in the Office of Development as Executive Director. Her direct supervisor was Bill Jenkins, now deceased."

"Did you find any connection between Bill and Rebecca before she started to work for HCU?" Dallas asked. Now, that would be something.

JW addressed her. "No, I haven't found any prior contact. But I'll keep looking." She glanced at Logan, then at Dallas again. "There is one thing that seems unusual."

Dallas' stomach had that sinking feeling predicting major shit ahead. "What's that?"

"Mr. Rice, are you close to your family?" JW said.

"Of course, we're one big crazy family."

JW was silent, pulling apart a croissant, then she spoke. "Mr. Rice, my investigation has found that after Rebecca Holland broke off with your cousin, she became involved with another member of your family."

"That's absurd," Logan said.

"No, it's not." JW countered. "Shortly after graduating from SMU, Rebecca began an affair with Billy's father, William, Senior."

"How in the hell did you discover that?" Logan growled.

Dallas squeezed his hand. "JW, are you absolutely certain this information is correct?"

"It's one-hundred percent verified. I know it's a shock to you, Logan." She flipped her long braid of hair to her back. "This affair with your uncle, while married to your aunt Flora, appears to be a very small blip in his life." She shrugged. "Everyone makes a mistake at one time or another."

Logan looked like he'd swallowed a frog so Dallas decided to go in a new direction.

"Thanks so much, JW, for all that research. Anything else this dramatic?" Dallas said.

"Not really." JW smiled. "Like I said, she started working for nonprofits and ended up at HCU. No marriages, no credit problems, no police record."

"She sounds boring," Dallas said. "By the way, have you accessed the passenger logs of international flight leaving from Las Vegas?"

"Rebecca left last night on a flight to Newark, then boarded a midnight flight to Rome."

"Rome. Why in the world would she go there?" Dallas asked.

Logan looked at her with a trace of frustration. "Remember our discussion about hiding out in the open? Rome is full of tourists, plenty of Americans to blend in with. It's a good place to hide with all the luxuries." He pushed his chair back from the table, looking like he was about to pounce on the closest bad guy. "I've heard the Italians are a bit more difficult for the American authorities to deal with than other European countries."

Damn. Now Dallas had to go to Rome. She looked at Logan. "We need to get back to Houston ASAP."

"Why so quickly?"

"Even I know the answer to that." JW spoke first. "She needs to go home to pick up her passport. It's a requirement for boarding international flights." Her glee-filled eyes turned to Dallas. "Right?"

Dallas threw up her hands. "Fine. You caught me. I need to use a computer to check for flights." She was getting ahead of herself. "But first, JW, what else do you have for us?"

"The flight arrives in Rome at four-twenty this afternoon, Rome time. I couldn't get a hit on a hotel reservation. Be very discreet in approaching the staff of any hotel in Rome. They're notorious for protecting their guests." She retrieved a stack of papers from her backpack and placed them in front of Dallas. "This is a copy of what I've learned thus far. My open list includes deeper research into the twenty-year period after college for Rebecca, her personal connection with anyone from HCU, including Bill Jenkins and Scooter Taylor, and any past or present connection with the Bridge Foundation."

"We're pleased with your investigation. Thanks for being so quick," Logan said.

"You have my phone numbers and my e-mail address. Please forward any further information via e-mail. That should be easier than dealing with time zones once I'm in Italy." Dallas stood and held out her hand. "Thanks again for all that you've done. Please send your bill to the university. We'll settle up with the Bridge Foundation." She walked JW to the door of the suite while Logan pulled out his cell phone. "Let me know as soon as you have more information."

"I should have another update by tomorrow morning." JW turned and quickly entered the elevator. She turned back to Dallas. "Good luck in Rome."

$ $ $

Dallas didn't travel to Rome alone. Once again, Logan made all the arrangements.

He'd literally drug her back to Houston on the Rice family jet to pick up clean clothes and passports. Little did she know he'd made all the flight arrangements and Rome hotel reservations before they lifted off from Las Vegas. She tapped her foot at gate E-15, Atlanta Hartsfield Airport, ready and waiting to board a Delta flight to Rome. And, she was thirsty.

Where the hell was Logan? Surely their boarding group was about to be called. She squinted and scanned the gate area. Finally, he came in view, casually sauntering toward her, a drink cup in each hand with his carry-on bag banging against a hip. He looked cute. Maybe it wasn't so bad having a man do errands—Dallas got what she wanted and he felt all manly and useful.

She slurped a good dose of iced tea then nodded toward the gate. "They should be calling our boarding group any minute. Did you get a call from JW?"

Logan shook his head, looking vaguely out of sorts. "I doubt we'll hear from her until tomorrow, like she said at breakfast. You never did tell me what you learned from Roddy earlier today."

Roddy had called while Dallas packed her clothes. "They haven't made any headway with the Swiss bank. Still don't know the name on the private account where the money was transferred from the Caymans. He said the FBI is negotiating with the Swiss authorities."

The gate agent finally called their group number so they queued up and were soon seated in first class with a glass of chardonnay

Dallas tapped her glass to Logan's then tasted the wine. "Here's to a very successful journey to Rome. What was I telling you before?" She wrinkled her forehead. "I remember now. Roddy said the Swiss privacy laws are just as tough as ours so we may have a problem. He'll let me know when he hears. Also, they forwarded Rebecca's picture and description to Interpol."

"Maybe we'll get lucky this time." Logan stretched out his long legs. "Once we're settled, we can e-mail Roddy and JW the hotel's address and phone number."

"Sounds like a plan." She was relieved to have a few hours

of no contact with anyone related to the theft. She was accustomed to occasional stress—her children were girls after all—and sporadic overtime at work. But this intense concentration of hunting for a person she didn't even really like was overwhelming.

She turned her head toward the window, closed her eyes. Logan squeezed her hand. She heard him open a newspaper. He really enjoyed keeping up with the news. The drone of the airplane's engine was surprisingly relaxing.

She woke two hours later with a clearer head and hunger pangs. Great timing as the flight attendants were beginning the dinner service. Logan had his nose buried in a book. She nudged his arm. "Good reading, Mr. Rice?"

He closed the book and placed it in the seat pocket "Yes, it's a murder mystery. I'm glad you napped. Would you like a drink or a glass of wine?"

"Hmm, a glass of cabernet would be nice." She felt considerably better after cheese, crackers, and red grapes. Another glass of wine accompanied the main course—filet mignon, garlic mashed potatoes, Caesar salad—just like home.

Between bites, they shared stories. Logan asked about how Dallas came to work for the University.

"Are you sure you want to hear this?"

He nodded, "I really am interested."

"Okay, you asked for it. I started taking college accounting classes when I was married. I worked part-time at a church doing their books. After my divorce, I went to the University of Houston and eventually got my degree and worked at an oil company downtown. But the overtime took its toll and I moved to HCU as Accounting Manager and after four years I was promoted to Controller."

"Sounds like a hell of an accomplishment considering you were raising two daughters at the time."

She grinned. "I'm good at multi-tasking."

"I bet you are." He winked. "Billy has an accounting degree, too."

"By the way, did he ever tell you about his college relationship with Rebecca?"

"No, he only mentioned Rebecca reminded him of a girl from college. Guess his memory was better than he thought." He looked down the aisle of the plane, hesitated for a moment then turned back to Dallas. "Do you suppose their relationship and break up was the motivation for the theft?"

Great minds do think alike. "The thought had crossed my mind. But it seems farfetched, more like the plot for a soap opera. People date and break up in college all the time without holding a grudge about it for twenty years."

"You're right. The fact they dated is simply a coincidence." Logan drummed his fingers on the lap table. "I do wonder about Rebecca's affair with my uncle though."

The flight attendant arrived to clear their dishes. She soon came back with raspberry soufflés and coffee and liqueurs. Dallas chose Kahlua and Logan opted for Amaretto to spike their coffee. First class was definitely the preferred method to fly. Good food and good alcohol.

She tasted her coffee. "This is great. By the way, thanks for handling all the reservations. I'm the one who usually does that."

"My pleasure. Surely it's not a major problem for you to have someone help with all the details." Logan's grin was charming.

She thought about that for a moment. A single mother for almost fifteen years with twin daughters, yeah, she was damned good at handling the details.

"No, of course not. It's nice to have someone around who I can depend on." Although she sure as hell didn't know how comfortable that made her feel.

The lights dimmed. A current blockbuster movie started on the video screen in the back of the seat in front of her. She finished the coffee, patted Logan's hand, and placed the sleep shades over her eyes. If she was lucky, she'd have four hours to sleep. Logan kissed her on the cheek and whispered in her ear to nap like a Cheshire cat. Huh?

Two glasses of wine and a decent dose of Kahlua didn't

immediately lull her to sleep. The past week kept spinning like a tornado through her head. Bits of clues and fragments of information were thrown out for a second then sucked back in the storm's narrow neck. Nothing seemed to stick or make sense. Eventually she'd figure out how the bits and pieces fit together.

$ $ $

This was Dallas' first visit to Italy and she was in love from the first sight of an ancient column next to a modern overpass on the highway. The car ride from Rome's Fiumicino - Leonardo da Vinci Airport to the hotel passed through an industrial area, skirted huge apartment buildings, and swept by the southern lawns of the Villa Borghese. The driver provided commentary while driving along what must have been the scenic route. She had purchased a Rome street map at the airport and attempted to follow their progress without much success.

The car turned left at a wide boulevard and after a block swung into the circular driveway of their hotel. A massive arched red door led to the immaculate lobby and reception desk of Albergo Santa Chiara.

Within minutes, they were ushered to their room, no suites available—one beautiful room and one very large bed. Dallas stared at the bed as her purse slipped off her arm to the floor. She must have had a look.

"We were lucky to find a room in Rome this time of year. It's tourist season." Logan tipped the bellman, then moved to where she stood. He picked up the purse and handed it to her. "It's a big bed, we can sleep on opposite sides or I can sleep on the chaise lounge. Whatever makes you feel comfortable."

Her eyes bored into him. Comfortable? He was nuts.

On the other hand, she was so tired she'd sleep with a python if it didn't snuggle too close. "I'm going to take a nap before I say something stupid. Feel free to join me in the bed." Her face froze, yet Logan simply grinned. "To sleep, that is," she added.

She slipped off her shoes and jacket, used the toilet, then

slipped between the sheets.

Logan was on the phone, then completed the call. "We have a wakeup call in five hours. Okay with you?" He shrugged off his sport coat.

"Hmm, yes." Dallas closed her eyes. The sheets felt relaxing, soft and cool. "Then I'll be ready for real Italian food."

It was weird. She was in a strange bed, in a strange country, with an almost strange man, and had no qualms about him sleeping beside her. Perhaps her brain was already warping due to a lack of Houston humidity.

FIFTEEN

Sunday, 4:05 p.m.

DALLAS' EYES FLUTTERED. Her elbow hit a wall. *What?* She jerked back while her hand stroked the wall. She came fully awake pawing Logan's very muscular back. It felt hard and warm, soft and cool—too much. She withdrew her hand and rolled to her back. The bed began to jiggle like a three-year-old playing with Jell-O worms.

She grabbed a pillow from behind her head and threw it. It lodged against his head and the bed's backboard. He pushed it off and flipped onto his back, with his hands behind his head.

"You called?" A grin sliced across his face.

Caught red-handed, she felt heat race from her chest and shoot straight to the ends of her hair. "Did you sleep well?"

"Yep." He reached out and squeezed her hand lying on the blanket. The warmth of his skin against hers was comforting.

"I wasn't trying to manhandle you." Her heart performed a thump-da-thump. Why did this man make her so damned nervous?

He pulled her hand to his mouth and gently kissed it above the knuckles. "Not to worry. I'm sure you're not accustomed to waking up in strange beds in strange countries with semi-strange men." He squeezed her hand again, then quickly rose from the bed. "I'll shower first. You relax a bit longer."

Dallas had to give it to Logan, in addition to being gorgeous, single, and wealthy, he was a gentleman with a wicked sense of humor. She liked him. In fact, she was semi-attracted to him. And, it had to stop. She didn't need a man in her personal life, whether she was lonely or not.

Business was different. Men were an inescapable part of the landscape. A person couldn't avoid them, like the flu during a really cold winter.

She couldn't figure Logan out. Since she'd laid eyes on him, he had been one step ahead of her in the search for Rebecca. Normally Dallas was the one ahead, the one who thought the quickest, the one who had the most original ideas. Of course, she didn't have the financial backing of an old, distinguished, and wealthy family as he did. No holding it against him. She hated to admit it, but bottom line, she needed his help.

$ $ $

After a shower and a taste of Logan's scotch procured at the duty-free shop in Atlanta, Dallas felt as perky as a pair of newly implanted double Ds. They left their room for the hotel lobby to forage for food.

But first she purchased an e-mail credit card and she sat at a guest computer to check her messages. Nothing. What the hell were Roddy and JW doing? She shook off the disappointment and remembered Logan telling her to be patient. Right. Okay, she'd do her best to be patient.

They left the hotel and strolled towards the Pantheon. The narrow street was busy with tourists. It was easy to understand why Rebecca had selected Rome as the spot to disappear. Americans were everywhere, easily identifiable in their white sneakers. Dallas mused the city had thousands of buildings holding thousands of hiding places. It dawned on her that it would be damn near impossible to find Rebecca without some local help.

"Logan, I was thinking."

"About what?"

"Rome is huge. I've overestimated *our* ability to actually find Rebecca. I haven't a clue where to start."

"Hmm . . . we'll talk later."

He grabbed her hand, led her around the corner of a yellow

building and there it was . . . the Pantheon—tall, round, gray stone, and aglow from the early evening sun. Dallas' very first Roman antiquity. She stopped walking and ogled the structure, her mouth open.

"Earth to Dallas." Logan waved a hand in front of her face. "Come back to me."

Oops, she'd zoned out. Being immersed in two thousand years of history was exhilarating. She squeezed Logan's hand.

"Sorry, I love history and get carried away." She walked a few steps ahead of him, raising her arms. "Rome is awesome. I want to see everything." She looked back at him. "After we find Rebecca."

Logan sauntered over to her. "Good idea. Let's walk over to the Piazza Navona. It's just a few blocks and well worth the effort."

"Why so?"

"After a fabulous dinner, we'll share a dessert called death by chocolate." He studied her out of the corner of his eye, his mouth twitching.

"I'm in," Dallas said, chocolate being one of her favorite food groups.

They walked along the west side of the Pantheon to a small piazza and turned left at Via Giustiniani. Buildings with a variety of colored facades and huge double wooden doors, lined the narrow cobblestone street. Quaint shops were sprinkled among the structures. They passed a plain-looking church and shortly the narrow street that opened to Piazza Navona and Bernini's Four Rivers Fountain.

"Logan, it's incredible." She pointed to the sculpture. "Look at the four river gods holding an Egyptian obelisk. The rivers are the Nile, the Ganges, the Danube, and the Rio de la Plata—water of the world gushes everywhere. In fact, Bernini added horses to—"

"Okay, Miss Roman Tour Guide, you officially have the night off. Let's eat. Tre Scalini is on the other side of the piazza."

"Sorry. Guess I'm excited being here. I'll keep it under

control, I promise." Like that would happen. Nana had a great story about Dallas at the Alamo in San Antonio.

"Let's eat. Tré Scalini is on the other side of the piazza."

She trotted ahead of Logan, searching for a sign across the piazza that read Tré Scallapini, uh, Scala . . . whatever. And there it was, dead ahead, across a narrow grassy area filled with street vendors. Logan had called ahead and they were seated immediately. He was a one-man reservation machine. Dallas hated to admit she liked it.

They sat at a patio table bordering the grassy area of the piazza. A clean-shaven young man, sitting a few feet away, picked at an acoustical guitar and started on a melody of Beatle songs. She never could have imagined *Hey Jude* being sung on a piazza in Rome.

Logan ordered bottles of vino rosso and water before they concentrated on the menu. Hmm, pasta or pizza? Easy. That decision being made, Dallas launched into her Rome agenda.

"First thing tomorrow, I want to buy a phone credit card at the hotel to call my family and Roddy. Ruthie, too. I forgot to call her in Atlanta." It was weird not being able to pull out her cell phone and punch in a number. Rome was her first experience of a seven-hour time difference and being out of touch. "You know, this past week has been . . . wild."

Logan nodded and chuckled. "Let's see. Today is Sunday and I officially met you last Wednesday and we've spent every night together since then. That's definitely a first for me."

The waiter arrived, pulling attention away from the heat infusing her neck and face. He poured the wine and glasses of water. Logan recited their dinner orders and they were once again left alone, eying each other over a raised glass of water. Logan's last remark stayed between them, floating in the Italian air.

Dallas did her best to avoid eye contact with him. She watched the street vendors conduct a brisk business while tourists roamed around the makeshift tables and easels of artwork. The melody to Paul McCartney's *Yesterday* spiraled toward them. It was one of her all-time favorite songs and always a mood booster.

She decided to take the plunge.

"This past week has been a first for me as well." She tilted her head, examining the man sitting across from her. "But now that I look at you, I definitely think it's been an exceptionally good week." Why in the hell did she say that?

Logan appeared to consider her words. His entire face smiled. "Back at you." He leaned forward, placing his elbows on the table. "My guess is we won't be searching for Rebecca every waking moment. Thus, we'll have ample time to explore Rome."

Huh? "I may love history but this trip is to find Rebecca, not play tourist."

He looked surprised by her statement. "Okay, but this evening we are off duty."

Dallas raised her glass and tasted the wine. Very nice. "I'll relax tonight but tomorrow the search is on."

Their dinners arrived and the next few minutes focused on tasting the authentic Italian cuisine. Dallas wasn't disappointed. The pizza with chicken and artichokes was delicious. She made a mental note, to pick up a cookbook before going home. That reminded her of Nana and Bill. An Italian wedding gift for them would be perfect—but what to buy for a seventy-something couple?

"Logan, we'll have time for shopping, right? I'd like to pick up a wedding gift for Nana."

"I'm sure we can add shopping to the agenda. So far, we have finding Rebecca, visiting the historical sites once we find her, and shopping in between." He counted off the items on his fingers, humor lighting his eyes. "Anything else?"

"Hmm, I think that's about it. First things first though, we need to visit the main police office in the morning. Surely they'll help us."

"My guess is that depends on whether the FBI or the Houston police have contacted them yet, or Interpol."

"I'll e-mail Roddy tomorrow."

She tapped a finger on the table. "I wish I knew more about Rebecca's personal life in Houston."

"Was she good friends with anyone at the university?" he asked.

"Let me think." She emptied her wine glass and Logan refilled it. Dallas thought about campus events Rebecca had attended—monthly staff luncheons, all-employee campus meetings, lectures. Who did she hang with? At last year's staff appreciation luncheon Rebecca had been chummy with Nancy Sims, who worked in the president's office. A couple of times, Dallas had noticed them having a drink in the campus coffee shop.

"I have a name I'll send to Roddy. Who knows, he may have already talked to her. I can't believe I hadn't thought about Nancy before."

"You're so hard on yourself. You're not a trained investigator. Lighten up."

"But I am good at details and I should have told Roddy about Nancy last week." She countered, somewhat embarrassed. "I need to concentrate on what I'm doing here. No telling what else I've missed."

Logan shook his head. "You are one stubborn woman. But I like you anyway."

She had a moment to think about Logan's last comment while the waiter cleared the table. For an eligible bachelor, he was surprisingly open about his feelings, much more so than her. Whatever feelings she had about him were closed to discussion. She had long ago admitted to herself that she wasn't good at relationships. And that was that.

"My goal in Rome is to concentrate on the HCU theft and tracking down Rebecca."

"I know that. But right now, let's order dessert. Tre Scalini is famous for its Tartufo." The corners of his mouth turned upward. "Death by chocolate."

"Are you trying to fatten me up?" She sucked in her stomach. Italian food was so heavy on the calories.

"Live a little. We can split an order." He motioned to the waiter.

"I'll suffer through a chocolate dessert . . . *just for you*." She patted herself on the back for being so agreeable. Perhaps she could sneak in an early morning run to burn off the extra calories.

$ $ $

The dessert was fantastic—a ball of dark chocolate gelato surrounded by a shell of dark chocolate rolled in cocoa, then topped with whipped cream—at least five thousand delicious calories. They took a more circular route back to the hotel to walk off the extravagant treat.

Dallas' nerves started twitching as they ventured closer to the hotel. How would they handle the sleeping arrangements? Could she carry it off without making a fool of herself? First, she wasn't accustomed to having another person in her bed, and second, what if Logan expected more than sleeping?

The hotel was just ahead. She took a deep breath, told herself to remember she was a mature adult with mature one-bed-hotel-room-etiquette.

Back in the room, the bed had been turned down and her anxiety returned. She attacked her luggage, hanging clothes in the closet, putting things in a drawer. Logan meanwhile excused himself to the bathroom. She appreciated the time alone and sat on the bed. What the hell was she doing in a hotel, in a foreign country, with a man she hardly knew? No turning back. She had to complete this pursuit to its end, regardless of the current situation. She took a deep breath and calm returned.

The bathroom door opened. Logan appeared, carrying his shirt. Oh, my.

"All yours." He yawned, draping the shirt over a chair. "I'm bushed."

Dallas gathered her things, stepped past him. He stopped her with a light hand on her arm.

"I'm with you one-hundred percent in this search. We'll find Rebecca, one way or the other."

"I know." A single tear rolled down her cheek.

Logan scrutinized her face. "What's wrong?" His finger

wiped the tear away, then he gently kissed the cheek.

"I'm fine, just tired and overwhelmed and uncomfortable."

"You mean one room, one bed?"

No mincing of words. She turned away, pulling her toiletry bag against her chest. "Maybe." She moved toward the bathroom. "I'm tired, that's all."

She changed into her pink pajamas covered with kittens, performed the normal nightly routine. She mentally readied herself for Logan in the bed, probably close to naked. She couldn't picture him as a jammies kind of guy, more like a boxers or briefs kind of guy. Her imagination refused to go any further than that.

She had nothing to worry about as she found Logan under the bedclothes, on his side, and asleep. She tiptoed to the foot of bed, leaned over to look at him. He was a sight—long lashes brushed his cheek, hair tousled, and a muscled chest sprinkled with curly light brown hair. Hard to believe a smart debutant hadn't reeled him in.

The bed sheets were cool. That surprised her considering a hot male was not a foot away. Dallas fluffed up the pillow under her head. Logan moved. Oh dear, maybe it was time to readjust her thinking on men and relationships. She *could* take a break from her no-men rule, maybe for a week.

$ $ $

Monday morning, Dallas and Logan piled into a cab at the hotel's entrance and headed for the U.S. Embassy along Via Vittorio Veneto. Logan had yet another friend of the family who had advised this course of action instead of going directly to the Italian police. With her nose pasted to the window glass, Dallas watched the fountains, monuments, and beautiful buildings pass by.

The streets weren't any worse than Houston on a weekday morning, other than the honking. After fifteen minutes, the taxi stopped in front of a tall yellow building with barricades in front of its driveway entrance. A line of people snaked down the block from the main doors with several U.S. Marines monitoring the progress.

Logan jumped out of the taxi and spoke to a Marine next to the barricade. He showed the soldier something from his billfold, probably his driver's license. The Marine talked on a cell phone, then nodded at Logan.

They scooted around the barricade and entered the embassy through its main doors, heading to a large ornamental desk. It sat under a sign—U.S. Citizens-Special—and was situated to the side of the reception area. Italian citizens seeking visas queued in lines on the left side of the open space.

Logan stated his name and asked for the legal attaché. Surprisingly, the young man behind the desk greeted Logan by name, asked for their passports, and directed them to sit and wait. They sat on a red paisley couch against a wall, providing a clear view of the lobby.

A few minutes later, a young woman entered from a side door. She handed them their passports and asked them to follow her. Logan and Dallas trailed behind her to a smaller reception area and then to a government-issue office at its far end.

A man sat at a metal desk facing the door. He stood at their arrival and came around to greet them.

"Good morning, I'm Agent Brown. I understand you're visiting Rome from Houston." He motioned to straight back metal chairs facing the desk. "Please, have a seat."

They complied and waited.

Agent Brown glanced first at Dallas, then Logan. He smiled and said. "How may I help you? Americans don't normally visit the U.S. Embassy without an agenda. Usually it's a lost passport or a theft of some kind."

She looked at Logan, who nodded.

"Agent Brown, thank you for seeing us without an appointment. Mr. Rice and I are in Rome specifically to find another U.S. citizen."

"Really?" Agent Brown said, sounding skeptical.

"Yes. She's my co-worker at Houston Cullen University. We believe she stole $25 million from the university."

Agent Brown picked up a fountain pen. "What's the name of your co-worker?"

"Rebecca Holland. I have notes for you and a picture as well." She placed the notebook and picture on the desk.

"Give me a minute while I review these." Agent Brown began scanning the notes.

Dallas worked at not fidgeting or tapping a foot. Logan stared into space, looking handsome and thoughtful. She envied his composure.

"Your police contact in Houston," Agent Brown glanced at the notes, "Roddy Phillips. Has he told you the name of his FBI friend?"

"No, he didn't. But I e-mailed him an hour ago, told him we were coming here, and asked for the agent's name. We figured you'd want confirmation that we're not wasting your time." She glanced at Logan, then dug in her purse. "Here's Roddy's card so you can contact him."

"Thanks." Agent Brown looked from Logan to Dallas, then smiled. "I'm glad you came here rather than going to the Italian police. Your friend gave you good advice, Mr. Rice. We liaison with local law enforcement in cases like this."

Logan uncrossed his legs, then said, "So, bottom line, what do you suggest is our next step?"

"At this point, you wait. I need to contact our field office in Houston as well as the police." Agent Brown leaned over his desk. "I'm sure you understand."

"What do we do in the meantime?" Dallas asked. Play tourist or shop? Both a waste of time with Rebecca on the loose.

Logan touched her knee. "Be patient."

"I know. But seriously, can we check out anything, do surveillance?" The instant the words were out of her mouth, a blush covered her face. She felt ridiculous and childish.

"That's not necessary. I agree with Mr. Rice. You must be patient." Agent Brown had the look of talking to his eighty-year-old grandmother. "Where are you staying in Rome?" he asked

Logan provided the name of their hotel. "I assume we're on

hold until we hear from you?"

"Correct." Agent Brown stood. "I'll contact you at your hotel once I receive confirmation of the theft and information on the search for Miss Holland." He ushered them to the door then shook their hands. "Enjoy Rome until I get back to you. Don't try to play detective while you're here, Miss Wells. That will only lead to disaster."

She murmured, "Yes, of course."

They exited the embassy through the front door. Back on the street, she stopped.

"That was intense. Do you think he believed us?"

Logan shrugged. "I don't see why not. He knew we weren't deadbeats before he even talked to us. Once he checks out all the details, he'll contact us."

"I'm glad you're so positive. Me, I'll wait and see." She scanned the street. "We need to talk."

"Let's get a coffee while we chat." He grabbed her hand. "There's a pizzeria on the corner."

They ordered coffee Americano then sat back to enjoy the sunshine and the spring morning in Rome—for about three minutes. Dallas' guilt at being in Rome, on university business and enjoying anything other than slapping Rebecca's wicked little face, had her thinking about their next step. She frowned.

"Dallas."

She jerked. "What?"

"I know what's bothering you."

"Oh yeah, what?"

"You're torn between being a good little HCU employee while at the same time enjoying the wonders of Rome."

Logan, a clairvoyant?

"That was five minutes ago." It was comforting to realize another human being, other than Nana or Ruthie, understood her. On the other hand, the fact that Logan could so easily read her was spooky. "I suggest we target our search to the typical tourist sites. She doesn't know we're here so I bet she'll play the wealthy American tourist game."

"I agree. Pull out your map and we'll plan our route."

She pulled the tourist map from her purse and spread it on the table. All of the tourist spots were highlighted and easy to identify.

"Logan, we're close to the Spanish Steps. Let's start there. It's supposed to be a magnet for Americans."

"Great idea."

They spent several minutes enjoying their coffee and people watching. Dallas could be still for only so long. She emptied her cup and again studied the map.

"Let's go," she said. They rose and stood on the sidewalk. "We need to walk down this street to the next corner and turn right." At least she thought so. She read the street name on the side of a building, located it on the map to be safe. She was seventy-five percent sure they were walking in the right direction. Close enough.

SIXTEEN

Monday, 11:56 a.m.

THE PEDESTRIAN TRAFFIC INCREASED in the block before the Spanish Steps. Cafes and pizzerias were open for lunch and buzzing with activity. Dallas and Logan worked their way to the top of the steps. A huge white church with twin towers, Trinità dei Monti, loomed above and behind a high wall on the right, while an outdoor market spread out on the left.

They split up. Logan moved toward vendors displaying their wares on moveable shelves—key chains, postcards, the usual. Dallas walked down a row of artists and tables holding easels showing off beautiful Italian landscapes in water color or pastel chalk. Tourists roamed slowly around the market scoping out the merchandise, but no Rebecca.

Logan found Dallas at the top of the white, thirty-foot wide marble steps that numbered one-hundred thirty-eight to the street. The stairs angled to the right then to the left with six foot landings after fifteen steps or so. Pots of red and white flowers bordered either side and along the middle of the steps. People of all ages reclined on the marble and blocked an easy descent.

"I'll go left and you go right," Logan said. "Take a good look at any blond women."

"She might have changed her hair color," Dallas said and decided to look at any female older than a teenager.

Logan nodded and started down the stairs. They each meandered among the bodies, stopping at the second landing for a breather. Logan waved and continued descending. Dallas followed but at a slower pace.

Logan waited for her at the bottom, Piazza di Spagna. She joined him a couple minutes later, thankful she hadn't trod on anyone. The people in the piazza were milling around, mostly blocking forward movement. Most seemed to be tourists, she heard French, German, and lots of English.

Logan touched her arm and motioned his head to the left. "Let's sit on the steps."

They found a vacant spot about ten rows up with a nice view over the throng at the bottom. The sun was bright, the sky blue, and the temperature enjoyable—perfect weather for people watching.

"This is fantastic. As much as I love Houston, we don't have views like this at home," Logan said.

"I agree. We have skyscrapers and freeways and Rome has buildings hundreds of years old. The sense of history is overwhelming."

"What's the next tourist site?"

She pointed to her map. "The Trevi Fountain is a few blocks away. It looks like an easy walk."

"Did you see the movie?"

"What movie?"

Logan laughed. "*Three Coins in the Fountain*. It popularized the fountain back in the fifties. The sculptures are beautiful and we can throw in a coin."

Dallas swung her head around to him. "You've been to Rome before?"

"Yes, several times."

"Why didn't you tell me?"

"It never came up."

She turned away from him. It bothered her this wasn't a first experience for him. Had he visited Rome with another woman? Why was she even thinking about the women in his life? His love life, past or present, was none of her business. And since she wasn't in the market for a steady date, she didn't even have an opinion on the subject.

She focused on the tourists loitering around the piazza. A

blonde woman appeared through a break in the bodies. Dallas rose to search for the face in the crowd below. "Logan, did you see the blonde in the blue dress? Come on, let's go." She nudged his shoulder and started down the stairs, quickly reaching the street.

"Where did you see her?" Logan said, joining her.

"Over to the left, by the corner of that yellow building." She pushed through the swirling bodies in what she hoped was the right direction. Everything looked different at street level.

They reached the building and Dallas turned a slow circle, hoping to see a blonde wearing blue. She circled again. Nothing.

"Dammit, I don't see her." Dallas roasted in the sun and was frustrated with this whole mess. "Why can't I find her?" She jerked away from Logan and leaned against the building, wiping sweat off the back of her neck.

Logan stared at her. "What is with you?"

"What is with me?" She threw her hands up. "Isn't it obvious? I couldn't find a blonde bimbo in a whorehouse."

His mouth curved into a smile before he burst out laughing.

"What is so damned funny?" She raised her chin, crossed her arms, and tapped a foot.

After a moment, he placed a hand on her shoulder.

The pressure was reassuring, comforting.

"Dallas, you've got to get a perspective on all this. I know you're frustrated. But we're civilians trying to act like the police. It's a long shot at best that *we'll* find Rebecca. You have to be patient until we hear from the FBI."

"Be patient, my ass. I want to find Rebecca and wring her stupid southern belle neck."

Logan put his arm around her waist and pulled her away from the building. "You're totally justified in feeling like that." He paused, looking around the corner. "Lunch or the Trevi Fountain?"

"Trevi Fountain." Dallas pulled away from Logan and squared her shoulders. Dammit, she'd find that bitch and in Rome.

She consulted the map and they started off in the direction Logan suggested. The upscale shops bordering the street reminded her of the shops in Houston. Rome was definitely cosmopolitan. After they found Rebecca, she planned to shop and play tourist.

"I think we're going in the right direction," Logan said after ten minutes. "Look for a sign that says Trevi Fountain."

"Yes, sir."

They soon came to a wide boulevard, Via del Tritone, and sure enough, a street sign pointed straight ahead to the Trevi. They walked down another busy street and followed the signs to a small piazza, shadowed by the buildings surrounding it. The Trevi Fountain rested at the juncture of three streets marking the terminal point of an ancient aqua duct.

The backdrop of the fountain was the Palazzo Poli. It looked like the front of an ancient building with Corinthian columns and a bunch of sculptures of Neptune and ladies holding urns and cups that spilled water into a huge square basin filled with coins. They walked along the upper perimeter of the fountain gazing at the visitors. No one resembled the southern belle.

They moved down a couple of dented stone steps to the lower level of the basin, which was bordered by a stone ledge occupied by visitors.

Logan grabbed Dallas' hand. "Let's walk to the other end and back and then sit for a while."

They looked at all the tourists directly in front of the water. No one was a Rebecca clone.

Dallas pulled Logan to an open spot on the uneven stone ledge. She took a deep breath and allowed her body to bask in the incredible sense of history surrounding her. She knew the fountain was completed in 1762 and included work by Bernini. He sure did get around Rome back in the day.

They sat in silence for several minutes, watching the water cascade, enjoying the ambiance, and continually glancing at the people surrounding them.

Logan nudged her arm. "History buff, you up to throwing a coin in the fountain?"

"You bet. Doesn't a coin ensure a return to Rome?"

"That's what I've heard," Logan chuckled.

"I'm throwing a U.S. quarter." She pulled two coins out of her wallet, handed one to Logan. "Here's one for you."

"Throw it over your left shoulder."

She counted, "One, two, three." Squeezing her eyes shut, she tossed the quarter over her shoulder. For some odd reason, the symbolism of this simple touristy act washed a flood of comfort over Dallas.

She glanced at Logan. His sunglasses were on the top of his head and his eyes were trained on her. They had crossed an unspoken boundary. The warmth of his gaze filled her with hope. Hope that what lay ahead wouldn't bite her in the butt. But at that moment, the planets in her world were in perfect alignment.

For several minutes, they watched the water dance over the sculptures. The eclectic crowd reminded Dallas of why Rome was a perfect location for Rebecca to hide. A change of hair color, a new cut, and a different style of clothing and she would be nearly impossible to recognize among the thousands of tourists. How in the hell could Dallas find her?

With her shoulder pressed against Logan, her chin collapsed to her chest. Dallas closed her eyes. She didn't want to admit to herself that the trek to Rome was probably a waste of time. But she'd see it to the end.

$ $ $

Along with the incredible monuments titillating a history buff, Rome was a goldmine for a serious shopper. Logan and Dallas left the Trevi Fountain and meandered their way back toward the Pantheon. Logan used the map to guide their route and Dallas kept an eye out for a children's store. After a couple of blocks of spectacular window shopping, she found one.

The window displays were adorable. Child size mannequins wore colorful cotton hats, tee shirts, and blue jeans. They were surrounded by blocks, puzzles, and an assortment of soccer balls. She pulled Logan into the shop. The interior stopped her short.

The upscale décor with painted blue, pink, green and yellow rainbows and balloons covering the walls reminded her of a children's store she had frequented at Houston's Galleria Mall.

With Logan tagging along, she zeroed in on the infant section with visions of something very soft and cuddly for her first grandchild. Searching the shelves for less than a minute, she spotted the perfect gift, a white cashmere baby throw. She lightly rubbed her hand over the velvety surface, then draped it over her arm. She purposely didn't look at the price tag. A few Euro's wouldn't stop her from buying a beautiful gift for her first grandchild.

"I like it," Logan said. "How about a stuffed animal?"

"Just what I was thinking."

They moved to the other side of the store and caught the attention of a salesclerk, or at least Logan did. He stopped to chat while Dallas riffled through shelf after shelf of pint-sized furry creatures. She settled on a brown monkey, a white lamb, and a golden teddy bear. Each was made of cut chenille and just as soft as the blanket. She placed the trio in a line on the shelf, then caught Logan's eye.

"Sweetheart, I need your help with the grandbaby gift."

Ah, the salesclerk did speak English. She backed off and Logan moseyed over to grandma.

Dallas pointed to her new friends. "Who's your favorite?"

His entire face smiled. "You know how many times I've made this same choice for nieces and nephews?"

She shook her head, thinking the lamb was the best choice.

"What the hell, get all three. I'm sure we can stuff them into a suitcase."

"Stuff them?" She looked at him and saw the twitching mouth. "Too funny, but you're right. I'll get all three." She gathered the baby animals along with the throw and settled them at the checkout desk. The sales clerk was the model of efficiency. Very nice, indeed. Dallas didn't look at the total Euro's on the charge receipt. That surprise could wait until she was back in Houston.

She accepted a shopping bag and grabbed Logan's hand, making certain he exited the store with her. The salesclerk blew him a kiss. How sweet.

Back on the street, they turned to the right and continued their trek toward the Pantheon and the hotel. Dallas' heart was a warm fuzzy after accomplishing one of her two shopping goals. A wedding gift for Nana and Bob would require much more thought.

While walking, she marveled at Rome's sophistication. Yes, the city was soaked in history, but it seemed comfortable in its modern twenty-first century skin. She liked the notion of that. The best of both worlds melded together into one enthralling city. A shiver raced up her spin—Rome was simply too cool.

She checked her watch, three o'clock, and asked Logan for the street map so she could verify their location. They were on Via del Sabini with a major cross street just ahead.

"I think we have time to check the interior of the Pantheon," she said.

They soon crossed Via del Croso. Delivery trucks clogged the street's curb, irritating the taxi drivers who responded with a loud honk of their horn.

Even with the noise, the walk was pleasant. They passed many business people. Dallas noticed the men were very attractive. Most wore dark suits fitted at the torso, soft leather shoes, and dark sunglasses. The picture was so nice on the eyes, minus the cigarette sticking out of their mouths. She concentrated on any female over five feet tall. No one reminded her of Rebecca.

They kept on the lookout for Via de Caravita and found it after ten minutes. After rounding a corner, Dallas had an attack of conscience. There she was, guiding Logan all over Rome with her trusty tourist map, while he should have been back in Houston taking care of Bridge Foundation business. She was selfish. She stopped forward motion, moved toward the window of a wine store.

"Logan, I'm so sorry."

He stared at her, placed a hand on her arm. "Sorry? For what?"

"I'm sorry for dragging you into this mess, first Las Vegas and now Rome." She pushed back a strand of hair. "I'm sure you have more important things to do than chaperone me in my search for Rebecca. It was a mistake involving you in this mess."

"Hold on, Dallas. I am involved in this mess. Don't forget the money Rebecca stole came from my family." He pointed a finger at her chest. "We're in this fifty-fifty. I told you before, you didn't drag me along. It was my choice to accompany you."

She threw up her hands. "Okay, all right, I was feeling guilty dragging you all over the place. I really am sorry, it won't happen again." She started down the narrow street.

Logan grabbed her arm, forcing her to stop.

"Dallas, the theft isn't the only reason I'm in Rome."

"Really?"

"I came because of you and your, uh, dedication to this mess. I'm here of my own accord."

"Thank you."

He enveloped Dallas for a quick hug. "I like you. You're fun to be around."

"Wonderful." Her heart skipped. *He liked her.*

"Let's check out the Pantheon. Rebecca might be touring there this very minute." He kissed her forehead and led her down the street.

They passed another piazza with a fountain holding a fair maiden spilling water from an urn. One frustrating thing about Roman streets was that they were short and changed names at an intersection or piazza. They'd be walking in circles if not for the map and Logan's memory. Dallas would never again complain about Houston streets.

They came upon the Pantheon from its left side. The piazza in front was filled with people and the cafes along its sides were busy as well. Just like Las Vegas, always busy. They meandered around the edge of the square then faced the monument.

The façade of the structure included eight tall and what she assumed were granite Corinthian columns. Dallas pulled out her tour guide for details. Yep, they were granite and supported a rather large pediment which appeared too heavy for the columns. Apparently, the builders ran out of stone so the columns didn't end up as tall as originally planned.

"Let's go inside." She touched Logan's arm.

This was her first experience roving around a building nearly nineteen hundred years old. They passed under the portico, columns on either side. The bronze doors were huge and were once plated in gold. They journeyed into the interior of the dome.

Dallas' breath hiccupped as pure beauty filled her eyes. At this rate, she'd be crying buckets by the Sistine Chapel. The lower interior wall was richly decorated in colored marble while the upper part was unadorned concrete. Extraordinary.

She moved with Logan to the left and soon came upon the tomb of Raphael, the well-known artist of the fifteenth century. Above the sarcophagus was a statue called Madonna of the Rock. The female figure held a small child and rested a foot on a boulder.

Rome was a mecca for art lovers. Threading around tourists, they came to the center of the monument, directly under the open oculus, or Great Eye.

"What happens when it rains?" she asked.

Logan pointed to the floor. "See the holes? They built a drainage system."

"Very cool," Dallas said, studying the floor. She raised up. "I don't see Rebecca. Should we walk to the next monument on the list?"

"I'm pooped. How about a rest and then something to eat?" Logan said.

"Okay. I'll plan our schedule for tomorrow."

"Don't forget, we're waiting on the FBI to officially locate Rebecca."

"Whatever you say."

$ $ $

After a five-minute walk back to the hotel, Dallas and Logan stretched out on the bed and promptly fell asleep. A few hours later, Logan's voice poked at Dallas' subconscious and started the wheels to turn. She rolled over toward his voice.

"That'll work. Thanks." Logan clicked off his cell phone.

"What will work?" she said.

"You're awake. I made dinner reservations."

"Great, where?"

"I thought we'd check out Rome's night life. Never know who you might run across. We have reservations at eight. You'd better get ready."

She checked her watch then jumped out of bed, just enough time to shower and dress. She made herself proud. In forty-five minutes, she was dressed in an aqua baby doll top, a black denim skirt, and gold sandals.

"I'm ready. Are we walking or taking a taxi?"

Logan rose from the chair. "Taxi. One should be waiting for us."

Within ten minutes, they arrived at an ambiance-loaded restaurant, Ristorante la Carbanara, near Camp dè Fiori in the heart of Rome. They elected to sit on the patio. It was lit with fairy lights and bordered the street, providing an excellent view of the strolling foot traffic.

The food and wine were excellent along with the conversation. Dallas blabbed to Logan about her marriage. Normally, she would never mention it to a man, but he asked.

"I got married soon out of high school. I was attending the community college but the fun life kept getting in the way. I met Jonathon at a club. He was older than me and very mature or so I thought. He had money to throw around, thanks to his father's string of auto dealerships. I was impressed by the family business and he was impressed by the cup size of my bra. Truly, a match made in heaven."

Logan nodded in understanding—sympathy, or horror?

"Why did you divorce?"

"That's an easy answer. Once his father retired, Jonathon became the general manager. I went to his office one evening with a surprise picnic dinner and the surprise was on me."

"How so?"

"I found him in his office all right. He was showing his parts to the Parts Department receptionist. I called him a not-so-nice name, slammed the door behind me, and hired an attorney the next day."

"Ouch."

"Actually, it was the best for both of us. We didn't marry for the right reasons. The twins were the one right thing we did. He made most of the school events and dance recitals."

"Sounds like a stand-up guy."

Dallas smiled at that. "He always knew just the right birthday and Christmas gifts because his girlfriends were so close in age to the twins."

Logan chuckled. "At least he had talents."

"I make fun of him but he has been a good father."

"And you're a good mother to be honest about that. Ever get close to marrying again?"

She looked at him with wide eyes. "Are you kidding? I told you before I'm a bad picker. The 'till death do us part' gene bypassed me. I don't have what it takes "

"Have you considered he was simply the wrong man for you?"

"Maybe, but I won't take the chance of going through another breakup." She drained her wine glass.

"I'm sorry you had to go through all of that. There aren't any winners with divorce."

Now that was an intriguing comment. "I thought you'd never been married."

"I haven't. Billy went through one five years ago. It was really ugly. He hardly sees his little girl," Logan said. "It changed him. But he's remarried now and happy with his wife and step-kids. How about dessert?"

She begged off more food. "Why don't we walk back to the hotel and get a coffee along the way?"

They paused on the sidewalk, deciding which direction to walk. After a short discussion with the restaurant hostess, they had directions to the Pantheon. They turned right on the busy street, following her suggestion.

Couples strolled arm in arm while shoppers laden with bags weaved through the crowd. After a couple of blocks, they turned onto Via del Corso. Street lights were abundant so it was a pleasant walk even with the heavy pedestrian traffic.

"Rome is busier than Houston at night," Dallas said as their pace slowed. She was acutely aware of the bodies moving around her—much worse that the Vegas Strip.

"Houston doesn't have all this foot traffic," Logan replied. "Being outside at night is a nice change. I like to walk."

"Me, too, the view of Rome is better on the street than in a taxi."

The crowd on the sidewalk became even more constricting. Dallas attempted to clutch Logan's arm as she sensed someone right behind her, too close. Then she heard someone whisper in her ear. The next moment she was hugging the sidewalk with Logan shouting at her. Someone had pushed her from behind, causing her to fall. Damn it to hell.

"Dallas, are you okay? What happened?"

She placed her hands over her ears. With eyes closed, she whispered, "Please stop yelling at me. I can hear you."

"Sorry, do you think anything is broken?"

"No, no." Her eyes opened straight into Logan's concerned face. The focus was a little off. "Help me up, please." She raised an arm to him. "I want to go back to the hotel."

Logan's eyes focused on Dallas as he placed his arms under her armpits and pulled her to her feet. She swayed for a second then found her footing.

"Thanks." She moved a step, discovered a pain or two she hadn't felt sixty seconds earlier. "Hmm . . ."

"Can you walk or should I get a taxi?"

She didn't like the idea of bending her body to enter a car and then unbend it to get out.

"I can walk. It's only two or three more blocks. Just hold my arm, okay?"

Now she knew what it would be like to walk down the street as an eighty-year-old. Thank heavens, Logan was with her. She couldn't have made it back without him. His presence at her side was becoming a habit.

SEVENTEEN

Tuesday, 12:25 a.m.

"IS THE WATER TOO HOT?" Logan turned off the old-fashioned faucet handles. The deep tub could float a small whale, or, in this instance, Dallas' sore and bruised body. Logan had dumped in the entire bottle of complementary bubble bath so suds nearly shampooed her hair.

She blew a clump away from her nose. "It's fine, really." She needed him to get out the bathroom so she could sink into the water in peace.

"I'm going to order room service. What would you prefer to help you relax? Coffee, wine, my scotch, or Kahlua?"

Scotch sounded terrible. Alcohol was the only legal drug they could obtain just then since she refused to see a doctor. She ordered Kahlua and vodka.

"I'll call it in and you take it easy." Logan half shut the door to the bathroom, offering her the opportunity to moan when she moved her legs and back. Her knees were scrapped a bit, along with her right forearm. She must have first fallen to her knees then rolled on her right side. Her body felt every contact with the concrete sidewalk on Via del Corso. The balmy water was soothing.

Semi-dozing in the warm room, she heard a knock, a murmur of voices, then silence. She soon sensed Logan and a draft of cold air.

"Dallas, the water has cooled, time to get out and put on your pajamas."

He held a huge cream-colored towel in front of his body,

hiding his face. "Do you need help to get out of the tub?"

"I'm fine." She could do this. Her muscles were warm enough that it wasn't too uncomfortable straightening up and gingerly stepping out of the tub into the fuzzy towel. He wrapped it around her.

"I'll let you finish," he said. "Call if you need me."

Dallas managed to smooth cream over her face and hands after pulling on a pair of old-lady pajamas. Ruthie was her supplier for birthdays and Christmas. The current ones weren't too bad—pink and white stripes plastered with bright-colored martini glasses and red buttons up the front.

She hobbled with pride out of the bathroom. Logan rushed over to her.

"Let me help you get settled in bed."

Dear, sweet Logan held her arm as she maneuvered onto the bed with as much grace as she could muster under the circumstances.

"There now, take it easy. I'll get you that drink."

He moved to the desk and returned with a glass in one hand and a box in the other.

"What's that?" she said, pointing to the box.

"First aid kit." He sat on the edge of the bed, opened the box. "I need to take a look at your legs."

He pulled out a tube of ointment, rolled up the pajamas, and gently rubbed it over the bruised skin of her knees. She sipped her drink.

"Where else?"

She showed him her right arm and continued to drink. He tended to her injured skin, pulled up the covers, freshened her drink, and settled beside her on the bed.

"Are you comfortable?" he asked, pulling the covers over his pajama covered legs.

"I'm okay. I'll be stiff in the morning though."

"I'm so sorry this happened to you." Logan squeezed her hand lying on the blanket. "What actually occurred on the street? One minute you were next to me and then you were flat on your face."

Dallas wouldn't classify herself as one of those women who cried at the slightest provocation. Her pride usually kept her in check. Right then though, she surprised herself as tears rolled down her cheeks. She sipped the drink then brushed her cheeks with the back of a hand.

"Dallas?"

"It just happened. It was weird. For at least half a block I sensed someone real close behind me. I figured my radar was on because the street was so busy." She chewed on her lower lip. "Something brushed the left side of my neck and then the guy hit my back, and I slammed to the sidewalk." She raised her shoulder, winced. Damn, it hurt.

Logan moved closer to her. "Why didn't you tell me sooner about this?"

"You never asked." Her head wobbled to the side. "I think I'm tired."

He slid an arm around her waist and pulled her toward his big strong chest. "Poor baby, I'm sorry you're hurt. Don't worry about a thing." He kissed the top of her head.

Logan's arm around her felt good. She snuggled into the strength of him. This was a secure setting and she didn't have one concern at that moment. For once, being at peace was just right. She settled her head against Logan's shoulder, and closed her eyes.

His hand smoothed her hair.

It felt good having someone to lean on. The last ten years had taught Dallas that self-reliance was the key to survival and a crisis-free life. Leaning on a man was not in her vocabulary, until now.

Her eyes flashed open. Her brain skidded into a wall. What? Lean on a man? No freaking way.

She pulled away from Logan or attempted to. He imprisoned her with a very strong arm.

"Don't even think of trying to move away from me."

"Sorry, a little uncomfortable." Most of her was one dull

ache. Or at least that's what her soggy brain conveyed. The alcohol had done its magic. Her concern about leaning on him was a physical thing, not a real-life kind of thing.

Logan's hand stoked her hair and he gently turned her face to his. His nose was two inches from hers as his gaze searched her face for—acceptance, approval, a go-ahead sign?

He apparently liked what he saw. Booze did the trick for her.

Logan's lips lowered and easily found Dallas'. His hand brushed hair off her face as his lips moved over it with small kisses. She floated on a cloud of deep sensations spiraling around her middle while her brain enjoyed an out of body experience. She snuggled deeper into his strength. His hand stroked under her pajama top, learning the curve of her breast.

"Hmm, nice, so long since a man has . . ."

$ $ $

A Tuesday morning in Rome, one word—incredible. Then Dallas rolled over and last night's episode screamed for attention as the entire right side of her body throbbed. She relived her stumble to the sidewalk. She squeezed her eyes shut, forcing the memory the hand on her back from her mind.

She tugged the blanket but it was stuck. She raised her head and saw the problem. She was still in the same bed as Logan, in the same hotel room, in Rome.

How could she forget?

Her brain was on the fritz, the lack of Houston humidity was taking its toll. Brain cells were literally drying up. She breathed deeply and rolled slowly to the other side. Ouch, her back was sore and her head hurt. The jerk who hit her must be laughing his ass off right then. Dammit.

Her eyes opened and she *really* noticed Logan. He lay on his back, hair mussed, in need of a shave, one arm behind his head, the other flat handed on his chest. Ah, yes, that chest—muscular, tanned, and a good dose of hair disappearing beneath the sheet at his waist. It had been a long time since she'd been so close to a man's chest, or any other part for that matter. Her stomach rolled like a drunken sailboat on a calm sea.

"Good morning, Dallas."

Her gaze moved from his chest to his face. His eyes were bright and eager and spoke of his hopes, whatever they might be. She couldn't think because her head hurt.

"Morning. Do you mind if we call down for coffee and aspirin?" She didn't have a prayer of carrying on a decent conversation without caffeine in her system.

Logan bounded out of bed like a colt taking a first jump. "Your wish is my command." He called room service then leaned over the bed and kissed Dallas on the cheek. "You rest while I take a shower."

She followed orders and dozed off. The next she knew, Logan was two inches from her face, whispering her name.

She placed a hand on his chest and pushed. "Geez, I'm awake. You don't have to keep repeating my name."

He straightened up with dignity. "For your information, I don't repeat. Breakfast is here. That's why I woke you."

"Good, and thanks."

"No problem." He sat at the small table in the corner and poured coffee.

"I'll be back in a minute." She rolled slowly to the side of the bed, swung her feet to the floor, and sat up. The old body was sore but not as bad as she expected. Good. She wouldn't be forced to waste any time in searching for Rebecca.

She was even more determined to find the psychopath bitch. Her instincts about Rebecca had been right from the very beginning. What Dallas didn't know for certain was why Rebecca had stolen the twenty-five mil in the first place. Hopefully, JW would turn over some nugget for the motive, or maybe it was revenge against the Rice family.

Dallas stood, held onto the wall. Her legs and back were stiff, and her arm was sore. Other than that, and a hangover, life was good. She could deal with a few aches and pains. Finding Rebecca was much more important. She hobbled to the bathroom, determined to get on with the work at hand, sore body or not. Ten minutes later she joined Logan.

"Great coffee." She nibbled a croissant after swallowing four aspirin. "What's the plan for today? Should we go to the embassy again?"

Logan spread jam on a roll. "Actually, I have an appointment this morning."

"What time should we leave?"

"Dallas, I'm going by myself. You stay here and take it easy."

"I don't need to rest. I'm fine."

"Of course, you are." He looked at her, half-smiled. "Regardless, my appointment doesn't include you."

She felt like she'd been slapped. She wasn't accustomed to being told "no" and she sure as hell didn't like it. Hmm, this wasn't like Logan. She watched him eat a bite of melon and drink coffee, too nonchalant. He was up to something. She could play that game, too.

"You're right. I'll stay here and rest. My head still hurts. When will you be back?" She already had a plan.

"After twelve o'clock." He rose and grabbed his cell phone from the desk. "We can continue with our search when I return."

"Sounds good." She rose clumsily and kissed him on the cheek before ushering him to the door. "I'll be ready when you return."

Damn straight she'd be ready, but first, she had work to do. She took a shower, spread ointment over the scrapes, gulped down more aspirin, and retrieved the Rome phonebook from a drawer in the nightstand. Last, she dug out the English-Italian dictionary from her purse.

Dallas poured another cup of coffee then sat in the middle of the bed with the phonebook and the dictionary. She looked up the Italian word for "hotel" . . . duh, it was "hotel." That was easy. The phonebook contained fourteen pages of hotel listings. She'd get through as many as she could before Logan returned. He wouldn't happy about her calling hotels in Rome asking for Rebecca. But it was quicker than visiting each one in person. And, too bad if he didn't like it—he wasn't her boss or her father or her whatever.

She opened the phonebook and set to work. Using the dictionary, she asked *Parla Inglese?* If they didn't speak English then *Sa dirmi se Rebecca Holland is a ospite?* Can you tell me if Rebecca Holland is a guest?

She began calling at the top of the list, then decided to contact every other listing. That way she'd cover the alphabet faster, ha-ha, like it would give her a better chance of hitting the right hotel. She left a message at each hotel with Logan's cell number just in case someone remembered a guest who might be Rebecca.

The coffee urn was empty before she hit the second page. It was slow going and after two hours, she was batting zero. Her efforts were frustrating, yet Dallas clearly understood her chance of locating a hotel with Rebecca as a registered guest was one in a million—the same as finding her at a monument or on a Roman street. She scooted off the bed, stretching her legs a bit before standing. She hobbled at first but the stiffness wore off the more she paced. As long as she kept moving, she'd be okay.

What would she do if she were in Rebecca's position? First, she would have gone to a location more secluded than Rome and certainly less cosmopolitan. But Rebecca *was* in Rome. Dallas could feel it in her gut and she had to locate her. There was no other choice. The memory of Nana in that hospital bed was an excellent reminder.

Perhaps Rebecca registered under another name, an alias, like her friend Nancy Sims' name or the name from the slot competition in Vegas. What was it? She thought back to the Paris Casino and slamming into the cocktail waitress. They talked to the security guy and Logan made that stupid comment about PMS. Dallas snapped her finger, Holly Roberts, that was the name.

She checked her watch, not yet eleven o'clock. She had a good hour and half before Logan returned. She retrieved both the phone and the phonebook off the bed and plopped them on the desk. Maybe the chair would help her back and lady luck would throw in a dose of good fortune.

EIGHTEEN

Rome, Tuesday Morning

A TAXI WAITED FOR LOGAN at the hotel's entrance. The ride to the U.S. Embassy gave him a few minutes to review the past few days. He smiled. Dallas was a whirlwind going ninety miles an hour and a hot one at that. He couldn't remember the last time he'd been so intrigued by a woman. A woman who was four years older, had grown children, and would soon add grandmother to her list of roles. The HCU theft did have a bright side, and that was meeting Dallas.

His initial distrust had evaporated slowly, like the morning fog over a Louisiana marshland dissipating with the first rays of warming sunshine. If she were the thief, she would never have shown him the Gregory James e-mail message. And when Billy had her checked out, nothing came up.

She had no idea of his interest in her. Sure, it was out of his normal comfort zone. He'd never, ever fallen, no not fallen, teetered on the edge of the romance cliff so quickly. He had to give it to Gram, though. She had told him more than once that when the right woman appeared on the landscape of his life, he'd know it immediately. Gram was right. That didn't make it any less discomforting. He rubbed his jaw, maybe the right woman had finally come along. Billy would be laughing his ass off if he knew. Roddy, too.

If Dallas knew, she'd be laughing as well. She had a blockade around her heart the size of the Great Wall of China. She had this silly idea that she was a disaster at relationships. Just because her ex-husband was a jerk didn't mean she was a bad picker of men.

Logan was certain she was fighting with herself.

He had seen desire in her eyes a couple of times before her brain took over. That kiss last night had been phenomenal and her body knocked it out of the park. He'd keep chipping away at her wall, even consider it a challenge. Logan had no problem with that.

The embassy was the same as yesterday, lines of people waiting to get inside for visas, U.S. Marines guarding the entrance. He showed his ID and went through the metal detector before entering the building. He was in Agent Brown's office in less than five minutes.

"Bob, long time, no see." Logan shook the agent's hand.

"Isn't that the truth? You're the last person I expected to see yesterday." Bob motioned for Logan to take a chair.

"Sorry for the surprise. Coming to Rome was a last-minute decision." Logan smiled lamely. "But how have you been? It's been what, ten years since we worked together in DC?"

"Life is great. Enjoy the job here and I'm engaged." Bob pointed to a picture on his desk. "Getting married this Christmas."

"You old dog," Logan said with a grin. "You're the last person I'd imagine tying the knot."

"We're not getting any younger. What about you? I assume Miss Wells isn't your girlfriend."

"I'm working on that."

"No kidding. She doesn't know you worked for the Bureau?"

"No, and I don't know how to tell her." Logan shrugged.

"I doubt she'll be happy you kept it from her."

"She'll be pissed as hell." Logan didn't even want to think about it. Dallas would be beyond furious. She had no idea he'd done a background check on her or that he had law enforcement experience. She was so damned cute when she talked about doing surveillance. He'd simply make her understand that she had been in charge of the search for Rebecca, not him, and that his interest in her was the real deal. Dammit, he'd make her understand. "What have you found?"

"I've spoken to both the police and FBI offices in Houston.

They're certain that Rebecca Holland is the thief."

"She's one bitch of a woman and clever." Logan grimaced.

"That's putting it nicely," Bob said. "Her apartment has been searched. Nothing from that yet."

"Any confirmation from the Swiss bank on the account name?"

"Not yet. You know how the Swiss are. They close up shop faster than a raided whorehouse."

Not only was Rebecca a nasty bitch, she was a smart bitch. "Did you get a positive ID on her arriving at the airport?"

"We checked the security cameras. There are a couple of people who might be her. We don't know if she's changed her appearance. But we're trying to track down the two women."

"What about hotels, taxis?"

"Yep, that's covered, too," Bob said. "We believe she's still in Rome."

"At least we're making progress."

"That we are. I trust you and Miss Wells will continue to enjoy the sights of Rome and let us do the searching," Bob said.

"Dallas is hell bent on finding Rebecca."

Bob stood, shook Logan's hand. "Well, old buddy, you're gonna have to keep her busy with something else."

NINETEEN

Tuesday, 12:40 p.m.

OOPS—DALLAS QUICKLY REPLACED the phone as she heard a key turn in the lock. Logan was back. She threw the phone book in the desk drawer and rose, composing a smile on her face.

"Hi, Logan, how was your meeting?"

After shutting the door, he surveyed the room. "It was fine, the usual. Did you rest?"

"You bet. I've been, uh, sitting around, taking it easy." That was mostly true, the sitting part.

He narrowed his eyes briefly, then smiled. "Good. How are you feeling?"

"A little sore, but good to go."

"You're sure?"

"I'm ready."

"Let's go then. We have a reservation." He opened the door.

"Where?" She gathered her purse, swallowed a wince, and walked in front of him. His answer to her question was a pat on the butt as she passed him. She wasn't sure the pat was appropriate but let it go. He was so damned earnest.

He intertwined his fingers with hers in the elevator. It felt good, as though she had an anchor.

They hailed a taxi outside the hotel and headed in the opposite direction of yesterday morning. Being a nosy girl, Dallas pulled out the tour map. Logan shook his head.

Was it a crime for a person to know where she was going?

Her best guess fixed their destination as the Coliseum. She wouldn't spoil Logan's surprise and kept her speculations to herself.

Out of the blue, she remembered she had missed a dinner with Jane and her new beau. She hadn't checked in on Liz or Nana either. As soon as she returned to the hotel she'd send each of them a news filled e-mail and tell them all about the visit to the Coliseum.

And, my heavens, she had a bunch to tell them.

She was right; the taxi stopped along the street in front of the monument. She nearly skipped as they walked to the ticket office.

"Did you know the Coliseum was completed in 80 A.D.?" Dallas asked as they waited in line.

"How do you know that?"

"From a movie . . . can't remember which one."

He chuckled and kissed her temple, then purchased their tickets.

An elevator whisked them from the ground floor to the upper level. This was the level holding the expensive seats back in the gladiator days. From the circular aisle surrounding the amphitheater, stairways led upward to less privileged rows of seats. Every surface was travertine stone. Half of the outer wall was gone—damaged in earthquakes and pillaging of the stone and bronze for other Roman buildings.

The actual floor was gone, revealing narrow troughs, now overgrown with grass and weeds. The passageways had housed animals and humans in a waiting area before they climbed up to the arena floor. Guess a gladiator would have been in a fix if he were claustrophobic.

They spent two hours trudging over every available walking surface, hoping to run into Rebecca. One clone sighting was the only excitement. They had no better luck touring the Forum.

Logan suggested they visit the Victor Emmanuel monument. It was up the boulevard and very popular with tourists. After a ten-minute walk, they stood on the sidewalk and stared at the site, built to honor Italy's first king.

"Holy cow, this is something else," Dallas said.

"No kidding. I've not been here before," Logan added.

Known as the "wedding cake" due to its ultra-white marble, this mammoth site housed Italy's Tomb of the Unknown Soldier with an eternal flame. Dallas declined to climb two hundred forty-two steps for a grand view of Rome. She sat on the base of a column facing the street while Logan wandered along a wide corridor toward the monument's interior.

She soaked in the sunshine and the ambiance of Rome for a few minutes. While studying the people around her, she noticed a woman standing near the street. Her stance seemed familiar. The woman stood next to a man. Dallas rose and made her way toward the busy street, moving around tourists while keeping the man and woman in view.

A white sedan arrived and the couple stepped toward it. Dallas tried to move faster but was blocked by a baby stroller and an irate mother.

"Rebecca, stop," she shouted.

The woman turned her head toward the monument as she entered the car. The door shut and the vehicle moved into traffic. Dallas ran, then limped, a few feet into the street as the car changed lanes and sped up.

"Damn, I'm sure that was Rebecca." She turned around to hunt for Logan. She found him coming down the stairs and explained her sighting of the HCU thief.

"Don't go after her alone again. She could be dangerous."

"She's not dangerous," Dallas said. "She's a black-hearted thief."

"Did you get the car's license plate number?" he said.

"I didn't even think of that. How stupid on my part."

"Most people don't think of it either." Logan pulled out his cell phone. "At least we think we know she's here and playing tourist. I'll let Agent Brown know about this."

After making the call, Logan mentioned stopping for an early dinner. He seemed to enjoy planning Dallas' social calendar. He was considerate too, as they walked slowly. The soreness in her arm and back continued to lessen, so as long as she kept moving. Although regular doses of aspirin helped the cause.

She soon spied the Pantheon and had a good idea of their location. Logan led her to a small "diner" in the corner of the piazza in front of the monument. A red door led to the restaurant. They settled at a table situated in an inner courtyard. Subdued lighting provided a canopy of intimacy.

Logan once again ordered Dallas' meal and it didn't bother her. If nothing else, they had food in common. That led her to an entirely new train of thought. Was it possible for her to truly have something in common with a man as fantastic as Logan? She couldn't imagine the two of them fitting each other. The fact they enjoyed the same food and wine was a coincidence, not a declaration of being soul mates.

He suggested dessert and Dallas declined. Since she wouldn't be able to run for a few days, she didn't need the extra calories. They enjoyed a leisurely stroll back to the hotel. Her legs were better for the exercise and her shoulder almost felt normal.

Logan suggested they stop at the hotel bar for a nightcap. She waved him off to the bar then went directly to a computer cubby to check her inbox. There were two messages, one from Roddy and one from Jane. Jane said she was sorry Dallas had missed the dinner with Jared but they'd plan another once Dallas returned home. Hmm, the beau's name was Jared—Jane and Jared, their names together had a nice sound.

Roddy's message wasn't nearly as pleasant.

He yelled at her for running off to Rome, thinking she was the HCU version of Wonder Woman and for dragging poor Logan into her half-assed shenanigans. She ignored that, Logan was a big boy.

He said they were certain Rebecca stole the $25 million; he'd provide the details later. There was no evidence linking her to Bill's murder. He didn't mention Scooter's death.

Dallas joined Logan at a small table in the bar with an excellent view of the lobby.

"Since we declined dessert and its calories, I'm feeling bold. How about a nice chardonnay?" Logan said with a lopsided grin.

She thought about that for a moment, glanced at her watch.

Eight o'clock. Oh, what the hell. She had nothing better to do and a glass would help her sleep.

"When in Rome, do as the Romans." She said, a warm glow filling her chest. "Chardonnay sounds perfect."

$ $ $

One hour and one bottle of wine later, Logan locked the door of their room. He stood perfectly still, his back against the door. Dallas sat on the edge of the bed, watching him.

A window had been opened by the maid and a breeze blew in sounds of the night—faint voices on the street below, an occasional car engine, music from the bar on the corner. Moonlight lit the carpet between them. He couldn't see her face but he could hear her breathing and smell her perfume. She rose from the bed, faced him.

They met in the middle. She placed a finger on his lips. "I'm not sure I'm ready for this."

Her touch had the sizzle of a lightning bolt. He took her finger and licked it, then released her hand. He stepped back, giving her space to escape from his reach. She remained still while he studied her face. He sensed a battle raging in her. After a moment, the confusion cleared from her eyes, she moved forward and leaned into him. Her tongue flickered across his closed lips.

She stepped closer, her breasts pressed against his chest, while her arms circled his neck. His head was spinning. His arms enveloped her slender body while her gentle kiss told him she was on board for his more than roommates plan. He couldn't hold back a second longer. His lips crushed against hers, his tongue darting into her mouth. She tasted like fresh rain, like roses, like the woman he loved.

He wanted more. He ached to run his hands over every inch of her body yet he imagined what Dallas might be thinking and sought to neutralize it. "Let's not analyze what's happening between us."

She moaned in reply. That was all the encouragement Logan

needed. He backed her slowly toward the bed, his arms on her shoulders, a grin splayed across his face. The only thought in his mind was getting Dallas naked as quickly as possible

After a couple of steps, she hesitated, pulled away from him. "Wait, let me catch my breath."

Logan's heart stopped and he couldn't think or breathe. Dallas sucked in air. Her eyes locked into his. He waited for her to say something, to do something, to tell him to go to hell.

After a beat, she took his hand in hers, her lips curved into a gentle smile. Logan's heart fired again, like an engine revving for the Grand Prix. Relief and anticipation swept through him.

"Come to bed with me," she whispered.

He pulled back. "Are you sure?"

She nodded and moved closer to the bed. "Here we are."

"Yes, here we are."

"Maybe we should talk for a minute," she said.

He brought her hand to his lips and kissed her fingers. He sensed her hesitation. "Let's not worry about anything but this moment. Right now, all I want to do is kiss you."

Logan picked her up in his arms then gently laid her on the bed, her head rested on the pillows. He settled beside her. He bent an arm and propped his head in his hand. His other hand brushed a strand of hair off her cheek then trailed along her jaw line to her neck.

- - -

Dallas held her breath as his hand moved to her blouse. She released a sigh when he began to unbutton it. Her mind was in turmoil. Is this what she wanted? Dare she subject Logan to her terrible history with relationships? A memory of Jonathon telling her she didn't know how to make love fluttered across her mind. Then she remembered this was Logan with her and snuffed out the thought.

The blouse was unbuttoned and his hand stilled. He looked into her eyes. She saw longing in his and her uneasiness shot straight to her heart. She had nothing to offer him. She was damaged goods. How in the world could this work? The words to tell him to stop never escaped her lips as his hand brushed her breast. Without warning, her anxiety crashed into her chest like a heart attack and she jerked from the pressure.

Logan's thumb rubbed over her cheek. "You okay?"

She nodded, not trusting her voice. She wanted to cry. Why was she so unsure of herself? Dallas' doubts evaporated with the touch of his lips on hers. The taste of him sent a blast of heat to her toes and mimicked her very first kiss. The power of it rushed through her and had her mind reeling. But right then she didn't want to think, only to feel—to feel his mouth on hers and his hands on her body.

She shivered.

He pulled back and tipped his forehead against hers. "Are you nervous?"

"A little." A whole lot nervous she thought. "We've never done this."

"With each other, but we're not amateurs," he said, his mouth twitching.

They looked at other each other, smiled like old friends meeting after a long absence. Soon their shirts were off then slacks, a skirt and shoes and his hands were all over her and hers all over him. Sensation followed sensation, hard muscles, soft flesh, remembering the curve of a hip and the sensual touch of a hand. Dallas' mouth explored the landscape of Logan, the hardness of his chest, the stubble of his beard, the dimples above his buttocks. She made a memory of every inch.

"Uh, Logan, don't want to spoil this but uh, do we have protection?"

"You're right." He jumped off the bed and rummaged in a suitcase. Within fifteen seconds, he had resumed his position.

Finally, their need became urgent and they came together, need matching need—their union so perfect that tears glittered in Dallas' eyes. Logan rested on top of her, his warmth caressing her body, his breathing heavy. She massaged his back with her palms, knowing this would be the last time she'd touch him. She would not assume they could mesh their very different lives together.

She squeezed her eyes shut.

Logan nuzzled her neck. "Thank you."

"For what?" she whispered in his ear.

"For trusting me." He brushed her cheek with his lips. "Why the tears?"

She opened her eyes, shook her head. She couldn't tell him the truth, that there was no tomorrow for them. "Mascara got in my eye."

He eyes narrowed for a moment then he chuckled, ran his hands along her hips and thighs. "Well, darlin', let's try this again."

And that's just what they did. Dallas once again shut down her brain and made another memory of Logan loving her and her loving him. In the far reaches of her soul, she knew the memory would have to last for rest of her life.

$ $ $

Wednesday morning dawned late. The remnants of an erotic dream floated on the horizon of Dallas' brain, delaying her normal early wake time. She blew hair off her face and opened her eyes a slit, the dream hadn't been a hallucination. It was real.

Logan lay on his back next to her. Memories of kisses filled her head—Logan, last night, mind blowing sex.

Holy shit.

She rolled to her good shoulder and hugged the edge of the mattress. She had participated in glorious, stupendous sex with Logan Rice without a care in the world. And, she couldn't use too much wine as an excuse, although it had created a nice buzz. What in the hell was wrong with her? Sleeping with Logan Rice could prove to be the dumbest move she'd ever made. Could she do anything else to make a bad situation worse? Apparently, she didn't know the depth of her talents in that department.

What a mess.

She sensed, then heard, then felt Logan stir beside her and didn't want to even consider what he must think of her. They were traveling together on business and then she had to screw up their relationship by having sex with him.

A hand patted her hip then gently slapped her butt. Uh-oh— he was in a good mood.

The mattress squeaked as Logan rolled toward her. His breath teased her ear before he kissed her neck.

"Good morning, sleepy head," he whispered. "You smell nice."

She smelled like sex and he damned well knew it. Fine, just fine, she could handle this situation. Granted, she didn't have much, hardly any experience with morning after sex conversation with a man who wasn't her husband. Since the divorce, there had been a guy or two, but they had left her townhouse after the deed was done. She felt like such a nerd, unsure of how to deal with Logan.

Her mouth found its voice. "Uh . . . thanks. Can we order coffee?"

She must have hit the after-sex-motor-button. Logan vaulted over her and out of the bed, landing on the floor. How could a forty-year-old adult do that?

He hurried to the phone and promptly called room service.

Whew . . . she needed coffee to negotiate any decent interaction with him.

He leaned over her, smiling.

"You relax. I'll be out of the shower in fifteen minutes." He trotted off to the bathroom and shut the door.

What was she supposed to do now?

Nothing.

Then, she understood.

Manifesting calmness, Dallas filled her lungs with the peace of the day. She could handle this. Sure, the situation was a bit out of her comfort zone, but she could deal with a happy man who enjoyed really good sex, with her. And, no question, it was good sex.

But . . . could she deal with herself?

TWENTY

Wednesday, 11:32 a.m.

AFTER THREE CUPS OF COFFEE and a croissant, Dallas clomped downstairs alongside Logan to check her e-mail. Nothing additional from Roddy but Liz was holding on, feeling like a whale.

With no word from Agent Brown, Logan and Dallas continued with their list of Roman tourist sites. They took a taxi to the Vatican and St. Peter's Basilica. They arrived on the side of Piazza San Pietro or St. Peter's Square. It was huge and flat.

Logan was in a fine mood. He nudged her shoulder and directed her onto the square.

"Come on," he said. "Let's look around."

"I suppose you've been here before."

"Yes, and I know the perfect spot for a kiss."

She rolled her eyes and followed him.

They walked to the center of the square, which was actually a circle. Columns bordered the sides. The colonnade was composed of two hundred eighty-four columns and eighty-eight pillars in a quadruple row, symbolizing the "gathering of Christianity." Dallas liked that. They walked to the center, marked by an Egyptian obelisk, and he kissed her. It was quick and sweet.

"That's something I've wanted to do for twenty years," he said. "Thank you for being here with me."

"You're welcome." She gave him a hug, then walked around the center of the square, tracing the outline of the obelisk. "Isn't there a special spot of some sort in the center?"

Logan moved to her side. "Yes, here it is. See this marble

stone? If you look at the columns from here, you'll see one row rather than four."

She squeezed against Logan on the stone. He was right; what an optical illusion. She hugged him again, then pulled back. "This is so cool. Can we go in the Basilica now?"

They observed everyone on the square as they made their way to the church—no Rebecca.

The entrance to St. Peter's Basilica, possibly the largest church in Christianity, was huge. The façade was over three hundred seventy-five feet wide and nearly half as high. One of the doors to the basilica was called "Door of the Dead." As they reached the center of the portico, Logan's phone rang. He answered and handed it to Dallas with surprise in his eyes. "It's for you."

What?

"Ms. Wells, this is Stephano from the hotel. I have a message from Hotel Alimandi Vaticano."

Did this mean what she thought it meant? "What is it, please?"

"The concierge called. They have a guest named Nancy Sims and she fits your description," Stephano said.

"Did he say anything else?"

"No, miss, that was all."

"Grazie very much."

She handed the phone back to Logan, performed a quick jig in front of the "Holy Door" at the Basilica's entrance.

She tugged on his hand. "We gotta go. I've found Rebecca."

$ $ $

They ran along the curve of the buildings facing the square then cut through the columns to a gate exiting the Vatican property. A taxi stand was conveniently placed on the corner.

They jumped in the backseat of the first taxi in line.

"We need to get to the Hotel Alimandi Vaticano." Dallas had no idea where the hotel was located, but the driver understood she meant quickly, *velocemente*. He gunned the accelerator and off they roared, for a block. Traffic blocked the street in front of the taxi.

"Oh, crap," Dallas shouted.

The driver again understood and veered off to the right, narrowly missing a Lexus and nearly clipping a Smart car. She gripped the edge of the car seat. Logan braced against the corner of the seat back, throwing her a "what the hell?" look, yet he didn't ask one question, which was comforting. They abruptly turned left at a wide boulevard.

The taxi made several more turns then after fifteen minutes swung into a small circular drive in front of the hotel. Dallas bounded out and rushed to the hotel's main entrance.

"Come on, Logan," she shouted over her shoulder. "It's show time."

She rushed straight to the registration desk. Logan skidded to her side after paying the taxi driver. She took a deep breath and counted to five.

"Good morning, I'm, uh, we're here to see Nancy Sims. Would you please call her room?"

The grey-haired woman behind the desk stared at Dallas before turning her attention to a computer screen. Her fingers raced over the keyboard. She squinted before turning around and running her fingers along the edge of wooden boxes with horizontal numbers. She stopped at a box with the number 327. A key filled the slot.

"Miss Sims, she is not here."

"Do you know where she went?" Dallas pushed back her hair. "How long ago did she leave?"

The woman pursed her lips, raised her arm, and pointed to what Dallas guessed was the concierge desk just past the entrance. They marched over and asked the same question.

"Miss Sims left a few minutes ago for lunch."

Out of the corner of her eye, Dallas noticed Logan palming a Euro bill from his pants pocket. He slid it across the counter. "Lunch, where?"

The bill disappeared under a travel brochure. "She has a reservation at Ristorante da Fortunato."

"Located where?" she asked.

"Go left at our driveway. Down a couple of blocks, turn right."

She pulled Logan's hand. "Let's go."

They exited through the front door and followed the drive to the left, turning at the sidewalk. They hurried along the street amid the noon hour crowd of local shoppers and gawking tourists. Within five minutes, they had covered two blocks and stopped to catch their breath.

She looked right, left, then at Logan. "You think the restaurant is to the right?"

"That's what the man said." Logan squeezed her shoulder. "Let's go find Rebecca."

They set off down another Roman street. Without a fountain, a basilica, or a monument to mark the spot, the streets were beginning to look the same. Dallas scanned the buildings looking for a restaurant sign titled Ristorante da Whatever. Logan's eyesight was better and pointed to a sign at the end of the block. They stopped under a green awning.

"Now what?" He put his hands on her shoulders. She didn't flinch at his touch, even though the right shoulder was still sore.

"Let's agree on how we're doing this," she said.

"How about we get a table like any other hungry couple?"

"Good idea." She suspected Logan considered this latest goose chase for Rebecca to be silly. "I'm hungry anyway. I can watch for Rebecca without being conspicuous."

Logan walked behind her to the reception stand and mumbled. "You, bring attention to yourself. Never."

"Be cool, we don't want her to notice us." A waiter seated them at a corner table with a perfect view of the dining area.

Logan leaned over the table. "By the way, she probably doesn't know I'm with you."

"Right." Dallas hadn't considered that. "Block me from view if I give you the high sign."

"The high sign?"

"Just follow my lead. You'll know if I spot her."

"How?"

"Stop being so hard-headed, you'll figure it out." She opened the menu. Pasta, again?

They ordered and waited for water; no wine today. Dallas closed her eyes for a moment and took a deep breath, praying for strength to end this chase for Rebecca.

"What's your plan?" Logan asked. "Will you confront her or hang back?"

"Guess I, er we, should have a plan." Dallas groaned in frustration. "I've been so intent on finding her that I haven't given any thought to what I'll do once we're face to face."

She sipped the water just poured. "Guess it's just you and me for now."

"Not sure that's a good idea."

There's no one else to help. This was it, now or never, the whole enchilada. "Face it. We're on our own. Roddy's not here and the official Italian help hasn't appeared." She pointed her index finger at his chest then at her own. "You and me . . .we need to bring down Rebecca."

"Bring her down?"

"Good grief, Logan, get with the program. We need to confront and uh . . ." What should Dallas do once she glared at Rebecca's headed-for-prison face? She considered her options, snapped her fingers. "We make a citizen's arrest."

He sighed and rolled his eyes.

"You have a better idea?"

"I've a hunch a citizen's arrest isn't all that common in Italy. Let's go with Plan B." He had the nerve to grin at her.

The restaurant's tables were filling up, a crowd milled around the entrance. She did her best to concentrate on Logan while inspecting the face of every female at a table or waiting for one. Most likely Rebecca had changed both her hair color and style and her mode of dress. That's what Dallas would do.

Did she have a Plan B? No. Logan's face came back in focus.

"You tell me, what's our plan if we spot Rebecca?"

His eyes avoided Dallas. Fine. Whatever. He didn't have a real plan either. This wasn't a crisis . . . yet.

"Dallas. . ."

"Uh-huh?" She turned an ear toward Logan while canvassing the restaurant a second time. She studied each female, hoping to catch even a slight resemblance to Rebecca—pointed chin or high cheekbones or full lips.

"Dallas, I need to tell you something—"

"Hold it." She held a hand over the table, palm down. Bingo. "I've spotted Rebecca." Dallas squinted to get a better view of her, to verify her initial reaction was correct. Yep, the woman was the black-hearted, southern belle Rebecca. She stood at the reception desk as cool as a vanilla gelato. Her hair was darker and the cut shorter—her cheekbones gave her away and those pink glossed lips.

"Be cool and don't turn around. She's standing by the hostess desk, light brown hair, yellow sun dress. She's talking to a young guy." Dallas squinted again. "He's cute."

Logan dropped a napkin, bent to the side of the table. "You're right, that's her." After a moment of silence, he said, "Where is she now?"

"Still up front. We never did decide on Plan B."

Logan pulled out his cell. "Guess we'll have to wing it."

"Whatever. I think she saw me." Dallas scrambled up from the table and rushed toward the entrance.

$ $ $

Dallas was out of her comfort zone. Logan seemed to be in his.

They followed Rebecca and friend out of the restaurant and watched the pair climb into a white Mercedes. Logan immediately found a taxi going the opposite direction. It performed a U-turn in the middle of the street and pounded to a stop at the curb where they waited. They jumped in the backseat and Logan spoke Italian to the driver.

The Mercedes was three cars ahead when it turned left. The taxi quickly made the same turn, Rebecca's car was still in sight but increasing the distance from the taxi. It had picked up speed. Rebecca must have realized she was being followed.

"Logan, should we call the police to set up a road block or something?"

He looked at her like she had bubble gum for brains. "Let's see how this plays out, then I can make a call."

What should they do once the Mercedes stopped and Dallas confronted Rebecca? She had imagined this scene with Roddy at her side, HPD badge in one hand and pistol in the other. He'd take care of the bad stuff. Dallas would yell at Rebecca and probably slap her.

She'd yell at her because Rebecca was just plain stupid and a terrible example of a woman who had so much—looks, smarts, a good job, and people around her who thought she was wonderful. Why was Rebecca so damned stupid? Stupidity was a crime of the highest order in Dallas' world.

The taxi stayed behind the Mercedes for another ten minutes as it made random turns.

All of a sudden, the Mercedes slowed down, pulled along the curb. The taxi did the same, half a block back.

"What do you think she's doing?" Dallas asked, her heart thudding like she'd run the Boston marathon.

"Playing with us," Logan said, cool as a cucumber.

She looked at him. He concentrated on the Mercedes.

"A door is opening," he said.

The back door of the Mercedes along the sidewalk had opened. They watched for a few seconds. Nothing else happened.

"This is silly. I'll go talk to her." She placed her hand on the door handle. "It can't hurt anything."

"Dallas, no. Do not open that door." He caught her arm. "I'll talk to her."

She looked him in the eye, recognized concern.

"And say what? She obviously wants to talk with me." She quickly slid her arm out of his grip and pushed open the taxi's door. "Don't worry, I'll be fine." Her brain ignored that fact that Rebecca might have killed Bill and/or Scooter.

Dallas stood by the car, noticed Rebecca waving at her by the Mercedes. Dallas waved back, then heard a very loud car backfire and noticed Logan rushing around the back of the taxi.

Her left arm developed a spasm and people dropped to the sidewalk in front of her. She noticed the Mercedes moved back into the traffic of the narrow street—strange, it moved in slow motion. Dallas collapsed to the sidewalk, blood seeping through her blouse. She saw Logan high above her before darkness slithered like a fog over his face.

TWENTY-ONE

Thursday, 11:33 a.m.

TWENTY-FOUR HOURS HAD PASSED since Dallas collapsed on the sidewalk in front of Logan. Her arm hurt like hell until the pain meds had kicked in. A huge bouquet of yellow roses sat on the table next to her bed. The room wasn't all that different from a hospital room in Houston. Other than the fact, she was stationed in a bed with a gunshot through the fleshy part of her upper left arm, and she didn't speak the language. A sling held her arm immobile.

Logan had just left to gather their belongings from the hotel. She'd be leaving Rome not as a conqueror, but as a semi-cripple. She was the HCU point person who chased the bad guy from Houston to Las Vegas to Rome—did she bring in the bad guy? No, hell no. Rebecca got away from them just as easily as she stole the money in the first place.

Dallas adjusted the sling, her arm felt tired to the bone. She wanted to go home. Home to Sugar Land and her townhouse and her family and escape the fact her liaison with Logan was kaput. What did they have in common other than enjoying the same food and walking upright? Nothing. He was class and money, and well, she was basic middle class.

She was done. Done investigating Rebecca. The police were the targets for bullets, not Dallas, the civilian. She was tired of everything and longed to get back to her normal life. Logan had promised, soon. After a few minutes of feeling sorry for herself, her eyes closed and she dozed off.

$ $ $

"Are you comfortable?" Logan searched Dallas' face, attuned to any sign of pain or discomfort she might exhibit. Sweet baby, he was being such a good nurse.

"I'm fine. I just slept five hours, my arm is immobile, and the pain meds help."

"You've only taken three pain pills in the last twenty-four hours."

"I know. But I'm not big on pills and my arm feels fine." She tried to smile, although it wasn't one of her best. She still felt out of sorts, more mentally than physically. "The doctor in Rome was great. She said I'll be back to normal in a few days."

Logan kissed her cheek, moved to the seat across from her. The Bridge Foundation jet had arrived in Rome a few hours ago and was now zooming across the Atlantic to Houston.

"Gunshots can be tough but the arm wound you have is one of the easier ones to recover from," he said.

"You're like an encyclopedia. How do you know that? Have you ever been shot?"

His face went blank, turned pink, then back to normal, all in ten seconds. His eyes moved away from her and told the story of his discomfort at her question. She found his reaction strange. He remained silent.

"Again, have you ever been shot?" She leaned over across the aisle and shook his knee. "You can tell Auntie Dallas anything."

His mouth opened, closed, opened again. "Yes, I've been shot before."

Now that was interesting. "Really? When and why? Other than myself, you're the only person I know who's been shot. Coincidence, huh?"

"I was shot on the job several years ago."

"You're kidding. Did the Foundation have a break-in?"

Logan ran both hands through his hair. "I wasn't working for the foundation then."

She plumped the pillow behind her head. "Who were you

working for?"

Logan rose, paced the aisle a couple of times. Something was up. Dallas' stomach got that queasy feeling, signaling shit ahead.

"What?" she said, her voice softened with frustration. "Just tell me."

Logan stopped his pacing, knelt in front of her, his fingers moving over her free hand. His eyes bored into hers. "I was shot twelve years ago when I was a Special Agent for the Federal Bureau of Investigation."

She absorbed that for a split second, threw off his hand, pushed at his chest.

"FBI? You worked for the FBI and you didn't tell me?" She rose, a bit unbalanced, and pushed past him toward the bulkhead.

"Now, Dallas, I wanted to tell—"

"Tell me, my ass. You had plenty of opportunity to tell me you were a professional." She slapped her forehead with her palm. "No wonder you always knew exactly what to do."

"It's no big deal. My past didn't have any impact on your investigation."

"My investigation! Did you go with me to Las Vegas and Rome as my babysitter? Did Roddy give you the idea?" Her face was hot and her arm throbbed. Had Logan played with her to keep her out of trouble? Well, that backfired the minute she was shot. "And I trusted you," she muttered, adding another notch to her lousy-man-picker belt.

"I wasn't your babysitter," Logan said, his eyes snapping with frustration. "That's ridiculous."

"Whatever. You made a fool out of me." Her fist pounded the top of a leather seat. "I talked to you about surveillance." Embarrassment washed over Dallas. She stopped pacing directly in front of Logan, in the middle of the aisle of the Bridge Foundation jet, somewhere over the Atlantic, and poked a finger at his chest. "Did you enjoy humiliating me? Was it fun?"

TWENTY-TWO

Saturday, 1:05 p.m.

DALLAS HAD BEEN HOME FOR just over a day. It was good to be nestled in her humble townhouse, minus the nasty remark on her bathroom mirror. Nana and Jane had taken care of that little nastiness. And that reminded her of Logan. Nope, she wasn't going there. Nope, she wasn't thinking about him. He was history as far as she was concerned. He was a reminder of her arrogance, her stupidity, and her incredibly bad judgment in letting a man get to her. That was not happening again, ever, for the rest of her life. She was done with men, except for the newborn kind, in case Liz has a boy.

The doorbell rang. Rather than her family, a delivery person presented Dallas with a huge bouquet of yellow roses, probably two dozen. She assumed it was from HCU. The card read: "Thinking of you, love, Logan." Her initial reaction was to throw the vase in the garbage can. However, being a practical woman, she put them on the table by her chair. Only nerds throw away roses in anger. She had trashed her nerd persona on a sidewalk in Rome. Today was a new day.

The door bell sounded again, immediately followed by the door opening. She rushed to embrace Nana, the twins, and Ruthie—all her favorite people, in her house, at the same time.

"Mom," Jane said after a hug.

"Mom," Liz said after a hug.

"My sweet baby," Nana said with a double hug.

"What the hell happened to you?" She could always count on Ruthie to be the sane one.

They all squirted tears, even Ruthie. Dallas was blissfully happy. It was fantastic to see them all at one time, her girls. Her heart opened and felt just right.

"You need to sit down." Nana ushered her to the chair. "Ruthie, you keep Dallas company while we get lunch organized." Nana motioned with her head for the twins to follow.

Once they moved to the kitchen, Ruthie got down to business.

"Okay, tell me everything." She settled on the sofa across from Dallas. "What happened in Las Vegas and in Rome? What's the deal with this Logan Rice person?"

That's why Dallas loved Ruthie, no kibitzing, no flowery build up. Just get to the point, already. She wanted to hear the real deal, not a sanitized version.

"I don't know where to start."

"How about at the beginning? I haven't talked to you since you left for Las Vegas. That was a week ago last Thursday." She raised her eyebrows for emphasis, noticed the roses. "Pretty. From HCU?"

"No." Dallas sighed. "They're from Logan."

"Oh."

"I'll give you the summary version of the story." Dallas adjusted the sling on her left arm to a more comfortable position and took a calming breath. "The first disaster in Las Vegas was Scooter running away from me. The first good thing was hiring a private investigator. Naturally, Mr. Ex-FBI Agent Logan arranged that."

"Logan worked for the FBI?" Ruthie's mouth dropped. "That gorgeous man is a Fed?"

"How do you know he's gorgeous?"

"I looked him up on the internet. He's been in the society pages of the *Houston Chronicle*. Very nice package to travel with, if you ask me."

"Looks aren't everything. Anyway, the next bad thing was learning Scooter had been killed and Rebecca had flown off to Rome. I followed her with Logan tagging along."

"Not such a bad place to search for a crook." Ruthie said.

"What happened there?"

"Logan could only find a hotel room with one bed—"

"One bed? How'd you handle that?"

"With dignity and keeping my distance. Although now I wonder if he booked one room on purpose. Anyway, we went to the U.S. Embassy rather than the Italian police. What I didn't know was that Logan and the FBI agent there were old buddies." Dallas rubbed her eyes. "Just thinking about it pisses me off."

"Are you tired? We can talk about this later."

"I'm fine. Where was I? Oh yeah, I told Agent Brown the story about our search for Rebecca and gave him Roddy's contact information. We decided to search for her while he checked out our story."

"Smart. But what about the one bed in the hotel room?" Ruthie was persistent.

"Not now."

"You slept with him, didn't you?"

Dallas ignored the question and continued with her story. "Eventually, I got a tip about Rebecca's location. We ended up at the same restaurant. She ran, we followed, her car stopped, she got out, I got out, she waved, I waved." She blew out a breath. "I got shot and she escaped. Now you know the whole story."

"Incredible." She looked pensive for a moment. "I still want to hear all about you sleeping with Logan."

Lunch saved Dallas from answering. Nana came back to the living room carrying a tray, followed by Liz and Jane with iced tea and a salad bowl.

"Lunch is served, girls. Let's celebrate Dallas being home safe and sound."

The food was wonderful—a simple avocado/fruit salad, sourdough bread, and oatmeal cookies. The girl talk was light and fun. No questions about the HCU theft or Logan Rice.

"Dallas, did you notice Ruthie's engagement ring?" Nana said.

"I totally forgot about your engagement. I'm so sorry." She set aside her plate and went over to Ruthie, gave her a one-armed hug. "Let me see that ring."

Ruthie held out her left hand, wiggled the finger holding a stunning sparkler. She held Ruthie's hand, studied the ring from different angles. "It's a knock-out." She hugged her again. "Have you set a date?"

"We're thinking about Las Vegas the end of August. I've done some research and The Bellagio is at the top of my list. Did you go there on your trip?"

"It's a perfect location for your wedding," Dallas said. "What style of dress are you considering?"

Life was funny at times. Dallas had a terrible track record with men and now she found herself involved in planning not just one, but two weddings. Who'd think that either Nana or Ruthie would even want her opinion about a wedding? It's not that she was against marriage, she wasn't. But like she told Logan, she was a lousy picker and she certainly wouldn't want to subject herself or her family to another divorce.

They discussed dresses and wedding receptions for a while then Dallas yawned and the group began to pack up. Just as everyone walked out the front door, Roddy appeared on the porch. She introduced him to everyone and ushered him inside.

"How ya doing?" He settled on the sofa, crossed his legs, looking very comfortable in her living room. "Gotta admit, you getting shot isn't on the point person job description," he quipped with a sloppy grin. "You're a real trooper."

"That's me, going that extra mile to get the job done." The real problem was her overblown sense of responsibility. It was no more her fault than Santa Claus' that Rebecca had stolen $25 million from the University. Dallas had been nuts chasing after her. "How have you been? Your mother out of the hospital?"

"I'm fine, my mother's fine, but I'm not the one who got shot. How are you?"

"I'm okay. Ready to get back to work."

"I talked to Agent Brown. He gave me the run down on the events in Rome. It was a stupid move on your part to exit the taxi."

"In retrospect, you're right. But how was I to know she had a gun?"

"We're not sure she was the shooter. Did you see a gun in her hand?"

Dallas thought back to that day and how she exited the taxi. She remembered how Rebecca smiled and waved. Perhaps there had been regret in that smile. She'd never know.

"I don't recall her holding a gun."

"The FBI thinks the shooter was her traveling companion." Roddy pulled out his notebook, flipped pages. "One Curtis Otis Adams, a small-time thief here in Houston."

"Why would Rebecca get involved with someone like that?" Another ridiculous question as she had no idea why Rebecca did anything. She grinned. "Sorry, dumb question. I guess if you're going to steal millions of dollars, hooking up with another thief isn't that much of a stretch."

"Right you are."

"Do you suppose he was involved in Bill's death?"

"Don't have any evidence that points to him. It's another story with Rebecca. We found her DNA at the scene and a neighbor witnessed Rebecca leaving Bill's house around the time of death."

"I'm not surprised to hear that. What about Scooter? Do you really think his death was an overdose?" Dallas shivered at the thought of Scooter sticking a heroin-filled needle in his arm.

"The Vegas police did an autopsy and ruled his death a homicide. He had no trace of needle tracks consistent with a habitual drug user."

"That's something positive then." She rubbed her arm under the sling, it was itchy and hardly hurt, which was amazing, considering it had only been four days since the shooting. She'd be fit as a fiddle for work on Monday morning, ignoring the doctor's advice to stay home for a week. "Do you know anything about Scooter's funeral?"

"I believe it was this morning in Austin," Roddy answered in a quiet voice. "I'm sorry about your boss."

"Me, too, but I still don't understand why he was in Las

Vegas in the first place. If it wasn't a family vacation like he told Ellie, why was he there?" She mentally slapped herself again. "Sorry, another dumb question, he was there because of Rebecca." She was still tired. Her brain wasn't working at full speed due to an earlier pain pill.

"That's correct." Roddy was silent for a moment. "They were having an affair."

"Rebecca sure had it in for the HCU vice presidents. Was she involved with any of the others, or Dr. Arnold?" She cringed at the thought of Rebecca's involvement with Scooter. Maybe he had been going through a mid-life crisis.

"No, we speculate she plied her charms only to Bill and Scooter."

"And they're both dead." Dallas shivered again, poor Bill and poor Scooter, one a charmer and the other an anal accountant. "What about Rebecca? Has she been found?"

Roddy sighed. "She got away, again. The FBI is working with Interpol. They think she left Rome on a chartered plane not long after you found her."

"I hope she's found soon." Dallas yawned.

"I better let you get some rest. Don't worry about Rebecca, we'll get her." He rose and kissed her cheek. "You rest, take it easy, I'll call if anything turns up."

He let himself out the front door while Dallas leaned back and put her feet on the ottoman. She rubbed her eyes with her palms, blew out a breath, rubbed her itchy arm again. She needed to change the dressing and apply medicated cream. She sighed, closed her eyes, and a tear rolled down her cheek—feeling a bit sorry for herself.

The last two weeks had spun by like a whirlwind. Too much had transpired. Her life had changed, forever she feared. Would she be the same old Dallas or the woman who had slept with Logan Rice in a Rome hotel? The man who lied to her at a time when she was hell-bent on making decisions he was much better equipped to handle. He lied to her in making love like a man who cared for her. She didn't want to think about him again.

She'd go to work on Monday for an hour or two and her life would smooth back into normal mode. No surprises, no talk of the theft, and no thoughts that weren't good for her.

TWENTY-THREE

Monday, 10:00 a.m.

IN HER OFFICE, DALLAS SPENT two hours deleting e-mail messages and shuffling through business mail. Her arm was sore but nothing she couldn't handle. Ruthie called to check on her. Dallas assured her friend that she was back in the saddle and things were fine. As she hung up the phone, she heard a knock and found Dr. Arnold standing in the doorway of her office.

"Good morning, how are you feeling?"

"I'm fine." She smiled, moved her left arm. "No broken bones."

He shut the door behind him and sat in a chair. "Glad to see you're up and about. Although I'm not sure you should be back here so soon."

"Not a problem, I need to catch up with two weeks' worth of work. I've cleared all my e-mails. The revised budget is next." Unfortunately, Scooter wasn't there to review the proposed adjustments. "I'll work on it by myself for now."

"That's best," he agreed. "Detective Phillips brought me up-to-date on the investigation. Now we wait for the authorities to find Rebecca."

"That's all we can do." Her stomach clenched. She had worked her ass off to deliver Rebecca to the police and she failed.

"The police wouldn't be where they are if you hadn't figured out how the wire instructions were changed and discovered Rebecca wasn't ill. And, the Franks check . . . that was a stroke of genius." He smiled broadly.

"Thanks." Stroke of genius? That was a stretch, but she did

appreciate his praise.

"You're very welcome. There is something I must discuss with you." His face shifted to serious mode.

"Okay." She prayed he wouldn't fire her.

"I'm appointing you acting vice president of finance. I'll need to consult with the Board for a permanent replacement."

Holy shit.

Stay cool. Dr. Arnold didn't need to know the level of her excitement. She hadn't even considered that Scooter's position would be open. There were so many things she'd change in the Finance Office, starting with—

"Dallas?"

She floated back to earth. "I'm honored to assume the position as acting VP of finance." Her heart hurled toward reality. "Thank you for your confidence in me."

He rose, a smiled plastered on his face, and shook her hand. "It's well deserved. I've scheduled a Council meeting for tomorrow morning. Ellie has the details. She'll also provide you with a key to Scooter's . . ." He stopped, regrouped. "Sorry, to the VP office. I think it's best for you to go through the desk. Also, I'll send you the list of projects Scooter had been working on."

She had only one question. "Before you go, could you tell me why you wanted me to report my work with the police to you and not to Scooter?"

He appeared startled, then composed himself. "All I can tell you is that I was aware of Scooter's, er, out-of-the-office relationship with Rebecca. I felt it best to keep your activities more confidential."

That made sense. "Thanks. I'll see you tomorrow."

After he left, Dallas sat in her humble controller's office, in stunned silence. She hadn't expected this appointment, hadn't even thought about it, but she sure as hell wouldn't back away from it.

She needed to make a list of changes . . . hold on . . . wait for Dr. Arnold's list of current projects. More importantly, she needed to talk to her staff to let them know before the appointment was announced to the campus. She sent an e-mail for a meeting after lunch.

Ruffling through the stack of mail on her desk, she glanced up to find a cashier standing in the doorway, holding a large vase containing a spring bouquet.

"These just arrived for you," she said with a curious smile. "I'll put them on the corner of your desk."

"Thanks for bringing them in." Dallas smiled right back.

This was unusual, flowers delivered twice in three days. She hesitated before pulling the card from among the blooms. The flowers were beautiful and smelled delightful. She couldn't help but enjoy them. Chocolate or flowers as a gift was sure to improve a girl's mood. The card read: "Please forgive me, love, Logan."

She couldn't blame the man for trying but he was wasting his time and his money. Logan Rice belonged to her past. He had lied to her, well, technically, it was more like he had withheld the truth. Withholding an important fact about a person's life from another person equates to dishonesty. Logan didn't deserve her.

She smelled the flowers again, bright yellow and pink blooms, light and fragrant. They would fit nicely in her new, uh, temporary office. Her stomach growled. She grabbed her purse and headed for the parking lot. She'd pick up lunch at a drive through, not healthy but fast.

She called Ruthie once in her car.

"Guess what?"

"You received more flowers."

"How'd you know?" She was surprised at Ruthie's guess but flowers weren't on her mind right then.

"I'm psychic. Didn't you know?" Ruthie teased.

"Smart ass, also. Listen to this, Dr. Arnold came by this morning. He appointed me the acting vice president of finance. How about that?" Telling Ruthie made it all the more real. She was excited to have the chance to play with the big boys

"Congratulations. You'll do a great job. Is it scary though? Walking in your former boss' arena can't be easy."

"Definitely. I have a major case of the nerves right now. But once I get through my first Executive Council meeting I'll be fine."

"When's the meeting?" Ruthie asked.

"Tomorrow morning. I've never been to one so I don't know how they work."

"You'll do fine. Watch and learn the lay of the land."

$ $ $

After a grilled chicken sandwich, Dallas met with her staff and gave them the news of her temporary position. Their reaction was mixed, as she expected. She did her best to reassure them she'd be available just as before.

Ellie called an hour later, and Dallas found herself seated in Scooter's chair, ready to clear out the desk. She felt like a vulture. He'd just been buried and here they were, going through his things. But, life goes on and HCU had financial concerns and projects that couldn't be put on hold.

Ellie entered the office carrying packing boxes.

"Thanks," Dallas said. "We can gather everything that's personal. I'm sure Mrs. Taylor will want it."

A look she couldn't identify, irritation maybe, crossed Ellie's face.

"Dr. Arnold told me he'd deliver everything to her himself."

That surprised her as she had planned on doing it. "If that's what he wants." She pointed to the bookcase. "Why don't you go through that and take the pictures off the walls. I'll do the desk and credenza."

They worked in silence for several minutes. Dallas pulled files from the drawers, quickly looked them over, put the work ones in a pile on the top of the desk, the others in a box. It didn't take long. Next, she opened the middle drawer and wished she hadn't.

"Oh, no."

"What is it?" Ellie rushed over to the desk.

"Look." She handed Ellie a photo then pawed through

greeting cards and handwritten notes.

"Gross." Ellie smirked at the picture of Rebecca sitting on Scooter's lap, both wearing lopsided grins. "This proves it."

"Proves they were more than work colleagues." Dallas shuffled greeting cards into a pile. No need for Ellie to see them. She didn't want to soil Scooter's reputation any further.

"Poor Scooter," Ellie said.

Dallas gathered everything in a pile and found a large envelope. "I'll save this stuff for the police. I'm sure they'll want it as evidence."

After another thirty minutes, they were done. The Facilities Office picked up four boxes for delivery to Dr. Arnold's office. Now she didn't envy him taking them to Mrs. Taylor. Dallas looked around. Every wall was blank. Every indication that Scooter had previously occupied the office had evaporated.

She shivered. It was creepy. Just two weeks ago, he and Roddy and Dallas had sat at the conference table. So much had happened in those two weeks. She had no choice but to adjust to the changes. She turned around and watched Ellie take Scooter's nameplate off the door. So . . . that was that.

TWENTY-FOUR

Houston, Monday

LOGAN WALKED INTO THE RED BAR, his favorite watering hole, irritated and pissed off. His first day back at the office boiled down to a giant pain in the ass. First, Gram had cornered him about his trips to Las Vegas and Rome. She was mad as hell that Rebecca wasn't in police custody. Well, damn, he'd tried, hadn't he?

Plopping down at the oak counter, he ordered a double scotch, two ice cubes. He stared aimlessly at the liquor bottles behind the bar, rubbed his beard, wondered what the hell was wrong with him. Ever since he'd said good-bye to Dallas last Friday morning, he'd been in a foul mood. He wasn't ready to admit to himself that Dallas was the cause of his nasty mood.

He slugged down half the scotch, felt a hand on his shoulder.

"Billy, how's it going?" He motioned with his head. "Take a load off."

Billy ordered a beer, studied his cousin. Apparently, he didn't like what he saw. "You got a burr up your ass?"

"What's it to you?" Logan snapped.

Billy held up his hands like a traffic cop. "Nothing. Not a damned thing." The beer arrived. He raised the bottle to his lips for a long pull, then said the obvious. "You might as well tell me what's going on. I'll get it out of you sooner or later. My charm is legendary, you know."

Logan grinned, sipped his scotch, enjoying its flavor. But damn, his life was a mess. He rubbed his face again. Might as well lay it all out on the table. Billy was right. He'd eventually drag it out.

"Sorry for the lousy mood," Logan began. "It's been a rough couple of weeks."

"Rough? You were traveling around the world with a hot-looking woman. That's not rough to me."

"That hot-looking woman thinks I'm a piece of shit," Logan countered, feeling sorry for himself. Why had he allowed Dallas to get under his skin? He had always prided himself on his control. That was shot to hell now.

Billy grinned from the side of his mouth. "Piece of shit, huh? I know you're a good man so that means you did something to piss her off." He punched Logan on the arm. "Tell me what you did."

Logan stared straight ahead, considered his options. He could send a message by courier, send more flowers, turn up unannounced at her office, talk to her grandmother. He didn't have any options that didn't involve kowtowing. Maybe Billy would have a good idea.

"She thinks I lied to her."

"About what?" Billy looked skeptical.

"I didn't tell her I worked for the FBI."

"Why not? That's old news."

"I just didn't," Logan spat out. Dallas had been so sure of herself figuring out the identity of the thief and then searching for Rebecca. His voice softened. "I didn't want to bust her bubble."

"Bust her bubble? Man, you're screwed," Billy snorted. "You can't even make sense when you explain what you did to piss her off."

"Ah, hell, she was really into figuring out what had happened to the $25 million. I didn't let her know I was experienced at that kind of thing. I talked to Bob Brown at the Embassy in Rome without telling her. She says I humiliated her." Logan drained his glass, signaled for a refill and another beer for Billy.

"You gotta admit she has a point."

"Hell, I'm screwed." Logan realized he had to take action. "What do I do to make it up to her?"

"Is she important to you?"

Logan nodded, hesitated before he spoke. "I think I want to marry her."

"You are definitely screwed. I think groveling will be a part of your plan."

Logan groaned. Groveling *was* the plan.

TWENTY-FIVE

Tuesday, 9:54 a.m.

DALLAS' FIRST VISIT TO THE Cullen Room as a member of the HCU Executive Council began with a whimper. She arrived on time, along with Dr. Arnold's assistant, who arranged a tray of drinks. She poured a cup of coffee then found a spot at the conference table. Without knowing if there was a seating protocol, she decided to wing it and took a seat. Jill Bacon arrived. She worked in Development so Dallas surmised she was poor Bill's stand-in.

The academic and the student affairs VPs finally arrived. They were talking about the standings for the Houston Astros. Dallas nodded at each VP as he found a seat at the conference table. Damn, every appointed vice president was male. Jill and Dallas, both acting, didn't have a snow ball's chance in hell of being selected for the permanent positions. The Council was a boy's club and neither of the two women had the right equipment.

Dr. Arnold arrived and sat at the head of the table. Dallas stifled a chuckle; his location was too predictable. His assistant took a seat at the end of the table to record the minutes.

Dallas opened her meeting binder and scanned the agenda. The most interesting items were the final discussion for a property acquisition and the status of the $25 million theft. The most important item was a review of the admissions status for the fall term. None of them would have a job if students didn't fill HCU's classrooms.

She quickly surmised the real power in the group belonged to the academic and student affairs VPs. That didn't surprise her as

258 Karen Sue Burns

students were the product and faculty, the manufacturer. Finance was a necessary evil, the gatekeeper, the group who said "no."

Dr. Arnold went through the various agenda items down to the details of the property acquisition and asked Dallas to review the alternatives available to finance the purchase.

"Yes, sir." She made a note to find Scooter's file on the subject.

"The last item is an update on the gift from the Bridge Foundation. A representative from the foundation will be here any minute. Ah, here he is now." Dr. Arnold motioned toward the door of the conference room.

Damn . . . the representative was Logan. What was wrong with that foundation? They should have sent Billy.

Dr. Arnold stood to greet Logan, they shook hands. Logan then went around the table shaking hand, saving Dallas for last.

"Good morning, how's the arm?" Logan grinned. Damn him.

"Fine." She smiled brightly, disengaged her hand. "Thank you *so much* for asking."

Logan sat across the table from her. Why couldn't he have done a phone conference? Then she wouldn't have to look at him. And he did look good—rested, refreshed, so masculine in a dark suit, yellow tie. Her stomach rolled, a bead of sweat floated down her back. He looked too damn good. She looked away, focused her attention back on the meeting.

"Mr. Rice, I understand you have something to tell us," Dr. Arnold said.

"Yes." Logan looked around the table. "We had insurance on the funds that were transferred and have filed a claim. It will be a while before our claim is fully processed." He smiled, glanced at Dr. Arnold then at Dallas. "However, once we receive the claim proceeds, we will be transferring the funds to the University. To make up for those lost, of course."

A round of applause, at least the foundation was a first-class organization. She felt Logan's eyes drilling into her. She did not look at him. Rather, she focused her attention on Dr. Arnold. He was providing a high level run down of the police investigation and the search for Rebecca, then he mentioned Dallas' name. She smiled, pleased that he had publicly acknowledged her efforts in tracking down Rebecca. The academic VP had a couple of questions and a few minutes later the meeting adjourned.

Dallas was backed into a corner, literally. Logan stood near the door, the only exit. She considered sliding past him without speaking. Thankfully, Dr. Arnold pulled him over to the end of the conference table. She scooted around the other end and out the door, waving to Dr. Arnold. She hurried down the stairs and rushed to the sidewalk. Her office was only a couple blocks away. She'd be at her desk before Logan finished with Dr. Arnold.

After a block, she heard someone call her name.

"Dallas, hold up."

She stopped and turned. There he was, the jerk himself, jogging along the sidewalk. He halted in front of her.

"We need to talk," he said, not even out of breath. Damn him.

"Sorry, I'm busy, no time." She turned and started walking. Three steps and he grasped her good arm.

"Please, this will only take a minute," he said.

"Don't have a minute."

"Come on, Dallas, give me a break. I'm trying to apologize to you."

That pissed her off. Give him a break? Men are so stupid when they think it's all about them.

"You don't owe me anything. Keep your apologies to yourself." She raised her chin, glowered at him. "If you'll excuse me, I have real work to do." Her shoulders sliced the air as she turned and marched toward a life without Mr. Logan Rice. Of course, if it truly was the end of Logan and she had no reason to believe it wasn't, why had her heart split in two? There was that.

$ $ $

Dallas' refrigerator was devoid of fresh food. She needed to go to the grocery store but not tonight. This had been her second full day as the acting vice president of finance and she was pooped, one tired puppy. Her arm zinged a bit, reminding her she'd been shot less than a week ago. She'd lather it with the salve the Italian doctor had provided and go to bed early. But she was starving and called the local pizza delivery service. Forty-five minutes to wait before gorging herself. She poured a glass of merlot and went to the computer in the study to check her personal e-mail account.

She found five-hundred seventy-three messages. Wasn't she popular? Not really, most of the messages were advertisements. She started at the oldest message and looked at each one, hoping to come across a really good sale.

The pizza arrived around message number one-ninety-eight. She threw two double cheese and black olives slices on a paper plate, sprinkled them with parmesan cheese, and poured more wine. Back in the study, she munched the pizza, drank the wine, and read more messages.

She saved a few that advertised local sales. She whittled the list down to a dozen or so messages when she came to one with the subject line: "Please read - I'm sorry." She almost deleted it, assuming it was from Logan, but she hadn't given him her personal e-mail address. She didn't recognize the sending address but opened it anyway.

After the first couple of words, her breath caught in her throat, her heart thump-da-thumped. The message was from Rebecca.

She read it out loud. "Dear Dallas: I'm sure you're surprised to hear from me. Frankly, I'm surprised as well. But that's neither here nor there. I simply want you to know that I am truly sorry you were shot in Rome. It wasn't something I planned. It just happened. However, I am not sorry about taking the money from HCU. I had my reasons. Tell the police I cannot be found. They are wasting their time. Best, Rebecca."

Holy shit. This was incredible—Rebecca apologized for shooting her. She needed to tell someone about this. What was Logan's cell number?

Whoa . . . no, she would call Roddy as this was police business. She punched in his number, paced the study, prayed he'd answer.

"Phillips."

"Thank goodness you answered. I have—"

"Dallas?"

"Yes, I have—"

"Why'd you call me?"

Did he have the over-thirty-male-form of ADHD?

"Detective Phillips, please listen carefully," she said slowly. "I have something to tell you. Are you with me so far?"

"Uh-huh."

"Peachy." Her pacing stopped in front of the computer. "I'm going to read you an e-mail I received in my personal account. Are you ready?"

"Uh-huh."

What the hell was wrong with him? He sounded like he was distracted. Maybe he was . . . on a date.

"Are you with Lynne right now?"

"Uh-huh."

"Fine, I'll make this fast." She read the e-mail in a clear voice. "What do you think? What should I do about this?"

"First, forward it to me. Second, you do nothing. Third, talk to Logan Rice," Roddy said.

"Why'd you say that? Why did you mention Logan?"

"I don't have time for couple's counseling right now." Roddy sighed. "Send me the e-mail."

The phone clicked. He had hung up on her.

What was going on? Had Logan talked to him? Of course, Logan had talked to Roddy. The question was why. Whatever, she didn't care. She had nothing to say to Logan.

She returned to the computer, found Roddy's e-mail address and forwarded Rebecca's message. Dallas' investigation had concluded with Rebecca's message. She had nothing to be ashamed of. She'd been a good HCU point person. The police knew the identity of the thief. They knew how the wire instructions had been changed and now *they could find Rebecca.*

An hour later, as she washed her face, Dallas thought about Las Vegas and Rome and Logan. No, she wasn't going there. She had no desire for Logan's presence in any city on the planet.

She settled under the bed covers, turned on the TV to catch the cable news. She sighed a deep breath, recognized a queasy stomach and a heavy heart. Yes, she was lost when it came to Logan Rice, but she would admit it, only to herself, in the dark of night.

TWENTY-SIX

Rio de Janeiro, Wednesday

THE WATERS OF THE ATLANTIC Ocean were calm, gently lapping against the empty beach. The ebb and flow of the waves evoked a tranquility and serenity Rebecca Holland hadn't felt in thirty-five years. She surveyed her domain, the patio of a beach house just south of Rio. The blue mosaic of the floor perfectly accented the artful grouping of chairs and lounges spread among large ceramic pots of tropical plants and flowers. A slight breeze dusted the large leaves of the philodendrons and floated toward Rebecca with the delicious scent of hibiscus.

She sipped iced lemonade, raised her face to the sun, and reveled in the simple joy of the day. She put her arms across her chest and hugged herself. Life was good. No, her life was perfect. She closed her eyes and snuggled her back against the luxurious beach towel covering the chaise lounge she rested on. Life hadn't always been so good. Her mind traveled back to that one day when she was seven years old . . .

Rebecca's mother kissed her goodnight, pulled the Beatles bedspread to her chin, flipped off the light switch, and closed the door. A tree knocked against the window, forcing Rebecca to snuggle deeper into the bed covers. Rain pelted the window, then flowed down the pane in rivulets. She wondered where the rain drops went after they fell. Her mother told her that rain came from the angels crying. But why did angels cry? Rebecca didn't understand that. Mommy said she'd understand when she got bigger.

But how big was bigger? She figured it meant big enough to run away from home. Her one friend, Jenny, had an older sister who had run away. But the sister was a teenager and knew everything. She'd told Jenny good-bye before she left home. Rebecca wanted to be smart like Jenny's sister. You had to have a plan. As soon as she was old enough, Rebecca would have a plan, too. She just had to. Her life wasn't good and Mommy didn't know. No one knew except for Tommy.

Tommy was scary and he wouldn't go away, even when Rebecca cried. She wished he'd never come to live with her and Mommy. But he came with Mommy's new husband. She called him Mr. John, that's what he wanted. She didn't like him. He smelled like cigars and laughed too loud. Sometimes he hit Mommy on her bottom and said it was too big. Mommy just smiled, didn't tell him to stop. But Rebecca wanted him to stop.

Rebecca tried her hardest to stay awake but the rain lulled her to sleep. She dreamed of Daddy and the sailboat. She was too little to help with the sails but Daddy let her hold the wheel when she sat on his lap. He laughed and kissed her cheek and stroked her hair flying in the wind. Mommy laughed, too. But Daddy died. Then Mr. John took Daddy's chair at the dinner table. Rebecca wanted to tell Mr. John to go away, because that was Daddy's chair. But she didn't, she was too scared. She was too little.

Rebecca couldn't breathe. A big hand covered her mouth.

"Don't make a sound Little Shit. It's time for fun."

Rebecca nodded, her eyes bright with tears. She knew better. She promised herself that one day she'd kill Tommy and run away with Mommy. Yes, she'd take Mommy away from Mr. John.

Of course, that never happened.

Eventually, Tommy grew tired of her. She never told Mommy of his late-night visits or the toll they had taken on her. She immersed herself in school work and making her mother proud. She did her chores around the house and went to church as Mr. John expected. She never dated. She graduated high school with good grades and finally had her chance to run away. She went to college. Although Mr. John complained that a private school was too expensive even with her full scholarship.

Rebecca had her first date her sophomore year and her first boyfriend her senior year. He was wonderful, dear Billy Rice. Then she got pregnant and all hell broke out.

Rebecca moaned, sweat beading her chest. Her eyes opened, momentarily disoriented, she patted her chest with a small towel, tasted the lukewarm lemonade. She blew out a breath. The dream was a reminder of how far she had traveled. And that every underdog has its day in the sun.

She had given Billy Rice and his family just what she had always dreamed of giving Tommy and Mr. John. Hit them where it hurts. But they were both gone now.

She didn't have one qualm of guilt for stealing twenty-five million dollars from the Rice family. They could afford it and were no doubt insured. And, HCU? She didn't give a damn. What a sorry bunch of losers. All of the executives were men. Men who thought they were so smart and so much better than their female employees.

Rebecca had shown both Bill and Scooter they weren't smart at all. She couldn't believe how gullible both of them had been. And they thought she'd been interested in their sorry asses. She did feel somewhat bad about Dallas. Dallas getting shot wasn't part of the plan. That's why she had sent the e-mail yesterday. Now she had nothing to concern her. Not that she had a conscience about everything that had happened. But if she had, it was now clear as ice.

Hell, maybe she should go to Hollywood. After all, she was one hell of an actor.

However, it was Dallas' fault the police knew about her and the money. Being forced to obtain new passports and change her looks had been a pain in the ass. Dallas *was* the responsible party. Hmm, perhaps she should pay Dallas a little visit. It would soon be time to check on her mother at the house in Victoria, not far at all from Houston. Mother had no idea her daughter was a multi-millionaire. It would stay that way. Rebecca was good at hiding secrets. Even her mother agreed that was true. Now, what should she plan for sweet, boring, stupid Dallas?

$ $ $

Saturday, 1:35 p.m.

"I love your wedding dress." Dallas and Ruthie were taking a coffee break while window-shopping in Houston's Galleria Mall. They settled on an out-of-the-way bench.

"Me, too. It passed the butt test."

"That it did."

Ruthie patted the plastic bag draped over her lap. "I have a question. Change of subject . . . what actually happened in Rome with Logan?"

"I don't want to talk about him."

"At least tell me what it was like seeing him at the Council meeting." Ruthie looked at Dallas with glee-filled eyes.

"You won't let this drop, will you?" She resigned herself to giving Ruthie what she wanted to hear. Otherwise, she'd pester Dallas until she broke down from sheer exhaustion.

"Nope." Ruthie grinned, fully understanding she had won. "I want to hear everything. Start with Rome, no start with Las Vegas."

Dallas had spent so much time pushing Logan out of her mind, she wasn't sure she wanted to bring him back. Her heart clenched. She needed to do this or she'd never get him out of her system.

Ruthie patted her hand. "Take your time."

Dallas' mind was a jumble of images—Logan at the Bellagio craps table with that stupid blonde, Logan in the clown costume with the killer grin hiding under the jester make up, Logan wearing nothing but a towel and a fabulous chest in the Rome hotel room, and Logan kissing her like there was no tomorrow.

She sighed. "I'm glad you're pushing me. I need to resolve this once and for all." She fluffed hair off her neck. Her head was hot, as usual. "It's hard to know where to start. I was off my game the minute I stepped on the Rice jet. Then a limo met us at the Vegas airport and the hotel room at the Grand was a suite the Rice family owns. It was beautiful." She took another deep breath. "Logan was so cool and totally in control. He knew the damned security chief at the hotel."

"That makes sense if the family owns the suite," Ruthie said.

"Yeah, well, money talks," Dallas asserted. "He's not like that though. He was so nice and he really tried to help me figure everything out."

"Were you attracted to him?" Leave it to Ruthie to be right on target.

"Attracted? Sure, but come on, I'm divorced, with kids, and about to become a grandmother. He's a good-looking and wealthy bachelor. How could I be attractive to him?" A wave of heaviness slid down Dallas' spine. Her life was upside down and she had no control to turn it around.

"You are so hard on yourself."

"No, I'm honest. I told him I'm a bad picker and he was safe with me."

Ruthie rolled her eyes. "You're so dumb at times."

"Dumb? What the hell does that mean?"

"You think you'll never find love again because you made a mistake at eighteen. Jonathon was a one-man convincing machine and you were powerless against him. I say this with love, but . . . get over it."

Was Ruthie right? Had Dallas used her divorce as an excuse to hibernate and not date? Had she deliberately shut down her heart for the past ten years? She knew without a doubt the answer to each question was "yes".

Everything made sense. She had been using her lousy marriage with Jonathan as *the excuse* to stay away from a possible relationship. She was only forty-four, not eighty-four. She had plenty of time to fall in love and even get married again.

"What are you thinking?" Ruthie asked. "You've got that look you get when you're up to something."

"I'm not up to anything. But I have been thinking . . . and, you're right."

Her eyes rounded, big as saucers. "I am?"

"Yep, I've been using my divorce as an excuse. Don't get excited. I'm just saying it's time to turn over a new leaf."

"Fantastic." Ruthie clapped her hands. "Who knows, you may be the one to marry after me."

Dallas sliced the air with a hand in front of her chest. "No way, I'm not talking about marriage. I'm saying I'll go on a date with the right attitude."

"That's a start." Ruthie grinned, tilted her head to one side. "Would you consider going out with Logan?"

Dallas looked at her like she had fallen off an alien space ship. "Are you nuts?"

"All right, I get it." She changed tactics. "Did you take any pictures in Rome?"

"No. We weren't tourists."

"Hmm, did Logan enjoy Rome?"

"He'd been there before so he knew his way around, once he told me," Dallas said. "It's a habit with him."

"What? Knowing Rome?"

"Hell no, keeping things from me."

"You're talking about him being with the FBI?"

"Come on, Ruthie, wouldn't that tick you off?" Her chest tightened. "It's like me not telling him I have kids."

"I see your point. But . . . isn't it possible you're overreacting?"

"Overreacting! How can you say that to me?"

Ruthie stroked Dallas' arm. "Calm down, engage that analytical brain of yours. Just because he didn't tell you right off the bat doesn't mean he's a conniving jerk. Maybe he thinks it's immaterial now. It's not like he quit working there last month."

"True. He said he really enjoyed the work and wasn't happy about quitting. It had something to do with his grandfather dying and pressure from his grandmother," Dallas said. Maybe that's why he didn't tell her.

"So . . . isn't it possible your punishment doesn't fit his crime?" Ruthie smiled. "I think you should reconsider Logan and his flowers. Seems to me, he's working hard to apologize to you."

The flowers were beautiful and he was trying. And, Dallas screwed it up by pushing him away.

She blew a slow breath. "I doubt he'll try again. I was a bitch to him after the Council meeting."

"Did you tell him thank you for the flowers?"

"No . . . no, I didn't."

"There you go." Ruthie nodded, satisfaction beaming across her face. "That's your reason to call him. But you still have a problem."

"What's that?"

"Whether or not you tell Logan you've fallen for him," Ruthie replied.

Oh, yes, there was that.

TWENTY-SEVEN

Sunday, 1:42 p.m.

TWENTY-FOUR HOURS AND SEVEN minutes had passed since Dallas promised she would call Logan to thank him for the two bouquets of flowers. Had she called him? No. She'd picked up the phone at least a dozen times. She simply didn't know what to say. "Sorry, I've been such an ass" didn't sound quite right. "I want to jump your bones" sounded even worse. And the third option, "I really, really like you" would put her on the cover of *Psychology Today.*

Actually, there was no rush. Dallas would call Logan before the end of the day. Monday definitely.

That settled, she poured another cup of coffee and planted herself in the chair to read the Sunday newspaper. The phone rang. She pushed the paper to the floor and hurried to the kitchen. The caller was Nana.

"How are you feeling?"

"Good, my arm is hardly sore. How have you been? And, Bob?"

"We're both fine. That's why I called. I want to tell you we've scheduled the wedding for September. Bob's son, the one in Japan, can't get vacation until then and we want him to be here."

"That sounds fine with me." She snapped her fingers. "Nana, I forgot to tell you something. It's really good."

"Good, huh? Tell me. You know how I like surprises." She could hear the smile in Nana's voice.

"When I was in Las Vegas, I won a jackpot at a five-dollar slot machine and—"

"Oh, that's wonderful. How much?" Nana liked the details.

"That's not important. Your wedding reception is on me. Everything." Dallas felt proud that she could do this for her grandmother.

"Oh, sweetie, that's so kind of you. Are you sure you can't use the money for something more important?"

"Nana, there's nothing more important to me than you having a memorable wedding day."

"I accept then. I better run, I need to tell Bob."

As she replaced the receiver, the doorbell rang. She became entangled in her doggy slippers, kicked them in the corner, and hurried to the door and opened it, not expecting a visitor.

Her mouth opened then shut, her stomach plummeted to the floor while her heart galloped down the street.

Silence. No words were spoken as they stared at each other. Finally, her heart slowed and she recovered her ability to join words in a complete sentence.

"Logan, what brings you here?" Her cool and totally in control attitude returned.

He lifted a picnic basket in one hand and held a grocery sack in the other arm. He wore a sexy smile as well.

"I'm here to grovel."

"Grovel?"

"I need to talk with you and I brought lunch."

She stepped back, giving him room to walk in front of her, swaying when she caught a whiff of his cologne.

He moved past her toward the kitchen. She followed him like a Doberman stalking a thirty-two-ounce T-bone.

He pulled two bottles of champagne from the grocery sack.

Dallas raised a hand. "Stop."

"What?" He placed the bottles on the counter.

"Why are you really here?"

His jaw clenched, his eyes slightly narrowed. "I really am here to grovel, to explain myself . . . please."

She looked at his handsome face, licking her lips nervously. Could she trust him? "Why two bottles of champagne?"

"One for today and a second for a return visit." He stowed one bottle in the refrigerator.

She automatically opened a cabinet for glasses while he moved next to her. He kissed the back of her neck. "Hmm." Suddenly, she felt warm.

He backed off. "Good," he said with a satisfied grin. "We can have a glass before lunch." The cork made a soft pssfft as it exited the bottle.

After she rinsed two flutes, Logan poured the wine. The bubbles reminded her of their last glass of champagne together— on the Rice jet after leaving Rome and before she learned the truth.

He suggested they sit on the patio. It was cloudy and pleasant, most unusual for June along the Texas Gulf Coast. They relaxed opposite each other in rattan deck chairs.

Logan lifted his glass. "Cheers."

She did the same. "Ditto."

He looked around. "Nice patio."

"Thanks."

Silence, uncomfortable silence.

"Dallas—"

"Yes."

"So . . . what was your favorite part of Rome?"

Jiminy Christmas, that's all he could say? "I loved Rome, in theory, as I didn't have much time to enjoy the sights, looking for a thief and all. It was great, right up to the point on the sidewalk where I was shot." She tasted the champagne and looked at him, challenging him to top that.

"The shooting was certainly my worst part." He leaned forward, holding the flute in both hands. "I thought I'd lost you."

"Not to worry." She raised her left arm. "All healed."

He rubbed his fingers lightly along her arm below the red scar. Maybe she should tell him she loved the flowers.

"I need to tell you something." He looked so damned earnest, like a forty-year-old boy scout.

"But first . . . I want to say thank you for the flowers, both deliveries. I should have said it before. I'm sorry for being tardy with my acknowledgment."

Logan's face brightened. She must have said the magic words.

"You're very welcome."

"How's it going at work now that you're back?" Dallas asked.

"Work's fine, the usual. Nothing changes." He closed his eyes for a moment then looked at her. "I really am sorry I didn't tell you I worked for the FBI. I know I should have but . . . I screwed up."

"I know."

"You'll accept my apology?" He grinned as though he realized he had vaulted over the last hurdle of a thousand-yard race.

"Yes, I will." She grinned back at him. "But you're still a jerk for not being totally open with me."

"You're right. I truly am sorry. I'd like to put this behind us."

"Agreed," she said. Whew, the worst was over.

The sky had darkened while they talked. Thunder rolled across the sky, the hanging baskets began to dance and rain spattered the patio.

"We better get inside." Logan rose and opened the door.

They ended up in the kitchen. Dallas started to open the picnic basket, but Logan stopped her and pulled her into his arms.

"I've missed you," he whispered and kissed her, not gently, but with a sudden urgency that drew a startled gasp from Dallas. She wrapped her arms around his waist, remembering the solid feel of him. He nuzzled her neck and shivers tumbled over her abdomen. Her heart pounded, her blood warmed. She captured his mouth, enjoying the taste of champagne.

She pushed gently at his chest, kissed his jaw. "Let's go upstairs."

"Show me the way."

She took his hand and quickly led him to the master bedroom. The room was dark except for flashes of lightening visible through the half-open slats of wooden blinds. The storm had unleashed its fury. Rain pounded on the window and trees swooshed in the yard.

"Ooh, it's cold." She rubbed her arms.

Logan stood behind her and placed his hands at her waist while his breath feathered the back of her neck. His nearness overwhelmed her sense of balance.

Dallas turned around. "Logan, I, uh . . ." Her voice stopped at the tenderness of his smile. Its sweetness almost broke her heart in two. Her arms stretched up and wrapped around his neck. "I'm so glad you're here."

"Me, too," he murmured as his lips traced a sensuous path along her jaw to her mouth.

He smelled so good and his chest felt even better—hard and so very masculine. With her mouth under assault, she transitioned from chilly to toasty warm in a matter of seconds. She whimpered.

He understood perfectly and pushed her gently to the bed. Dallas peeled his polo shirt up and over his head, dropped it to the floor. Her finger traced the pattern of a heart over his chest, touching the skin ever so lightly. She felt his sharp intake of breath before she heard a soft whistle.

Logan's hand captured hers and brought it to his lips. "I really am sorry." He caressed the top of each knuckle with a kiss.

She couldn't think about his apology or anything else but the man who lay alongside her. "No more talking," she whispered.

His voice fractured with huskiness. "All right then."

The gentle touch of his lips on her mouth erased the last residue of anger. He drew her in with his hands and his mouth as her body pressed against his, eager for every point of contact.

A crash of thunder outside the window had them diving under the smooth yellow sheets.

Logan snuggled with Dallas once again, patted her hip, and tugged her against him. "My girl," he murmured against her temple.

Dallas' heart opened, this was all she wanted, had ever wished for. The sweetness, the heat, the possibility those two words offered. She felt dizzy from the cascade of feelings zigzagging inside her. She cuddled against his neck, breathing in the scent of sandalwood. His hand found the curve of her breast and her pulse spiked.

Within minutes, flesh warmed flesh and one beating heart pressed against the other. When she arched to meet him, she panted his name and lost herself.

After their breathing slowed and Logan again lay alongside her, Dallas realized she now knew what she wanted. But she wouldn't yet share the discovery with Logan—all in good time.

They rested, sharing a caress and a tender touch. Dallas tingled from the ends of her hair to her toes. Suddenly, Logan moved to the edge of the bed, pulled on his shorts, turned back to her with a devastating grin. "How about a cup of coffee?"

"Great idea." She scrambled off the bed and threw on a robe.

Five minutes later, they settled back on the bed, toasted each other with their mugs, and nestled under the covers.

Rain beat gently against the window. The thunder was in the distance now, the storm moving on down the road. Dallas gazed at Logan, unsure of what was next. Did this mean they were friends? Really good friends? Lovers?

Maybe just maybe, they were on the edge of something deeper than friendship. She honestly didn't know but she understood her girly genes were getting ahead of her brain. Her bad picker mentality sat on her shoulder, telling her to take it slow, not to jump off that relationship cliff, to be cautious.

Logan squeezed her hand. "Why so quiet?"

"Just thinking."

"And I know what you're thinking about." He rolled on his side, looked at her with a knowing grin.

"Sure, you do."

"I agree with you. We need to take this slow." His finger stroked her cheek. "In fact, I think we should go on a proper date."

Damn. "You mean where you call me, ask me out, and we go out to dinner or to a movie?"

"That's what I was thinking." He leaned over and kissed her hard. "We can have our first real boy-girl date."

She leaned over and kissed him back. "Deal."

The phone rang and she picked it up.

"Dallas, where have you been? I've left two messages."

The message light was blinking. They had ignored the phone. Dirk sounded excited.

"Is it Liz?" She sat up. "Are you going to the hospital?"

Logan scrambled out of bed, began pulling on his clothes.

"We've been here for almost two hours. She's in labor," Dirk huffed.

"I'm on my way. Tell her to wait for me."

"Just hurry."

$ $ $

Dallas ran into Liz's maternity suite just as a baby boy emerged, sucked in that first breath, and began to wail. It was pure magic.

"Sorry I'm late," she panted.

"Mom, finally," Liz whispered.

The baby was quickly placed in Liz's arms, pink and perfect. Dallas pulled a camera from her purse, and did what grandma's do, took a dozen photos of her new grandson. After a minute, a nurse took the baby away for a bath and measuring.

Dallas looked from Liz to Dirk and gave them a thumb's up. "You guys did good. He's adorable. What name did you finally settle on?"

"Cutter Phillip Holmes," Liz said. She was bright eyed and relaxed, hardly showing the stress from just giving birth. "We figure with Cutter, he'll be the only kid in school with the name."

The nurse poked her head around the corner of a short wall. "He's twenty-one inches, seven pounds eleven ounces."

Dallas patted Liz's hand. "Now that I know the details, let me go tell everyone that Cutter has arrived."

She hurried to the waiting room and found Logan deep in conversation with Nana while Ruthie listened. Bob was reading a magazine. Dirk's parents were standing by the window, coffee cups in their hands. Jane and a man she didn't recognize, sat side by side on a short couch with their feet on a table. She'd obtain the details on him later. Jonathon stood to the side, not sure of his place.

"We have a baby."

Eight heads turned to Dallas, anticipation in every pair of eyes.

She shared the details then grinned. "He's a looker, too."

Everyone jumped up at once, talking over each other.

"When can we see him?" Nana asked.

"In a little while," she said. "Let's give them time alone." She spied the picnic basket on the floor. "In the meantime, is anyone hungry? Logan brought lunch." She motioned to Jonathan. "Come over here, Grandpa, join us."

After twenty minutes, the basket was empty and Dirk waved in the group to see Cutter. He nestled in his mother's arms. Dallas took more pictures. Logan took a turn with the camera, capturing the entire family. They soon left to give the new parents a much-needed break.

On the way home, Logan asked Dallas if she wanted to go with him to visit his Grandmother. She declined as it was late and she had reading to do for a Monday morning meeting. He walked her to the townhouse porch.

"Don't forget I'll be calling tomorrow about that first date." He kissed her then patted her butt.

She grinned and waved good-bye.

Inside the townhouse, Dallas plopped in her chair and allowed herself the pleasure of a few minutes to relax.

She felt on top of the world. She had a grandson, a perfect little guy who had his father's nose and his mother's eyes, Dallas' eyes. Tears spilled. She was such a mush ball. She'd visit a toy store after work on Monday. Cutter needed a football.

She brushed away the tears, not appropriate on such a happy day. That brought Logan's face to mind. Handsome, kind, and smart . . . Logan Rice.

He had fit in just fine with Nana and the girls. Jane hadn't even given her the third degree about him. Ruthie must have talked. Oh well, it didn't matter.

Logan had become important to her. It was just three weeks since they had met—the beginning of her search for Rebecca. Her life was better for the adventure of chasing a wicked crook and almost catching her. It was up to the police now.

And, she had things to do. It was time to look for a new car—a red SUV to fit the new grandma—one with a good backseat for grandkids and car seats. The twins would say she'd had gone over the edge. No problem, her wings were working just fine.

TWENTY-EIGHT

Two Months Later

DALLAS COULDN'T COMPLAIN. Life was good, other than continuing to wear her controller bonnet along with the acting VP finance Stetson. The meetings were killing her—academia loved to talk. She'd started using her computer calendar just to keep up. Thank heavens Ellie managed to keep her on time.

Happy to leave the workweek behind, Dallas arrived home at six o'clock on a Friday evening in mid-August. She changed her clothes and checked her watch, where was Logan? He should be there already. He had insisted on bringing dinner, something healthy. She needed to run again. The HCU workload limited her time for exercise and her ass was spreading.

Logan arrived a minute later with flautas and enchiladas and all the fixings from Dallas' favorite Mexican restaurant. Healthy? She'd ignore her ass this one meal.

He spread the dinner on the kitchen counter then kissed Dallas thoroughly on the mouth. Even after the many times he'd kissed her, a butterfly still spread its wings in her stomach. This gorgeous man was her man.

"Did you have a good day," he said, rubbing his hand along the curve of her back.

"Good enough."

They made plates and perched at the counter to enjoy their meal.

"Babe, I told you about the tickets for tomorrow evening, right?" Logan said after a few minutes.

"Um, tickets? Oops, that's my cell." She hurried to her purse for the phone.

"It's Roddy, long time, no talk."

"Right, I haven't heard from you in a while." She leaned against the counter, knowing full well this call wasn't good news. Roddy wasn't a chit-chatty kind of detective. "Okay, what's up?"

"You're too smart for your own good."

"Right. What's up?"

Logan perked up and she motioned for him to be quiet.

"I miss playing detective with you, but something is up . . . per the FBI, Rebecca Holland left Brazil."

"Brazil?" Dallas rubbed her forehead. "That's where she's been hiding? Where'd she go?"

"That is the one fact we don't know."

"Why did she leave?"

"Don't know that either."

Rebecca must have a very good reason to leave Brazil. "My guess is figure out the why and then you'll know the where." She clicked off.

She found Logan on the couch in the living room flipping channels with the TV remote.

He took her hand and kissed the palm. "Hmm, you taste good."

"You smell good." She kissed him on the neck.

He looked at her with a serious face. "What did Roddy say about Rebecca? I hope she's not coming after you."

"Why would you say that?"

"Don't forget you're the one who set the police on her."

"Old news." Dallas didn't want to think about Rebecca and what she might be planning to do. As she'd concluded after the gunshot in Rome, running after Rebecca was the job of the police. She grabbed the remote. "What's on TV?"

She found an Astros baseball game and they settled in. "How about a glass of wine?"

"I'll get it."

How nice to have a man around the house to pour the wine.

Logan returned with two glasses and they settled on the couch side by side.

"This is nice," Logan said. "Something I could get used to."

"What? Drinking wine in front of the TV?"

"Yes, with you."

She patted his thigh. "Awe, you are so sweet tonight."

"I mean it. I think we should move in together."

She nearly choked on the wine, cleared her throat. "That's not something I've ever considered."

"I figured that. I've not either. But I think it's the perfect solution."

"Solution to what?"

"Your hang up about getting married again."

She scooted to the edge of the couch and turned to him. "Hang up? I do not have a hang up about marriage. It's perfectly fine for other people."

"That's exactly what I mean. Why won't you even consider it?"

"Because I'm lousy at it." She sighed and flopped against the back cushion.

"Do you hear yourself? You have a bad attitude."

"Maybe, maybe not. I think of myself as being honest." She did not want to continue this conversation.

"That you are. But I still think we should move in together and see how it goes."

"We don't know each other well enough. What has it been, three months?"

"That's plenty of time for me to know what I want."

Dallas patted his cheek. "Sweetie, you are so cute."

He captured her hand and gazed at her face, his smile a galaxy away. "Don't do that. Don't trivialize my feelings."

"I'm sorry, I didn't mean to." Dallas never wanted to hurt him, ever. "Okay, I'll think about it."

$ $ $

By the middle of the next week, Dallas had managed to put

Logan's words behind her, mostly. She did not consider herself the type of woman to trivialize a man's feelings or words. Yet, she wasn't ready to wrap her head around the thought of them moving in together.

Did that mean she was old fashioned? Maybe, probably. The truth—she was terrified of commitment. It equated to fun like watching a rattle snake slither out of a toilet bowl. You just never know when it might bite you in the ass. But . . . Logan deserved her taking his suggestion seriously and with some soul-searching on her part.

Dr. Arnold called and told Ellie he was heading over. It was almost two in the afternoon and Dallas had no idea what might be on his mind. She wondered why he hadn't summoned her to his office—good news or bad news? She had no clue how these things worked.

Before she could rationalize her last thought, Dr. Arnold walked into the office. She rose, walked around the desk to meet him.

She thrust out her hand. "Dr. Arnold, good to see you today."

He shook her hand, briefly she noticed, then sat at the small round conference table. Being quick on the draw, she seated herself across from him.

"I know this is unusual and you're still making the transition from controller to VP."

Transition? To VP? She assumed he was here to tell her a search committee had been set up for the VP position.

"Things have been easier this last month," she said, physically forcing her hand to stop smoothing her hair.

"I assumed that would be the case." Dr. Arnold smiled that small smile he had down to an art.

She never knew what he was thinking or his real opinion on a subject. Unlike Dallas, whose face was a neon sign flashing her thoughts.

"Thanks for your support," she said. How lame was that?

"Please look over these proposals." He handed her an envelope and rose. "The Board approved your appointment as VP finance. Congratulations."

Dallas' skin tingled—finally, it was real. She wanted to shout with joy, then noticed Dr. Arnold watching at her.

"Thank you so much. I'll do my best."

He smiled lamely. "I'm sure you will. The appointment includes a fifty percent salary increase. An announcement to the campus will go out this afternoon." He shook her hand and left.

Dallas mouthed "holy shit", performed a fist pump, then picked up the phone to call Logan. She replaced the receiver. This news, she'd tell in person, to observe the look on his face. She punched in her current pay rate on a hand calculator and computed her new salary. Nice.

$ $ $

Southwest Freeway, Texas

The road sign read fifty-four miles to Houston and a special surprise visit for Dallas Wells. Over the past twenty years, Rebecca had driven from Victoria to Houston too many times to count. The first time, on her way to college, had been in a second-hand Volkswagen, not via the luxury coupe she drove today. Unfortunately, that reminded her of why she had to leave in a hurry all those years ago.

Tommy brought it all on himself, damn him. It happened a week after her high school graduation. She was in her bedroom packing the last box of books for her drive to Southern Methodist University. She was starting college the summer term rather than waiting until August. She needed to get out of Victoria, to get away from Tommy.

During her last year of high school, Tommy had taken to dropping by unannounced, especially when Rebecca was alone in the house. Most times, he tried to touch her yet she was able to push him off or get out of his way. That last night, he had been drinking and wouldn't leave her alone. She could smell the putrid

*beer on his breath as he lunged at her. She slipped out of his grasp
and ran to her mother's bedroom.*

*She knew where her mother hid the handgun that had been
her father's. She rushed to the closet and pulled the box from the
back, behind shoes and a small suitcase. She tore off the lid and
felt the weight of the gun in her hand. She knew it was loaded. She
turned at a sound, Tommy had followed her.*

*"What are you doing, bitch?" He had a belt in his hand,
raised it over his head in a tease. "You come here or I'll beat the
shit out of you."*

*She stayed crouched on the floor, said nothing. He shuffled
closer to her, waves of anger radiating from his shoulders.*

*Rebecca pulled the gun from behind her, held it between both
hands, did her best to keep from shaking. "Stay away from me,
Tommy."*

*"Or what, you gonna shoot me." He cackled then whipped
the belt in the air, the tip catching her arm, leaving a welt.*

*She gripped the gun harder, took a deep breath, adjusted her
feet so she could move quickly. "You've touched me for the last
time. Come closer and I swear, I'll shoot your sorry ass."*

*He slapped the belt on the floor before lunging at her. She
pulled the gun's trigger and . . .*

Rebecca shook her head in an attempt to dispel that old
memory. She couldn't remember much else. Her mother had
rushed into the room and stared at Tommy crumpled on the floor.
She gave Rebecca one fierce hug and said "Don't worry, baby,
I'll take care of everything." Rebecca handed her mother the gun
then went to her bedroom and shut the door. She left for SMU that
afternoon and never asked her mother what happened to Tommy.
She only knew he was gone and would never hurt her again.

Mama was Rebecca's safe place. That's why Rebecca had to
take the chance to leave Brazil and visit Mama after her surgery
for breast cancer. It also provided the perfect opportunity to pick
up her father's gun. Of course, it wasn't that much of a risk. She
had multiple identities and passports—money could buy

anything. It was kind of like playing pretend and dress up, something she'd been doing since childhood.

$ $ $

Wednesday, 11:15 a.m.

Roddy shifted in the seat of his car, grabbed the phone from the dashboard on the second ring.

"It's Logan. I've been thinking about your call to Dallas the other night."

"Uh-huh."

"Have you received any information on Rebecca's location?"

"Nothing concrete."

"She could be anywhere, Houston even."

"That's a possibility. The FBI received a tip in San Diego at an airport rental car agency. A clerk called in a report of renting a car to a woman who sorta, kinda, maybe looked like Rebecca."

"San Diego, huh? Is the return there?"

"One way, return in New Orleans," Roddy drained the coffee cup. He wished he had a thermos.

"Houston's on the way."

"That's why I'm outside Dallas' office building."

"You want company?"

"Hell, no." Roddy nearly laughed. "Why don't you go back to the FBI?"

"It's complicated. Don't forget Dallas traded her Volvo for a red Jeep SUV."

"Thanks." Dallas' Jeep exited the parking lot and turned right at the corner. "Gotta go, Dallas is on the move. Do you know where she's going?"

"Probably lunch. Let me find out where. I'll call you back."

Roddy clicked off and concentrated on following Dallas. Calling would spook her. She was too smart not to ask why he wanted to know where she was lunching. She turned left, heading west. He stayed three or four vehicles behind her. He doubted she'd recognize his car but didn't want to take a chance.

After a few minutes of driving, she pulled into a strip shopping center anchored by a home decorating store. He parked several cars away. Dallas rushed into a bookstore. She came out after a few minutes carrying a shopping bag, backed out and pulled onto Richmond Avenue. He did the same.

He called Logan who hadn't been able to reach Dallas on her cell and no one answered her office phone. Logan said he'd keep trying. The traffic ahead slowed at a set of four uneven railroad tracks. The lights began to flash and the arms starting moving down.

"Go, asshole," he yelled at the car in front of him. The car braked as a white Lexus behind Dallas zipped over the tracks just before the arms fell into place. Dallas sped down the street. He pounded the steering wheel. "Dammit."

Roddy had no idea where Dallas went. Her car was long gone by the time the crossing arms opened and he crossed the tracks. He tried Logan again.

"Have you talked with Dallas?"

"No, but I left a message for her best friend, Ruthie. She might know where Dallas likes to go to lunch."

"You don't know that?" Roddy growled.

"No, I don't."

"Put it on your damn to-do list. Call me back as soon as you hear."

Roddy wanted to throw the phone at the windshield. Where the hell was Dallas? He had a bad feeling about that tip in San Diego. All he could do was drive around the area and look at cars in parking lots, hoping to catch sight of Dallas' red Jeep. He called the dispatcher, issuing a Be On the Look Out bulletin for all patrol cars in the Inner Loop area to look for Dallas' vehicle.

He prayed it would be a waste of effort.

$ $ $

Houston traffic hadn't changed.

For nostalgia's sake, Rebecca decided to take a chance and headed toward the HCU campus while thinking about when to deal with Dallas. Luck was on her side as Dallas turned right in front of her onto Richmond Avenue. She was lucky she'd so easily recognized the bitch in the new vehicle. After a minute of following the red SUV, railroad arm lights flashed ahead. Rebecca had no trouble darting safely over the railroad tracks behind her. Dallas was so stupid, she had no idea she was being followed.

After a few minutes, Dallas turned right at Sage Road. "I bet the twit is going to the Galleria," Rebecca muttered. She was getting tired of keeping Dallas' SUV in view. She wanted this over so she could get back on the road and head to Louisiana.

"Damn, I'm smart," Rebecca exclaimed.

Dallas made another turn then pulled into a parking entrance to the Galleria. Rebecca had to wait for a car to pass before she could turn into the garage. She gunned the car a bit to catch up to Dallas then had to brake as a long Cadillac backed out. The driver was a flipping idiot and didn't know how to make a sharp turn. The car moved forward then backed again.

Rebecca pounded on the horn of the Lexus. "Move, asshole," she shouted. The Caddy limped up the ramp then slowly turned onto the down ramp. She pounded on the horn again then darted around the car to the next level.

She looked from side to side, expecting to see Dallas' vehicle. Nothing. She turned onto the next up ramp and continued to search for Dallas. Then she saw her. Dallas was entering the Galleria on the third level.

"Damn, damn it to hell," Rebecca screamed. She repeated every swear word she knew then patted her purse on the seat beside her. The gun was a calming influence, her steel security blanket. "Just breathe," she said, willing her nerves to settle down.

She parked in the first open space and turned off the car. She sat in it, staring straight ahead. She thought about her mother and all she had endured in the years since her first husband's death. Daddy dying so young had changed everything.

One wicked thing after another had followed her from

Victoria to Dallas to Houston. All the ugliness stopped now. She breathed slowly, in and out, dispersing calm throughout her being. Taking care of Dallas would end it. End the wickedness forever. She grabbed her purse, sensed the power from the gun. It filled her with energy and strength. She headed for the door Dallas had just entered.

TWENTY-NINE

Galleria Mall, 11:47 a.m.

THE GALLERIA MALL WAS ALWAYS busy. Why didn't people work anymore? Dallas noticed a number of teenagers hanging over the railing, watching the ice skaters below. Then she remembered the fall school term hadn't yet started. The summer had gone by so quickly. Guess that's what happens when you're busy doing two jobs. Now that she was officially VP she could hire a new controller. Good news.

She strode toward the cosmetic store, intent on getting the make-up Ruthie had special-ordered for her wedding. It was ready and she was on her way in less than five minutes. She searched her purse for her cell to call Ruthie but it wasn't there. "Darn it, I left my phone at work," she muttered as she hurried back to the parking garage. She'd pick up a lunch salad at the deli on the HCU campus. Might as well help keep them in business.

$ $ $

Roddy called Logan again. "A black 'n white spotted Dallas' SUV in a Galleria garage. I'm going over there now to make sure nothing's going on."

"Which garage?" Logan asked.

"You don't need to go chasing after Dallas. We've haven't had a sighting of Rebecca in Houston."

"I want to make sure she's okay."

"She's gonna be pissed if you show up and ruin her lunch or shopping trip."

"I'll take that chance. Again, which garage?" Logan's voice was low and controlled.

Roddy shook his head, a grin on his face—true love. He rattled off the entrance number and headed for the Galleria.

He could pick up some take-out at the food court once he made sure Dallas was fine and dandy.

$ $ $

Dallas threaded her way through the crowds milling in front of the window displays of school clothes and electronics. She hurried to the glass door leading to the garage. She was eager to get back to the office to check her e-mail. Perhaps the announcement Dr. Arnold mentioned had already been released. She was eager to read how he described the circumstances around her appointment.

She didn't notice the woman glare at her as she reached the door or that the woman reclaimed an object from her purse and hid it between the folds of her summer skirt. She didn't notice the woman stand and follow her into the garage. She didn't notice the footsteps trailing behind her.

Almost to her Jeep, Dallas heard someone call her name. She turned.

A woman stood five or six feet away, in the middle of the ramp. She stood very straight and very still, with her hands hidden in the folds of a long skirt.

"I'm Dallas. Do I know you?" Dallas asked, apprehension fanning the back of her neck. This was strange.

The woman continued to stare. After a beat she said, "Yes, you do." As she spoke, she raised her right hand toward Dallas, it held a pistol.

Recognition flooded Dallas as her body stiffened in shock. Rebecca had returned to Houston and apparently to shoot her, again. Fear and anger knotted inside her. This whole situation pissed her off. She *would not* let Rebecca see how much the gun freaked her out.

"Hello, Rebecca, I see you've crawled out of your worm-filled hole. What brings you back to Houston, the scene of the crime, so to speak."

"Dear, dear Dallas, always the smart ass."

"What do you want? I need to get back to work."

"And then call the police?" Rebecca wiggled the hand holding the gun.

"I don't have a phone with me. Just leave and run back to your hole. I don't care what happens to you." The bravado in Dallas' words was false while the gun pointed at her chest was real.

"You don't want justice for HCU?" Rebecca snickered.

"Again, what do you want?"

"To get rid of you, everything is your fault."

Panic like she'd never known before welled in Dallas' throat. Rebecca was close enough to shoot her straight through her heart, now cloaked in ice. Her first thought was of Cutter. The notion of never holding her sweet grandson again nearly had her lowering to her knees and begging for her life.

No, no way in hell. She'd be damned if she'd let Rebecca see the anxiety that threatened to undo her. She *would not* allow Rebecca to inhabit her life any longer. She pushed aside her jitters. She needed to formulate a plan, and quick.

"You want to get rid of me?" she said with a false laugh. "You already tried that once."

"Let's give it another go." Rebecca again wiggled the gun. "Where's your car?"

Dallas sucked in air, fear spurting through her. She had to stay calm. She had two options—get away from Rebecca or get the gun. She looked down the ramp. The garage was empty. What happened to all the people inside the mall? She was on her own.

"My car? Nah, let's go inside the Galleria and have a glass of wine." Dallas' voice was shakier than she would have liked. She took one step forward. "We can talk."

Rebecca backed up a step. "Stop," she said with cold determination. "Don't move."

Dallas raised both hands in front of her. "Okay, no moving."

Rebecca was about seven or eight feet away. Could she dive towards her and knock her over? Or run behind a car? No, better to keep her talking until—

"You bitch, you never could follow directions."

"Why did you take the money?" Dallas watched the woman shift in platform sandals that looked uncomfortable. She made her decision to fight back.

"Because I could," Rebecca spat out.

"You're a smart lady." Dallas smiled, gritted her teeth and prayed for strength. "But not smart enough."

Dallas pushed off from the balls of her feet. As she rushed forward and toward Rebecca, the motion seemed slow as though it wasn't her body. Her arms pushed out, away from her body and the purse in her right hand contacted with Rebecca's left hip, pushing her off balance.

Dallas followed Rebecca to the floor of the garage. The purse went flying yet the gun remained in Rebecca's hand. Dallas landed on Rebecca's left side and pain shot up her back. She ignored it and focused on getting her hands on the gun.

Rebecca squirmed like a snake, attempting to push Dallas off of her. Dallas pounded her fist on Rebecca's chest then on the forearm of the arm holding the gun. The fingernails of Rebecca's free hand dug at Dallas' face as she leaned over Rebecca's chest.

Her cheek burned but she didn't release her hold. Dallas pushed the weight of her body against Rebecca, trying to force her to stop twisting from side to side. "You damned bitch, stop moving."

"Go to hell," Rebecca shouted, trying to buck off Dallas. "Get off me."

That pissed her off even more, so Dallas wiggled to the point she ended up lying full on top of Rebecca. She pushed her right forearm against Rebecca's throat and used her free fist to pound the arm holding the gun.

Instead of breaking Rebecca's grip, the gun fired, binging on the ceiling of the garage.

Dallas' mind reeled in momentary confusion. She stopped

beating Rebecca's arm.

Rebecca stopped moving.

Dallas glanced toward the ceiling and didn't notice the change in the angle of the gun. But she heard Rebecca grunt and turned her head away from the ceiling. The first thing she saw was the gun pointed at her face.

She swallowed hard and without thinking gripped Rebecca's hand to push it away.

"Stop it," Rebecca growled, pushing just as hard against Dallas. "You need to die."

Time passed in slow motion, yet Dallas realized it was only seconds since she'd tackled Rebecca. She had to end this game.

Dallas released Rebecca's hand and fisted her hands together, swinging them like a baseball bat toward Rebecca's face using every ounce of power and momentum she could gather together. Her aim was off and she pounded into Rebecca's jaw.

The exact details of what happened next were lost in the blur of a car nearly hitting them on the ramp, someone shouting her name, the gun being grabbed, and strong arms pulling Dallas upward.

"You've got one helluva punch." Roddy led her quickly to the side of the ramp as a security officer ran out the Galleria entrance door and rushed over to them.

"What's going on?" he demanded. "We have a report of gunfire."

"Under control," Roddy replied while displaying his badge. He threw a pair of handcuffs to the guard. "Here, put these on the woman on the ground." He then pulled out a phone and made a call. He gazed at Dallas and mouthed "You okay?"

She nodded and closed her eyes briefly.

Rubbing her jaw, Rebecca tried to sit up as the guard approached. She attempted to fight him with flailing arms, but the beefy guard easily flipped her onto her stomach. He tugged her arms back and expertly wrapped the cuffs around her wrists. He pulled her to a standing position.

"Put her in the back of my car for now," Roddy said. "A

squad car will be here any minute."

Dallas leaned against the back of her vehicle and watched the scene with her mouth open while rubbing her right hand. That last punch hurt like hell. Just thinking about their struggle over the gun had Dallas shaking. She pressed her palms over her eyes and sucked in a hard breath. *Stay calm . . . it's finally over.*

She didn't see Logan's car park behind Roddy's but she heard him call her name.

"I'm over here." She stepped away from the Jeep and rushed into his arms.

"Thank god, you're safe." He kissed her forehead then rocked her for a few seconds, his arms tight around her. He stepped back then stroked a finger along the side of her face.

"Ouch. Anything else hurt?"

"Just my hand. I tried to get the gun."

"She had a gun?" he said, his voice squeaking.

"Of course," Dallas said with more boldness than she felt. "Doesn't she always have a gun when I'm around?" She watched a HPD cruiser stop behind Logan's car. Roddy pulled Rebecca to it and shoved her in the back seat. *Good riddance.*

Roddy walked over to them. "You made good time getting here, Logan."

Logan nodded. "Can we leave?"

"In a minute." Roddy turned to Dallas. "You'll need to give a statement."

"I figured as much."

"Can't she do that at home?" Logan asked, clearly protective of Dallas.

"I'm going back to work," she said firmly.

"No problem," Roddy said. "I need to process a couple of things here then we can do it. Where?"

"My office."

"My house," Logan countered.

Dallas' hand was throbbing like a frog croaking at night. The smart thing would be to take it easy for the rest of the day. Nana hadn't raised a dummy so she decided to call Ellie and give her the news. "I'll be at home for the rest of the day. You can come by any time for my statement. Logan, may I borrow your cell phone?"

He grinned and handed her his phone.

Great . . . he could make lunch and open a bottle of wine. A celebration was in order.

THIRTY

A Friday in Late August

THE RICE FAMILY JET TOUCHED down in Las Vegas shortly before two o'clock in the afternoon. The stairway descended, a dozen people deplaned. Two limousines waited in the shade. Logan and Dallas piled in the second one along with his grandmother and Billy, and Jenny, Billy's cute as a button wife.

"Dallas, once the wedding festivities are over, we expect you and Logan to join the family on the tour of Hoover Dam on Monday." Grandma Rice smiled, knowing full well her wish was a command everyone in the family would comply with—power, plain and simple.

"Yes, ma'am. It's a date." She patted Logan's knee. "Right?"

Logan nodded. "We'll be ready at nine-thirty Monday morning."

The limo dropped Logan and Dallas off at the Bellagio. The family suite at the Grand was full so they opted to stay at the same hotel where Ruthie's wedding would take place. It was a much better idea than staying with the Rice family which could be awkward when it came to sleeping arrangements. Dallas respected Logan's grandmother and didn't want to create an uncomfortable situation.

After they settled in a beautiful suite, she called Ruthie to let her know they had arrived. The plan was to meet in the Bellagio bar for a drink then walk over to Spago at Caesar's for a pre-wedding dinner with the family.

"Okay, Logan, we have three hours before we meet Ruthie. What shall we do?"

He smiled suggestively, twirling a strand of her hair around his finger. "Let's take a nap."

$ $ $

Saturday morning dawned clear and warm. Dallas convinced Logan to run with her at seven o'clock. They ran the same route she had on her first visit. It was different though, running with another person next to her, matching her stride. She liked running with Logan. He could leave her in the dust, but he was too much of a gentleman to exert his superior strength. Another trait she admired in him.

She also appreciated his restraint. He hadn't pressed her about moving in together since he'd suggested it three weeks earlier. He deserved a response. Thinking about what she might say made her jittery.

After they entered the suite, Dallas grabbed her ringing cell phone.

"It's Roddy, how's it going?"

"How are you?" Logan threw her a towel. She caught it and wiped sweat off her face.

"Good. I told you I'd call when I had a complete story for Rebecca Holland."

"Yes, you did," Dallas replied. "Let me put you on speaker so Logan can hear." She handed her new phone to Logan. "Where's the speaker button?"

He grinned then punched one of the little square keys. "It's Logan. What have you got?"

"This is a quick summary as I've e-mailed a sanitized version of our report to both of you. By the way, your PI, JW McKenzie, provided good information for us and saved me a lot of leg work."

"She's cute, isn't she?" Dallas said.

Roddy chuckled. "Don't know about that but she's got a real knack for doing background work."

Logan rolled his eyes, impatience flaring. "Did you find out how Rebecca changed the wire instructions?"

"Her friend is a computer hacker. He did the coding and attached it to the black cat e-mail."

"I knew it! Thanks, Roddy," Dallas said. "Why did she steal the twenty-five million?"

"That I can answer," Roddy replied. "Part of it was to get back at your family, Logan, and the other part was plain old greed. She was tired of working and wanted the easy route to retirement."

She shivered. "A lot of people are tired of working but they don't kill to get ahead. It's disgraceful."

"You always look on the bright side," Roddy said. "You'll see in the report that she killed her stepbrother as a teenager."

"That doesn't surprise me," Logan said.

"He abused her for years and as you know, abuse has an impact on a person, especially young girls," the detective explained. "In fact, she's a tragic story."

Dallas heard a door slam before Roddy announced he had to go.

Logan handed the phone back to Dallas. "Rebecca has quite the history."

"Let's forget her. She's in jail and I'm glad she's out of my life."

"She is the reason we know each other."

Dallas smiled as contentment and relief filled her. Rebecca was truly gone. "I prefer to think it was destiny."

Logan's blue eyes flickered with amusement. "I'll go with that logic, too."

She kissed him on the cheek. "Go take your shower. I'll get coffee. I don't want to wait for room service."

"You're doing better. You can actually talk in the morning without coffee." He patted her butt on his way to the shower.

$ $ $

"And now, I pronounce you, husband and wife." The minister smiled his approval while shaking hands with Ruthie and her new husband. Ruthie looked beautiful. The green dress she wore showed off her slim figure. She'd curled her blond hair at the ends so it framed her face, which glowed with happiness and contentment and belonging. She and her new hubby were a perfect complement to each other—two peas in a pod who were so well tuned into each other that they could finish each other sentences.

Their relationship gave Dallas hope. Maybe the over-forty crowd could find that special someone, even after a nasty divorce. Ruthie sure proved that a second relationship could be better than the first. There's something to be said for maturity in choosing a mate.

Dallas gazed in blissful satisfaction at Logan. He was chatting with Ruthie's sister and her husband like they were old friends. He was comfortable talking with anyone, anywhere he happened to be. Probably due to all that interrogating he did as an FBI agent. He laughed as he talked, demonstrating his story with his hands. The glow of his smile warmed her as she watched him. Serenity washed over her as her heart made its final decision.

The photographer rounded up guests for wedding photos. The first shots were of the bride and groom. The Terrazza di Sogno (Terrace of Dreams) overlooked Bellagio's Lago di Como providing a beautiful backdrop. The Bellagio Fountains rose on schedule and added a magical touch to Ruthie's official wedding photograph.

After several group photos, Ruthie suggested one of Logan and Dallas for her wedding album. They stood along the balcony's edge with the fountains behind. Logan put an arm around Dallas' waist, drew her close.

"Smile nice, babe. You need to practice this."

"Practice smiling?"

"No." He kissed her temple. "Having wedding photos taken."

Her heart clenched. Wedding photos? "Are you kidding?"

He squeezed her waist, patted her butt with a familiar touch. "I never kid about my wedding."

"Okay, all right, we can move in together," Dallas whispered. "It'll be a test to see if we can get along in the same house."

He squeezed her even tighter then leaned over and kissed her mouth. "No problem with that. We can fix up a bedroom for Cutter, too."

That settled it. She'd say "yes" if and when he asked. Dallas' smile broadened as the Bellagio Fountains danced behind her. She gazed at the people around her on the terrace, her heart overflowing with joy and hope for the future. Yep, life was damned good.

THE END

Favorite Quiche Lorraine

6 servings

Ingredients
- 1 pie crust
- 6-8 slices bacon cut into 1/2" pieces and cooked
- 2 large eggs
- 2 large egg yolks
- 1 cup sour cream
- 1 cup half and half
- 1/2 teaspoon salt
- 1/2 teaspoon white pepper
- a pinch of nutmeg
- 1 cup shredded gruyere or Swiss cheese

Directions
1   Preheat the oven to 425 F. Place the crust in a pie pan, prick with fork and bake for 10 minutes, then remove from the oven.
2   Whisk together eggs, yolks, sour cream, heavy cream, salt, pepper, and nutmeg in a medium bowl.
3   Spread the cheese and bacon evenly over the bottom of the warm pie shell. Pour the egg mixture to 1/2" below the crust rim and bake for 15 minutes, reduce heat to 350 F and bake another 20-25 minutes, or until a knife blade inserted about one inch from the edge comes out clean. The center should feel set but like gelatin. It will finish cooking as it cools.
4   Transfer the quiche to a wire rack to cool and serve at room temperature.

Note: Dallas loves this quiche recipe so please enjoy! She adds 2-3 cut green onions with the bacon.

Thank You!

If you enjoyed **The Wicked Chase**, please take the time to leave a review via the vendor where the book was purchased. Reader reviews are one of the best ways for writers to gain new readers and gain feedback about their work. Thank you if you do post a review. Also, be sure to let me know via my website or on Facebook. I'd love to hear from you! Also, you can find a complete list of my books on my website.

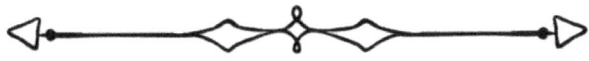

The Author

Karen Sue Burns has been a writer since 8th grade. Her former job as a CPA has provided interesting experiences: travel to Rio de Janeiro, London, and Oslo, auditing wine bottle glass molds in California, and taking a helicopter to a drillship off the Texas Gulf Coast. Now she spends her days living out her passion--writing political thrillers, cozy mysteries, and Texas ghost novels sprinkled with romance. She enjoys cooking and creating recipes so her heroines do the same. All of her indie anthologies and novels include one of her favorite recipes. Readers may contact Karen via the Bio/Contact tab on her website. Check out the Recipe tab while you're there.

Contact:
Facebook: https://www.facebook.com/karensueburns
Website: http://www.karensueburns.com

Karen Sue Burns